Diary Of A

Dieter

By
Marie Coulson

With my love
Marie Coulson

Diary Of A Dieter

Copyright © 2013 by Marie Coulson

<u>Editing</u>
Madison Seidler
www.madisonseidler.com

<u>Cover Design</u>
M. Coulson

<u>Model</u>
Michael Scanlon

<u>Image and Photography</u>
FuriousFotog
www.onefuriousfotog.com/

For all of my girls. The curvy girls, cake-aholics, and the men who let us slip through their fingers. This kitten got her cream.

Table Of Contents

<u>Chapter 1</u>

"I'm sorry. I think this line is bad. I must have misheard you because it sounded like you just said ..."

He exhaled loudly.

"I did. Look, Charlene, it's not you. It's me. I just don't know what I want from my life anymore, and to marry you while I figure it out, just isn't fair to either of us. I know this must be hard to accept, but I just can't go through with it."

I sat completely frozen on my slightly worn out rug. The phone was gripped so tightly in my palm that I could have snapped it. Brad and I had been together for four wonderful years and engaged for two. The church was booked, the reception was planned, and every last detail had been meticulously designed. January twelfth was meant to be my dream day—my happily ever after—and now Brad Mahoney was jilting me just three weeks before the big day! Most girls get jewellery or a nice sweater for Christmas. I got dumped!

"You're seriously calling off our wedding three weeks before the big day *and* doing it over the phone! Are you freaking kidding me?"

I got to my feet and began pacing around my small, but cosy, London apartment. This was a bad dream. It had to be.

"But you only left here two days ago! I don't understand. We ate, we kissed goodbye, and you headed to Ireland to see your family. What the hell changed in forty-eight hours?"

He groaned and almost growled at me.

"This is what I'm talking about, Charlene. You always think everything is about you. Well, maybe this time it's not. Maybe I'm just not ready to settle down. And let's face it, we've been headed for the rocks for months now."

I was stunned. Months? Months! We were on smooth ground as far as I was concerned. Steady, firm, and straight like my beautiful wedding gown, which was hanging in my closet, blissfully unaware of the horror unfolding in the living room.

"Not ready to settle down? You proposed, for crying out loud! You don't *accidentally* ask someone to marry you. And what do you mean months? Was I in a coma that you neglected to tell me about? Because I have no idea what you're talking about. *Months*. Christ, Brad. You couldn't have picked a better time to have a midlife crisis than three weeks before our *wedding*?"

I was becoming hysterical, and for me, this involved screeching at a frequency only dogs could hear. This was evidenced by the Afghan hound next door who had now begun a chorus of 'woe is me,' or at least that's what it sounded like every time the poor, pitiful animal howled across the street at my window. The tears were now streaming down my face, and the sobs coming from my mouth meant that the two of us, the hound and me, were now a duet!

"Charlene. Charlene, you're getting all worked up again. Calm down."

Calm down! Was he fucking serious? You know they say you go through stages of grief? Well, in the past ten minutes I'd gone from broken to completely pissed!

"Calm down? *Calm down! You* call me up, on Christmas day no less, and tell me you don't want to get married anymore! Calm down? I'm about to ram my heel through the phone and choke you, you arrogant son of a ..."

Buzz.

I stormed over to the intercom and picked up the receiver with my free hand.

"What?"

"Oh, erm ... Charlie?"

I rolled my eyes and exhaled loudly. "Yeah, Adam. Come on up. Join the party." I pressed the entry button and hung up before resuming my break up.

Awful, isn't it? I actually resumed the conversation where I was being verbally stomped on, and my whole life was tipped on its head. I was a glutton for punishment.

"Charlene, I should go. You have company."

"Don't you dare! You at least owe me an actual, feasible reason, Brad!"

He groaned again, and now I was really getting mad. He had no right to be fed up or irritated. *I* was the jilted bride around here. I deserved my diva moment!

"Come on Charlene, do you really wanna hear this? I mean, really?"

"Yes!"

"Urgh. Fine. It's not been right between us for a long time. We just don't connect the way we used to. We haven't even had sex in over a month. I have needs, you know. And let's be honest for a moment, you haven't exactly been ... taking *care* of yourself lately."

Taking care of myself? What the hell was that supposed to mean? I showered more than that hound got bones. But it was true that was the only bone that had been seen around here in a long time. But it wasn't for my lack of trying!

3

"What do you mean I don't take care of myself? I walk around once a month like I have a porcupine between my legs just because you like me to be waxed. I shower every damn day because you hate that just-got-out-of-bed smell. And after sex, I always make sure to change the sheets because you don't like them all sweaty and covered in, what was it you called it? Oh yeah, people juice!"

The door creaked open, and I could see Adam's thick, black-rimmed glasses before I saw the rest of him. I waved him in and held my finger to my lips to indicate he should keep quiet.

"What do you want me to say here, Charlene? You wanted the truth, and you got it. Besides, it has nothing to do with any of that. I meant … I meant you've, you know, put on a few pounds. Maybe twenty-eight or so. It's a turn-off. I can't get all sexed up while your handles are wobbling everywhere. It's … not my thing."

My jaw hit the floor, and I snarled back at him.

"Wobbly handles! You complete and total …"

And then it dawned on me. If Brad wasn't getting off on my jelly parts, then whose jelly mould was he filling instead?

"Oh. My. God. Who is she?"

Adam had taken a seat on my pastel pink couch, and his eyes were burning into me as I held my breath, waiting for the reply.

"What? What do you mean *who is she*?"

I grunted.

"Now who needs to be honest? I'm not an idiot, Brad. You're not fucking me, and I know you aren't self-pleasuring. We both know how you hate the mess and all. So don't bother pretending like you're not screwing some skank. I should probably get fucking tested. Do you keep your clothes on with her to avoid all the *icky* sex sweat, too?"

That seemed to just make him angry.

"She is not a skank!"

I knew it! I knew it, I knew it, I knew it! Oh, the arseholism knew no bounds! Not only was I jilted, dumped and fat, but I was also cheated! Merry Christmas, Charlene!

"You dick! You complete and total dick! How long? Who is she? I have a right to know!"

He breathed deeply, in a self-pitying way, as though it were hard for him to speak. Pfft. He'd get no sympathy from me. He'd given me a ring, and now I would give him the finger. Metaphorically speaking, of course.

"Uh, Charlie?"

I turned around and held my hand over the receiver as I snapped at Adam.

"Shhh. Can't you see I'm in the middle of being crushed? Can't a girl get dumped in peace anymore?"

He made a gesture as though he were zipping his mouth shut and leaned back in his seat.

"She's a woman from work. We went out for drinks one evening after work. We were celebrating a huge win on a case. One thing led to another and ..."

"And ... you had a minor memory lapse in which you forgot you were engaged? You are such an asshole!"

"I never meant for it to happen, Charlene. It just did. I'm sorry, and I would have preferred you to have never found out, but I couldn't marry you when I'm in love with Aneska."

The skank had a name. *Aneska.* Sounded like some sort of medicinal cream you rubbed on a bad nappy rash or irritation. Right now, that's exactly what she was. A pain in my arse!

"I hate you. I hate you so fucking much."

"Please try to understand, Charlene. I'm doing this for both of us."

I laughed.

"Oh, how silly of me. I should have *thanked* you for shagging your colleague for me. It was such a wonderful and sweet gesture for you to make. It's the best Christmas gift I could ever have asked for. *Truly.* But next year, I'd love for you to stick your dick in a live plug socket! It'll leave you just as shocked and burning as I am right now! It would be the best gift ever."

I cast my eyes at Adam who had crossed his legs and cleared his throat a little. He was clearly imaging how that sort of connection might feel. Shame Brad couldn't have done the same. If he had kept his fucking legs crossed, I wouldn't currently want to hack his dick off with a rusty kitchen knife. Meat and two veg, coming right up!

"Charlene, you are being unreasonable. I called to be kind, and all you do is get angry. I understand that you hate me, and I get it, I do. But whatever you choose to believe, I never wanted to hurt you. I care about you. I could never hate you enough to marry you for the wrong reasons."

I threw my head back and laughed hysterically with tears still streaming down my mascara-streaked face. Adam watched me in total disbelief and also, I think, a little shock. I must have seemed like a complete nut job. I was a straitjacket away from looking like a psych patient, who escaped while on a trip on the sunshine bus.

"I believe you, Brad. Hating me would require a certain degree of emotional commitment and evidently, you are lacking in that area. Hell, you're lacking in most areas! You wanna talk about sexual turn-offs? How about the repetitive sound of your socks scrunching against the mattress? Or that God-awful sound you make when you're about to come. How does it go again? Oh yeah, 'not on the sheets, not on the sheets' Oooh, sexy."

"Now you're just being childish. I haven't got time for this, Charlene. It's Christmas day, and I'm with my family. I think …"

I stopped him immediately. "It's Christmas day? Oh, I hadn't noticed. I completely bypassed the tree we decorated together. I totally forgot about the gifts that I wrapped and gave to you just two days ago, and I really should have realised what today was when my phone rang and my fiancé, instead of wishing me a Merry Christmas, decided now was the right moment to tell me he was fucking another woman!"

I sank to my knees in front of the couch, and Adam placed his hand on my shoulder.

"Charlie, come on, hang up. Or else I'm taking that damn phone from you and giving him a piece of my fucking mind."

I shook my head and swiped at my eyes.

"I'm sorry, Charlene. I really am. I wish there were something I could say or do. I know it's hurting now, but it will get easier to let this go. I promise."

I sniffed through my tears and snickered at him.

"Ha! Your promises are like your arse, Brad. Seems nice on the surface, but still full of shit!"

And before he had a chance to fire an insult back at me, Adam had snatched the phone from my hand and hung up. I would have told him off if I hadn't been a snivelling mess on the rug. My knees to my chest, I rested my head on them and sobbed. I sobbed shamelessly and completely lost control. My body shook like I had a vibrator shoved up my doodah, and I rocked back and forth like a woman possessed.

Adam slid down to the floor behind me and wrapped his arms around me tightly. His long legs were on either side of me as he pulled me close to his chest. I rested my head on it and let out a staggered and loud cry. The hound across the street joined me in a chorus of 'woe is me,' and I couldn't help but laugh at the whole sorry situation.

Adam gave me a confused look. "What's so funny?"

I leaned my head back to get a better look at my friend.

"Everything. My life ... is a joke!"

Adam gave me a squeeze. "It's not a joke. There is nothing funny about what that jizz stain just did to you! That arsehole is going to get what's coming to him, and if I ever see him around here again, I'll happily wipe his smug little grin off his dick-chin face! No one messes with my girl. Ever."

Adam and I had been friends since school. He was a chubby kid and found himself the target of a lot of bullies. James Hill was one of them. He was that really horrible kid who every adult loved to hate. He had a face only his mother could love, and somehow, he still managed to end up the most popular kid in school despite his dickery arseholishness. Anyway, one day we were in phys-ed and Adam, bless his heart, forgot his kit. He was forced to wear something from the lost and found, which naturally, was two sizes too small. Being only twelve, he hadn't really been able to protest to our very overweight teacher who told him to suck it up. And when I say overweight, I mean it. The man was clearly more accustomed to lifting doughnuts rather than barbells.

Our task was simple. Climb the rope. Easy, right? Wrong. For my poor, chubby Adam, it was Everest! He gripped the rope and pulled himself up to about a foot off the ground and just stopped. The teacher, of course, began yelling, screaming, and hurling abuse at him to 'get his arse up that rope like there was a bag of cupcakes at the top!' What a douche. And then he left—walked right off to his office, sat at his desk, and got his *Playboy* out!

Adam was left dangling, knowing the moment his feet touched the floor, Mr Doughboy would waltz right back in.

James Hill took full advantage to humiliate Adam in front of the whole class.

"Hey, fats, you heard him. Get your arse up there like it's on fire!"

Adam slipped slightly from all the sweat pouring from his palms. James edged closer, and I caught a glimpse of something shiny and thin in his hand. That little turd was about to prick Adam with a needle! Well, not on my watch. We weren't friends at the time, but I certainly wasn't about to let him get violated with a pin!

Just as the end of the needle was about to poke Adam, I stormed over, caught James in a headlock, swooped my foot on the floor and knocked him clean off his feet. We landed on the ground with a bump, and he let out a very loud and piercing screech. You see, as we had struggled, he'd dropped the pin, and as we landed … he'd sat on it. I released him, and he stood abruptly and danced around in agony. It transpired that the pin had managed to go through his shorts and enter the pre-existing hole in James's arse.

He waddled off to the nurse's office, and I managed to convince Adam to come down, considering Mr Doughboy had now followed James; I figured it was safe. He thanked me, and I told him he needed to learn to stand up for himself.

"I know. It's kind of hard when I'm only one, and then there's him, and his friends."

I rolled my eyes. "Don't you have any friends?"

When he shook his head, I swear, my heart did a little whimper for him.

"Well, you do now! Come on, let's blow this class and go hide out in the library."

The rest is history. We've been friends ever since. Adam Fitz was solidly my best friend in the whole world.

Buzz.

Shaking my head and coming back to the real world, I stared at Adam and growled.

"Who the hell is that? It's Christmas day, and I've just had my heart dropped in a wood chipper. Do people have no consideration for my turmoil?"

He shrugged and held me closer. "Want me to get rid of them?"

I nodded. "I'm not feeling very into people today."

He gave me a weak smile, got up, and answered the intercom.

I could hear the high-pitched rambling from where I was sitting. Adam held the receiver away from his ear and winced. Glancing back at me, he raised his eyebrows as if to say 'do you really wanna let them in?'

I rolled my eyes and nodded. I had to get this over with sometime, right?

Chapter 2

Adam handed me a cup of coffee. I had yet to move from the spot on the rug that I had now been occupying for a little over two hours.

"He's a shit, Charlene. I mean, I've met some real pricks in my time, but that one is a fucking cactus!"

Vanessa was pacing back and forth across the lounge, stomping so loud that I was surprised my neighbour from downstairs hadn't complained. Not that he ever complained. Or spoke to me. Or even acknowledged my existence. I didn't even know his name.

"I knew he was bad news. The moment I met him and he told me he was a solicitor, I thought *slug*, and it seems I was right. The slimy, oily, disgusting little worm! If I ever get my hands on him …"

"How did you even know he'd called?"

"He called *me*."

I turned and looked at my friend, Dana, who had finally piped up after sitting silently on the couch the entire time she'd been here. Ness had done enough talking for all of us. For a five foot three, slender, blonde-haired, real-life doll, the woman was a force to be reckoned with. When Ness got a bee in her bonnet, you ducked for cover because you could bet she was setting the whole hive on you!

"He called you? He didn't even have the decency to allow me to tell people myself?"

I began flailing my arms around as I yelled at the general insensitivity and barefaced arrogance of the man that, until about three hours ago, I called my fiancé. Adam quickly grabbed my coffee from me and placed it on the counter. Huffing, I threw myself back and lay on the floor. Dana shifted her feet slightly to avoid giving me a heel to the forehead. Her small frame and big green eyes were her arsenal. Dana knew exactly how to use them to her advantage. Sitting forward on the sofa, she gazed at me sympathetically with those gigantic emerald puppy dog eyes of hers.

"He thought you might need your girls. I'm not saying he isn't a complete and total arsewipe, but at least he cared enough to get you some backup."

I snorted at the idea. "Oh, what a prince! I can almost imagine how that went. 'Hey Dana, so, I've just dumped my fiancé, I'm fucking a woman who sounds as though she should come with a side effects warning label …'"

"Mainly 'May cause home-wrecking syndrome and caution, dirty slut is contagious,'" Ness interrupted.

Dana rolled her eyes in response. "It wasn't like *that*. He told me you two broke up, and he'd called it all off, but that's all. So I called Ness …"

"And I, of course, called Adam."

I gawped at Ness, and then snapped my head around at Adam.

"You knew! The whole time you were here … Wait a second. We were still breaking up when you got here so … that arsehole told my friends he was dumping me before he actually dumped me! Could I be more pathetic? This just keeps getting worse."

Dana and Adam gave me a sympathetic look while Ness's jaw practically dragged across the floor as she continued to walk around my living room. If she didn't stop soon, I would have bald spots all over my plush white carpet.

"That sick, twisted, scheming, cheating, man-whoring, kiss my tight yoga pants wearing behind, douchebag!"

We all stared at her as she ranted and cursed Brad, loudly and in beautifully bright and colourful language.

"My mum always said that you have to kiss a few frogs before you find your prince. I thought I'd found my prince, Ness. Turns out … just another fucking frog." I was slowly moving from anger into self-pity and deep sadness. I didn't like it, and it really wasn't in my nature to be the type to wallow, but I felt it was acceptable under the circumstances.

"Frog? Frog! He's a scum-sucking toad who should do everyone a favour and crawl away, taking his little bed-hopping harlot with him!"

Adam tried to interject, but Ness was on a roll. I shrugged at him.

"You need to cut that dick right out of your life, Charlene. And you need to do it right now. Throw his clothes into a pile and set them on fire, hurl his stereo out of the window, and rid this whole apartment of any *Brad* memorabilia. The man is a parasite, and he's been feeding off of you for years. Time to flick him off and stamp on the little fucker."

Ness and Dana had been my friends since college. We'd all taken the same music class. Ness was a very typical pop star wannabe at the time, and while working on a project together, the three of us had formed quite a bond. I don't think I could have gotten rid of them if I tried. And now, I wouldn't trade them for anything.

Sitting up, I sighed heavily.

"I cannot believe I'm going to spend Christmas day as an abandoned bride! There has to be some unwritten law somewhere about that. Like never dump on their birthday, or Valentine's Day, or the day their pet dies. You know, something like that. And then there's all the cancelling and telling everyone that I got dumped!"

I could feel the tears starting again. The thought of calling all my relatives and friends to explain that there would be no wedding after all was leaving my stomach in knots.

Adam sat down next to me on the rug and handed me a tissue.

"We'll do it all. I'll start calling all the services, the church, the reception venue, and the caterers after the holidays. I'll cancel everything and get as much of your money back as I can."

"And we'll call all the non-immediate family guests," Dana squeaked. I think she was feeling bad that she knew I had been dumped before I did. I didn't blame *her*, though. I blamed that nutfucker, Brad.

"You'll have to tell your mum and your family, but we can do the rest. What were your plans for today anyway?" Ness asked.

I held my head in my hands.

"I was meant to be going to Mum's for dinner and then flying out to Ireland to surprise Brad. My ticket is on the counter over there. God, I am such an idiot!"

Adam shook his head and wrapped his arms around me protectively. "You are not an idiot. He is. He had a great girl at home, and he decided to throw it all away for some cheap whore at the office. It's like dropping a diamond and picking up a rock. That's my male perspective, by the way."

Leaning on his shoulder, I nuzzled into the crook of Adam's arm. Letting out a long and staggered breath, I sniffed.

"I really don't feel like dinner at my mother's. Can you imagine how it's going to be? Once I tell her about this, she's going to be wailing and cursing all over the turkey and veg. And then there's my grandmother. I'm sure she'll have some wonderful advice for me like she did when I got engaged. Something along the lines of 'Well dear, when you're giving away the merchandise for free, no one wants to buy the store.' *Great*. Can't wait."

The three of them exchanged looks. They knew my gran well, and that that was exactly what she would say.

"I'll come with you."

I snapped my head up and stared at Adam.

"What?"

"I said I'll come with you. I'm not really missing anything at my family's place. I can come to yours and be ignored just the same. Besides, you could use the back up once your brother and his wife get there."

I smiled at him. I loved Adam. He was truly the best friend any girl could wish for.

"You are the best. You know my family loves you and would never ignore you. You're more likely to be hounded by my mother than left to your own festive devices."

He gave me a quick peck on the forehead. "So, go and get dressed because I don't think your robe and slippers are going to cut it. I know it's casual, but I think you need to show them all how strong you are, and that you will not be beaten by that arsehole. *I* may beat the shit out of him when I get my hands on the prick, but you are a princess and should dress like one. Go on, I'll take care of some stuff and wait in here."

Throwing my arms around him, I squeezed tightly. Ness and Dana quickly joined me, and before he could protest, we were a bundle of hugging bodies on the floor.

"Get off me! You will crush me, and I won't be taking anyone anywhere!"

Ness and Dana stood quickly, straightened themselves out, and smiled.

"Oh, man up you big girl," Ness teased.

"Vanessa, compared to you, I am a mere mortal. You are more man than all of us. Just lacking the equipment. Pre-op?"

She poked her tongue out at him, and I laughed. I *actually* laughed, and it totally took me by surprise. For one tiny second, I forgot about my impending torture at the hands of my family and just enjoyed a moment with the family I chose to surround myself with. My friends.

Hooking a hand each beneath my arms, Dana and Vanessa hauled me to my feet and marched me to my room.

"We'll help you get ready. God knows you need the help. I've seen your wardrobe. When are you going to let me loose in there?"

Vanessa was a stylist for one of the top magazines in the city. She had dressed hundreds of A-list celebrities, and we frequently used her and her excellent taste at the company.

I worked for the R.J. Littman Record Company. When I'd first started out there, I was an intern just making her way and trying to break into the music management business. And now, I held one of the most coveted positions in the entire organisation. I was the one that signed bands and made them 'public ready.' My boss, Regina Littman, was a doll. I mean a *real* doll. The woman was more plastic than the countless credit cards she owned! She'd been nipped, tucked, and stuffed more than a quilt, but beneath her enormous silicone breasts beat a heart of gold. I loved my job.

"You can style me when you can pay for it. I'm not yanking out the credit cards just so that you can go nuts in Donna Karan."

She tutted and rolled her eyes as she began rummaging through my closet. "Oh, ye of little faith. What the hell is this? Oh, this has to go. Cashmere should never be a skirt after the nineties, darling, and those shoes are out of the question! Do you shop blindfolded, woman?"

My clothes were being flung around the room as Ness began "filtering" out the inappropriate choices. Dana had already set to work on my hair. She owned her own salon and had a line of hair products available in all the best retailers. She was also someone we hired a lot in the company. I was relatively lucky that they were both so awesome at their jobs. When I'd suggested them to Regina, she had been sceptical, to say the least. Mostly due to the two of them being *my* friends, and I was still proving myself as a manager. Thankfully, they were both incredible, and Regina was so impressed she offered them both freelance contracts, which, of course, they quickly accepted.

"Ooh, what about this dress?"

I shook my head.

"Too small."

She groaned and threw it on the floor. "What about these jeans and that shirt?"

I shook my head again. "Hasn't fit in about three months."

Groaning, she stepped back and surveyed the damage.

"So, what does fit then?"

I pointed over to the closet between Brad's and mine. *Brad's closet.* Images of me setting it on fire and watching with menacing laughter filled my head.

Ness opened the doors and gasped.

"Oh good God, no. No, no, no, no. Oh, Charlene. *Why?*"

Picking up a long black roll neck sweater, she held it at arm's length as though it repulsed her. And by the look on her face, it did.

"What? I like it. Besides, it has some give since it's stretchy."

"It's horrific, and I forbid you to ever wear it again!"

I rolled my eyes at her overdramatic display. Holding her palm to her forehead, she continued to ransack my closet. I threw myself back onto my bed.

"Oh, Charlene, no! Your hair!"

I sat up quickly and gave Dana an apologetic look. She sighed and resumed her attack on my unruly mass of ginger hair. I was lucky enough to have had a Scotsman as a sperm donor father. My mother had met him in her twenties while on vacation. She told me they'd gotten drunk one night, and I had been the result of several hours of beer swilling. Romantic, huh? Anyway, a month later she'd gone back to tell him, and he'd informed her he was married. Nice. Seems I met a guy just like my father. He wanted nothing to do with me and left my mother high and dry. Just like Brad was doing now. Except, thankfully, I wasn't carrying his child. I shuddered at the thought. Imagining Brad during the birth was hilarious. All that mess and screaming, he'd have been likely to lose consciousness. That, or he'd have been frantically rubbing his hands with the alcohol gel they provided. How the hell did I fall for that freak?

"When you get home after the holidays, we are hitting the stores! We should have been hitting the wonderful boutiques of Paris, but now that the fucknut went and screwed you over ..."

I held my hand to my mouth and let out a little whimper. For my hen night, the girls had arranged a whole weekend full of fun and laughs in Paris. We were meant to stay in

Disneyland and have cocktails, ride roller coasters, and act like teenagers again. Now, I was going to be spending that weekend alone in my apartment with Jacob for company. Jacob was my cat. He got his name after I'd found him rummaging through my rubbish bags. He was licking some soured cream off one of my discarded 'Jacobs Creek Rose' bottles. I tried to shoo him off, but he kept crying at me in the pitiful little way he does. So, I took pity on him and allowed him to stay one night only. That was three years ago. Brad hated Jacob. He always hissed and snarled at him if he got up on the furniture. I should have realised then that Brad was a douche. I mean, really, who hisses at a cat? What a snake.

"Don't worry about it, Charlene. Paris isn't going anywhere. We could go this summer. Right, Vanessa?"

Dana glared at her and realising her mistake, Ness quickly relented.

"Oh, of course. Paris shmaris, right? We can have just as much fun seeing in the New Year here."

I rolled my eyes as Dana began to tease out the knot I'd created by rolling around the bed with half a can of hairspray on it.

"Oh yeah, that sounds like *so* much fun. Excuse me while I tie some concrete to my feet and hurl myself off the London Bridge. What could be better than getting drunk in the apartment and waiting for my ex-fiancé to turn up and collect his stuff? Awesome."

Ness huffed and stood with her hand on her hip. "Are you going to sit on that pity pot for the rest of your life?"

Dana's mouth fell open, and she snapped back at her sharply. "Ness! She just had her wedding called off less than six hours ago! Have some common courtesy." She was beginning to get riled up. The way she was pointing her curling iron at Ness made me uncomfortable. But then again, it was right next to my head.

"I'm just saying she can't mope forever. Hell, Charlene, you should be counting your blessings that the shit streak is out of your life for good. He really was no good for you. We tried to warn you."

Now, *I* was getting angry. I loved my friends, but Ness had a tendency to let her mouth run away from her.

"Okay, Vanessa. I get it. You all hated him. Can you drop it now? It's hard enough as it is."

She inhaled deeply and opened her mouth to speak, but a knock on the door silenced her.

"Are you decent?" Adam's voice came booming through the door.

"Never. But I'm clothed, if that's what you mean," I yelled back at him.

Opening the door, Adam stood with his phone in his hand and cleared his throat loudly. "Well, I cancelled your ticket to Ireland and got your money back."

I gave him a grateful smile and mouthed a thank you as Dana began tugging at a rather painful knot in my hair. He shrugged and turned his attention to Ness, who was almost completely buried inside my wardrobe. Her slender hips and black kitten-heeled shoes were all that was visible.

"We could push her in, lock the door, and tell everyone she moved. One shove. That's all it would take," Adam joked.

"Any excuse to get your hands on my arse. Oh, Charlene! This is perfect!"

Backing her way out of my wardrobe, she held up a long, black, roll neck sweater dress. I shook my head fiercely as soon as my eyes landed on it. "No. Not going to happen. Take it out to the trash."

The three of them gave me confused looks. Rolling my eyes, I exhaled loudly. "I got that for our honeymoon. Brad liked it. He liked that it didn't show any skin. I hate it. Throw it out."

"Skin? Honey, it's like two degrees outside. You can wear it with some skinny jeans."

Skinny jeans? Was she not paying attention? Squeezing into a pair of those would make me look like a sausage bursting out of its skin. I gave Adam a pleading look. It wasn't that I hated the sweater for what it was; just what it represented — oppression from a man who had just dumped me. I glanced at my wardrobe where my stunning bridal gown was hanging. That's right, vintage lace and ivory silk, we're not meant to be it would seem. Brad has screwed us both, and we're left with the bill.

Walking over, Adam sat beside me on the bed, earning him a grunt of annoyance from Dana who was still untangling my mass of hair. He placed a hand on my leg and smiled. "Charlie, it really doesn't matter what you wear. One, your mother will criticise whatever you choose. Two, you will tell yourself that even in a potato sack and belt, your sister-in-law looks better than you and three …" He pressed a kiss to my forehead and hooked his thumb beneath my chin, lifting it so that I was now looking right into his sweet, blue eyes. "… You look beautiful no matter what you wear. Now, get off of your arse and get dressed. You have to face your mother sometime."

I rolled my eyes and groaned loudly. "Can't I just run away?"

Ness shook her head violently at me. "Cliché and overdramatic, Charlene. You're a jilted bride and these days that doesn't allow you to go crawling under a rock and crying yourself to sleep."

I gave her a stern look and was about to respond, but Dana beat me to it. "And you'd know *what* about being a jilted bride? Or a bride. Hell, what would you know about being in a relationship?"

Fisting her hands on her hips, Ness glared back at Dana. "I know enough to know that I don't need nor want one—too much hard work, heartache, fights, fucking, and trouble if you ask me. I'm happy just the way I am thank you."

"Bitter, alone, and unsatisfied then?" Adam piped up.

Huffing, she threw one of my black pumps at him, barely missing his head. "Not that it's any of your business, but I am perfectly satisfied with my sex life. I get as much as I need. No more. No less. Besides, you're one to talk. When was the last time you had a girlfriend? Or even a friend with benefits?"

Adam turned pink and gave me an embarrassed look. "I'm not interested in one-night stands, and if I did meet the right girl, I sure as hell wouldn't tell you about her."

"Why not?" Ness demanded.

Groaning with frustration, he stood and towered over her. "Because you are so quick to give an opinion, piece of advice, or even a comment."

She gasped with, what I assumed to be, insult. "I do not!"

A loud snort of laughter escaped Dana's mouth behind me, and Ness was on her immediately, like a fly on jam. "What was that supposed to mean?"

Releasing my hair, Dana shook her head. "Oh come on, Vanessa. Tina, Gabriella, Hannah, and Tracy—they were all nice girls, and you had an opinion on all of them. You were obvious that you didn't like them, too."

Ness stared at me, hoping for my support, but Dana had a valid point. "Charlene? Back me up."

I shook my head. "I have enough drama of my own. You three can scratch each other 'til your bleeding. I'm purely an innocent bystander."

Turning to face him, Ness squared up to Adam. "I do not have an opinion on the women you date."

He laughed and began counting off the women on his fingers. "Tina, her head was too big."

Dana giggled behind me as Ness defended herself. "The woman looked like one of those bobbleheads you put in your car. I didn't know whether to shake her hand in case her whole body moved, and her head wobbled around like a boat in water. Besides, she was sleeping with her ex."

I nodded. "*That* is true. She called that one. Though, I don't remember her head being overly large."

"Okay, granted she was a cheater, but it wasn't like I was going to marry her. Gabriella was perfectly nice, and you scared her away in one shopping trip!"

Now *I* laughed. Ness, Dana, and I had invited Gabriella for lunch and shopping one afternoon. She and Adam had been dating for almost a month, and as his best friend, I felt it was my duty to 'assess' her suitability. Especially after what had happened with Tina. Everything had gone wonderfully until … we hit the stores. Naturally, Ness dragged us to every designer boutique in London. Dana and I were used to this and had, so far, been shopping with her countless times without buying a thing. Gabriella, on the other hand, was a learner. She oohed and ahhed over every dress, pair of heels, designer bag, and hat that she saw. It was at this point Ness asked a crucial—in her opinion, it was crucial—question. "So, Gabriella, what do you do for a living?"

And then came the answer that would end her relationship with Adam forever. "I work for a bank. I chase credit card and loan debts. You know, missed payments, etc." The horror on

Vanessa's face was unmistakable. You see, little did Gabriella know, Vanessa owed at least five thousand pounds on her credit card, and her payments were sporadic. She disliked the girl immediately and spent the rest of the day 'giving Gabriella her self-worth and confidence back.' What this meant was, she spent four hours telling the women she could do better than Adam, who was a mere med student with thousands of pounds worth of debt to his name. Not exactly husband material, she told her. She even went as far as to wind up the poor woman's biological clock! "You're not getting any younger, are you? And you look like the type to have lots of kids and settle down."

It was a sad day for womankind and a worse one for Adam. Gabrielle promptly dumped him over dinner that evening. I spent the next three days trying to convince him not to kill Vanessa, and that he was, indeed, marriage material.

"Okay, I may have had ulterior motives with that one, but I saved you a life of penny-pinching and purse-tightening. You'll thank me in the long run."

Adam rolled his eyes at her. "Fine. Let's say you're right, but what about Hannah and Tracy?"

I raised my hand to speak, but with a wave of her perfectly manicured hand, Ness silenced me.

"I did that for you. Those two were bad news. Hannah was clearly after the money she thought you had, Mr Doctor, and when she found out, you had none she left. I simply pointed her in the right direction. And as for Tracy … I'm telling you, that was the biggest voice box I've ever seen. It was an Adam's apple, and you know it. She had hands like Muhammad Ali! How you missed that, I have no idea."

Dana fell back on the bed, laughing, and I had to bite my lip to hide my own amusement.

"Tracy was not a dude! I inspected every inch of that woman. She was just … bigger than most."

Ness snorted a laugh. "Ha! Maybe she was an Amazonian in a previous life. Either way … your gene pool and hers were never made for mixing. I can see it now—huge, manly girls with glasses and braces. It's just cruel, and Mother Nature wouldn't thank you for it."

Adam scowled at her. "And what's wrong with my teeth?"

Finally able to control my laughter, I interjected. "Hey! Guys, enough. Adam, your teeth are fine. Ness, give it a rest. No matter what you two say, you love one another and would hate to see the other hurt, so kiss and make up so we can get back to what's important here. Me and my Goddamn miserable ex and the wedding I have to cancel."

Walking over, they both wrapped their arms around me tightly. "I'm sorry, Charlie. God, I wanna strangle and torture that arsehole for doing this to you." Adam had always been protective, but I always felt, deep down, that he really didn't think much of Brad. Though he never said anything, I was pretty sure that was to keep the peace and make me happy. Ness, on the other hand, had made it clear from the start how she felt.

"You're better off with that slug as far away from you as possible. He's a creep, and someone needs to throw salt on him and watch him sizzle away into a slimy puddle."

She always did have a way with words. "I know you hated him. I know you didn't like that I was marrying him, but I loved him. I was going to walk down the aisle, say I do, and live happily ever after. Well, as happy as you can be, I suppose."

Releasing me, the two of them gave me a sympathetic look. Dana's arms slid around my middle as she hugged me from behind. "And that's the reason you shouldn't have been marrying him in the first place, sweetie."

Glancing over my shoulder, I gave her a puzzled look.

"Happily ever after should mean *just* that. They make you so happy that you can't imagine ever being happy without them. They should make you walk on air, glide on air currents, and turn you inside out. You are worth far more than 'as happy as you can be.' You, Charlene Winters, are destined for an epic love story. You deserve one."

Tears filled my eyes as I gazed at my friend. Dana was a sweetheart. There was no doubt about it. Silence fell, and it was the most awkward of silences we had ever endured. Picking up my sweater dress, Ness held it out to me and gave me a weak smile.

"Come on, trust me. What have you got to lose?"

At that point … not a whole hell of a lot.

<u>Chapter 3</u>

The drive to my mother's house felt like an eternity, as I sat rigidly and wrung my hands together constantly. Adam placed a reassuring hand on my knee, which was jerking up and down like it was on springs.

"Hey, it'll be okay. I'll be right there with you. How are you feeling?"

I shook my head weakly. "My heart is broken, I'm exhausted from crying, and I'm wearing a sweater dress that was intended for my honeymoon. Also, let's not forget we are currently hurtling toward my overbearing and dramatic mother, who will no doubt blame it all on me and my 'career girl' desires. Can't wait."

He gave me a half smile. "You know what to expect from her at least. So, you can be prepared. Thick skin, baby girl, and for the record, there's nothing wrong with wanting a career. I love that you're independent, self-sufficient, and successful. She is too. Deep down. Like, really deep down. Your heart will mend. You know he wasn't right for you, right Charlie? I mean, the guy was a complete dick."

I exhaled noisily. "But he was my dick. I wasted four years on that man. Four years of washing, cooking, cleaning, and having sex with one man. If you can even call it sex. My bed was so clean after every session you could have performed surgery in there! It was probably more sanitised than your operating theatre!"

He winced. "Please don't talk about sex with him. It creeps me out. Not you having sex … just with him. He's so flat, plain, and stiff all the time. He was never the type you usually go for."

I gave him a confused look and raised an eyebrow, curiously. "I have a type?"

He chuckled and nodded, keeping his eyes fixed on the road. "Yep. Tall, successful, party boys. Work all day and party all night. They were all immature idiots, though. None of them were good enough for you. But, admittedly, I don't think there is a man out there that's good enough for you, Charlie."

Scooting over, I wrapped my hands around his bicep and rested my head on his shoulder as he drove. "I love you, Adam. I don't know what I would do without you. You're the best friend I never asked for and the one that's been there for me since."

He pressed a kiss on the top of my head and leaned his cheek against it. "I know. It'll be okay. Just give it time. I promise, I'm not going anywhere."

As we pulled up outside my mother's bungalow, I stared out the window at her impeccable little front garden. Rose bushes lined the edges, and her lawn was perfectly green even in the middle of winter. She always had been good at keeping a home—something I was reminded of every time she waltzed into my apartment and 'tidied up.' Something Jacob particularly disliked. He and my mother had a very strained relationship. He clearly considered her moving his little cat bed, food dish, and toys a grave injustice. After all, he'd spent over a year training me to leave his things exactly where they were. I had the scratches of honour to prove it.

The second the engine halted, my stomach churned loudly. I was sure Adam heard it, but if he did, he said nothing. Giving me a sympathetic look and a nod, he opened his door and got out. I gripped the handle on my side tightly, but I was certainly not willing to open it yet. It was safe in the car. As far as the rest of the world was concerned, I was still happily engaged and about to get hitched. And by rest of the world, I meant my mother. If you wanted anything to be spread around like a hooker's sexually transmitted disease, you told Cynthia Winters. My mother was the local gossip, motor mouth, Oracle, and know it all. Her curtains twitched more than my knickers did when Ian Somerhalder was on the TV. Say what you will about that man, but I was an addict of that smouldering man candy. But that's beside the point; the point is, my mother has a big mouth.

Adam clicked the handle up and tried to pull the door open, but I had a death grip on the handle.

"Charlie, what are you doing? Come, on. You have to do this sometime."

I shook my head and pulled on the door, trying to keep it firmly closed. "No, I don't. I could run away. Come with me; we'll run away together, and everyone can assume I dumped Brad to elope with you. It's foolproof."

He laughed as he gave the door a hard yank, pulling me with it and hurtling out of the car. Adam caught me in his arms and gripped me around the waist.

"That would be a very good plan, except no one would believe it. We've been friends for far too long for people to believe you suddenly fell madly in love with me and ran off to get hitched. It'll be okay. I'm right here with you."

I gave him a disgruntled look. Spoilsport. Dr Fitz always had been the sensible, level-headed, and rational one in our relationship. Most of the time it was refreshing, but right now, I hated it. I wanted to forget my problems, run, and hide under my duvet for a few months, burying my head in the pillow 'til it all just faded away. But clearly, this wasn't an option. Lifting me from the ground, Adam closed the car door and headed for the house. My feet were inches from the ground as I groaned and complained.

We hadn't even knocked when the door swung open, and my mother flung her arms around us both. "Charlene! Adam! What a lovely surprise."

I gave her a confused look. "Hardly, Mother. You went on and on for weeks about me coming for Christmas dinner. We both knew I would end up coming."

She rolled her eyes and ushered us inside, gripping Adam by the elbow as he ducked his head to fit through my mother's tiny front door. "Adam, darling, it's so wonderful to see you. You look more and more handsome every time I see you. How is work? Charlene tells me nothing these days. I feel like a stranger to you both, and I practically raised you alongside one another."

Giving Adam a slight smirk, I dropped myself onto the large, plush, brown sofa. He ran his fingers through his hair and slid his thick black glasses up his nose with his middle finger. "Uh, it's fine. Busy, but fine. The house looks great as always, Mrs W. And dinner smells amazing."

She patted him on the arm and gestured toward the lounge, where I was now deeply engrossed in the latest edition of *The Cotswolds Weekly*. My mother and her dreams of a country cottage were clearly still in full swing. The woman had Harrods taste and a purse full of mothballs, but she had held onto that dream for years. It was probably the reason she had gone through so many husbands. I'd had two stepfathers growing up. The first was the man I called Daddy. Henry was my world. A city banker, he met my mother through a mutual friend, and they married when I was three. I adored him. We were as close as any normal father and daughter could be, and I was smitten. When he was diagnosed with cancer, I was devastated. I watched as my mother ignored the problem one moment and then wailed and howled the next. I attended countless family therapy sessions at the hospice and Dad had even sat me down to talk about what to expect. We made a plan, and together we composed a memory book filled with pictures, stories he wrote about us, and mementoes from places we'd been. But nothing prepared me for losing him. He died the following spring, just after my twelfth birthday, but my mother soon got over her loss and married his brother. Uncle Tony had been a great comfort to her while she cashed in my father's life insurance. The holiday in the Bahamas probably didn't do much harm either.

Unfortunately, Uncle Tony decided that the merry widow of his dead brother was bringing him a lot of unwanted attention, and he was open to gossip wherever he went. The pressure of his celebrity status in our small town became too much to bear, and he soon divorced my mother and moved to London. Last I heard, he had re-married and had a couple of kids. I still got a Christmas card every year, and this years was a simple message: *Happy Holidays. Best Wishes. Tony.* It was brief and not what you would expect from someone who had raised me through my teenage years, but it was perfectly acceptable for the two of us. We weren't close, and we certainly weren't family in my eyes.

Slumping down at the other end of the sofa, Adam gave me a knowing look as I rested my feet in his lap. He nodded toward the kitchen where my mother was busying herself with every tray, pot, and pan in the house by the sound of the clanging echoing through.

"You need to tell her. Better to do it now than when your brother and his wife get here."

I groaned and threw the magazine on the floor. "I don't want to do this. If I tell her, that makes it real, and I like being in denial right now. Denial is safe, and it doesn't hurt like a dagger through my chest."

Taking my right foot, he began to massage it gently. "Denial is not safe. It's dangerous, and if you stay there too long, you'll drown in that river. Get your arse in there and tell her. What are you going to do? Wait 'til you're at the church in three weeks and happen to mention it? Hey, Mum, guess what? Brad isn't coming. Do it now, Charlie. I know it hurts, but it's just like mending a dislocated arm. A quick and painful shove in the right direction, and it's done."

I winced at the thought. The sound of bones crunching and visions of limp limbs being shoved into a socket filled my mind. Yuck. Adam always did have the stomach for the gruesome. I was pretty sure it was one of the reasons he became a surgeon. Blood and guts were an afternoon treat for him. For me, they were a horror movie that would leave me keeping every light in my apartment turned on all night.

The last horror flick we'd seen had been particularly disturbing. Poltergeists and crazed murderers in masks were not my idea of an evening in. It was hell. We'd turned the lights out, snuggled under a blanket and watched the two-hour long blood fest. By the time it was done, I was adequately terrified of the dark; I was also on red alert. The slightest sound made my breathing quicken, my heart race, and my survival instinct was in full swing. So, as you can imagine, when I got up in the middle of the night to fetch a glass of water, I had every possible light on in the apartment.

It would have been fine had Jacob not suddenly meowed at me from between my feet. The sound along with the sensation of his fluffy tail on my leg sent me hurtling across the kitchen and climbing on top of the fridge. I sat there for a good half an hour glaring at him as he stared up at me from the floor. He had a particularly satisfied look on his furry little face, and it irked me. I didn't come down again 'til Brad came home from his 'boys' night out.' I should have realised, even back then, that he was being unfaithful. Men didn't like Brad. He didn't really have friends. He had colleagues. He was probably with her that night and every night that he claimed was for business or dining a client.

I shook my head as I thought about all the signs I had missed or chosen to ignore. I knew they said you could be blinded by love, but I had clearly been knocked unconscious by it. I wasn't blinded—I was comatose.

Adam nudged my leg. "Hey, daydreamer, come back to Earth. There's a very real issue you need to address, and I think you need to do it before—"

The doorbell broke his lecture, and I flung my arm over my eyes and groaned. My mother quickly rushed out of the kitchen and practically bounced to the door. Opening it, she squealed with happiness and excitement.

"Gareth! My darling boy. Oh, how I've missed you. Come, give Mummy a kiss."

My brother was a large man. Six foot three in height and built like a brick house pumped full of steroids. I wasn't overly convinced he wasn't pumped full of steroids. Going from matchsticks dangling from his shorts to huge, thick tree trunks in only three months was a little far fetched in my opinion.

I peeked out from beneath the seclusion and safety of my arm. Adam was staring at me with his 'I told you so' expression. I mentally cursed myself for not seizing the opportunity to tell my mother in private when I'd had the chance. Because now, I had an audience and that included …

"Nadine! Oh, you get more and more stunning every time I see you. I love your new haircut. And this dress is gorgeous. You always did have the best taste. Charlene, Charlene, doesn't Nadine look wonderful?"

I raised my arm in the air and gave her a thumbs up. I'd have preferred to give Miss Perfect a different digit from the same hand, but it would only have given me more trouble, and I had enough problems already. Adam quickly caught my eye and shook his head.

"It's not worth it," he mouthed. How the hell did he always know what I was thinking? I sometimes wondered if we were too close for our own good.

"Charlene! Come and say hello to your brother and sister-in-law. You are so rude." My mother gave me a hard stare before turning her attention back to Nadine. Huffing, I clambered off of the sofa and walked over to the door. I stood in front of my brother who towered over me.

"Hey," I offered.

"Hey," he replied. And that was pretty much our entire greeting. We didn't feel the need for long, warm, drawn-out hellos. It wasn't our style, and we lacked the relationship. Gareth was my mother's stepson. He was Henry's son, and you might think it would have made us close, but it didn't. Gareth had always been jealous of the bond I had with his father, and he made no secret of it. When Henry died, Gareth didn't speak to me for almost a year. You see, my father had left me a considerable inheritance, and Gareth's was not quite as large. Though mine did come with conditions. I had to use it for university. Gareth was already a senior at the local university, so giving him that sort of cash was pointless.

Besides, he'd only have blown it on fast cars and faster girls. Which brought me right back to his wife, who was dragging her eyes up and down my body.

"Nadine, how have you been?" I was being polite, but every muscle in my body tensed as the words left my lips. I hated this bitch. Nadine Langley was the most superficial, fake, boring, gold digger you could ever meet. Her long, golden hair, designer clothes and so much makeup, she could have been repainting the house with it, was simply masking her ugly personality. This woman was Satan.

She gave me a smile that was as fake as her oversized boobs. "Oh, you know how it is. Busy. If I'm not running the house, I'm running errands."

I gave her a confused look. "You have a maid. What running do you have to do exactly?"

She put on her best giggle and grinned. "Well, I supervise. Janine can't get it right all the time, and if I don't point out where she can improve, the poor girl will always be mediocre. I'm investing in her future, and she'll thank me for it someday."

I snorted a laugh. "Her future? Nadine, she's working for you to pay her way through law school. I think her future is solid."

Now she looked puzzled. "Janine? Law school? Are you sure?"

See, I told you. This bitch lived in la-la-land, and if it didn't directly affect her or improve her status, information about others was useless.

"Yes. Law school. She told me last time I came over for that God-awful dinner party you hosted."

My mother glared at me. "Charlene! I'm getting really tired of your smart mouth. It's Christmas, for goodness sake. And besides, if not for Nadine, your big day would be in shambles.

Thank God for your organisation skills." She gave Nadine a warm smile. I have to be honest. I was slightly jealous of the way my mother fawned all over her. She never looked at me that way.

"You're right, Mother. Thank you, Nadine. The wedding really couldn't happen without you."

Adam cleared his throat behind me, and I shot him a warning look. He shook his head at me and slumped back against the cushions on the sofa. Pushing past me, Nadine made a beeline for him. She leaned over the back of the sofa and wrapped her arms around his neck, giving him a peck on the cheek.

"Oh, Adam. It's so nice to see you. It's been far too long. I'm sure this one keeps you hidden away so she can keep you all to herself."

Raising an eyebrow and casting an eye back at me, he gave her a weak smile. "Uh, yeah. I guess it's been a while."

I rolled my eyes and turned my attention to my mother and Gareth who was hauling Nadine's designer suitcases from the car. A tapping on the backseat window caught my mother by surprise, and as she poked her head around the door, she groaned. *Excellent*. There was only one person in the world who could make my mother feel that instantly uncomfortable.

Running over, I pulled the door open and offered my hand. "Gran, Merry Christmas."

She took my outstretched palm and turned her nose up. "If you say so, dear. I've just spent two hours on a slippery leather seat, listening to Miss Too-Much-Money-And-Too-Little-Brain go on about her new jewellery. And all for some dry turkey, awkward conversation, and forced pleasantries with *you* people. I'd rather be stuffed myself and put my head in the oven. But if you insist … Merry Christmas."

Gran was my mother's kryptonite. I always got a certain amount of satisfaction whenever she visited. Okay, she was a cantankerous, miserable old bag, but she made my mother unhappy and that, in turn, made me happy. For all the criticising, nitpicking, bullying, and general backhanded compliments my mother gave me, my gran had some equally great ones for her own daughter. Karma was brutal, and so was my gran.

Walking over, my mother plastered on a smile. "Mum, good ride over?"

I had to bite my lip to stop myself from laughing as my gran gave my mother a snorted laugh and walked right by her. For an eighty-year-old woman with a cane, she sure could move. I looked at my mother and shrugged before following in after my gran. When I got there, I found her gripping Adam's cheeks like they were hard candy. "Oh, Charlene, why couldn't you have married this one? He's so cute, *and* he's a doctor."

I rolled my eyes. "You know why gran."

"Ah, yes, the member of our family that's not a member of our family. Maybe that's why you're the only one I can stomach."

Adam smiled at her before assisting her to her favourite armchair. My heart always skipped a beat whenever anyone sat there. It was Dad's chair. Coming up behind me, Gareth rested his chin on my shoulder.

"The old witch was a fucking nightmare. I had to pull over three times just so she could stretch her legs. This dinner is going to be a disaster." I giggled and glanced back at him. "I bet it won't be boring though."

He had no idea just how much of a disaster it would be. I was going to tell everyone the truth all together, at the same time. That way, I could get all the tears, tantrums, and comments dealt with in one swoop. And that was just my mother. God knows what the others would say. But I had a feeling one person would be thrilled at the news. Nadine. She had made no secret of the fact her wedding was the wedding to end all weddings. I was pretty sure that was her motive for taking such an active role in planning mine. The little tart just wanted to make sure I didn't out-do her. Well, I certainly wouldn't be now.

Fisting her hands on her hips, my mother sighed loudly. "Right, shall we make our way to the table for dinner and then after, we can do gifts."

We all nodded in agreement except Gran, who mumbled something under her breath as she rose from her squat on my dad's chair.

I walked toward the dining room, but Adam caught my elbow, halting me as everyone else left the room. "I told you to do it earlier. You realise this is going to be hell, right?"

I nodded. "Yes. But at least this way I only have to shove that dislocated limb back in once. Rather than doing it over and over again with each of them."

Giving me a half smile, he wrapped his arms around me tightly. "How are you feeling, by the way?"

I shrugged as I nuzzled my face into his broad chest. "Numb. It doesn't feel real. We've been apart so much recently that it just feels like another business trip or family thing taking him away from me. I'm angry at him, at her, but mostly at myself for not being smart enough to realise he was screwing someone else."

Gripping my arms, he gently pushed me away from him and stared at me. "This was not your fault, Charlie. That guy is a dick, and he doesn't deserve you. Look, sometimes we have to go through painful endings just so we can start a new beginning. You *will* get your happily ever after. Just not with him."

Shaking my head, I pulled myself from his grasp. "No, I won't. Because they don't exist. Come on, better get this over with."

Taking my hand, he laced our fingers together, and we took our seats at the table. I gave him a quick squeeze before settling down for what was going to be the most traumatic meal of my life.

* * * *

Dinner was uneventful. Nadine spent the whole meal bragging about her gifts from Gareth while he nodded and smiled where appropriate. My mother grinned at her while my gran rolled her eyes and tutted at them both. Adam and I had kept a dignified silence. That was until Nadine cornered me.

"Charlene, I've been meaning to ask you—your bridesmaids, will they be wearing the same sickly shade of pink you chose for the flowers? I'd hate to wear pink and look like I was part of the wedding party."

Bitch.

I shook my head. "No, they won't be wearing pink. In fact, they won't be wearing anything."

My mother gasped. "Charlene! I will not have my daughter being one of those new radical brides who make a mockery of marriage by throwing one of those awful themed weddings. And nudity is certainly not acceptable."

"It would make the whole sorry mess more bloody interesting than that *ones* was." My gran pointed over at Gareth and Nadine, and I had to hide my enjoyment.

"All ice sculptures, harps, and fancy food that I wouldn't have fed the dog. I was so hungry after that meal, I had to snack on the awful tasting crisps they put in the middle of the table."

Nadine gave her a confused look. "Crisps? We didn't put out crisps."

Gran rolled her eyes. "Of course you did. You know, those funny coloured ones that went with the flowers."

Almost choking on the gulp of water he'd just taken, Adam immediately burst out laughing, and I couldn't contain my own giggles any longer either. Patting her arm, I spoke breathlessly through my fits of hysterics. "Gran, those weren't crisps. That was potpourri."

Gareth grinned and held his hand over his mouth as my mother bit her lip, staring down the table at my gran.

"You ate my centrepieces? Good God. Gareth, it isn't funny." Nadine nudged him, but all that did was loosen his hand, and a loud guffaw escaped his mouth. The three of us roared with laughter as Nadine huffed and puffed like the big bad wolf.

"Well, if you had put on a proper spread, I wouldn't have been forced to eat it. No wonder my shit smelt like roses for two days," Gran stated.

That piece of information caused my mother to crack and throwing down her napkin, she threw her head back and laughed. Tears were streaming down our faces as Adam, and I caught each other's eyes. It hardly seemed like the right time to bring up my bad news, but was there ever a good time?

Once the laughter had subsided, and Gareth adequately calmed Nadine and his incessant petting of her ego, my mother cleared her throat loudly. "Well, I think it's safe to say we shan't have any potpourri at your wedding, Charlene."

Adam's hand slid beneath the table and gripped my knee. I stared at him as he nodded slowly at me.

"Mum, there won't be any potpourri. There won't be any flowers at all."

She interrupted me before I could continue. "Oh, Charlene, why must you be so difficult? This wedding is going to be very dull if you keep changing things and at the last minute, too! How are we meant to make arrangements if you cannot stick to the original plans? Nadine, do you have your planner?"

Urgh. Nadine and her damn planner. That filo-fax followed that woman everywhere. Inside were detailed specifications for every aspect of my big day. The big day that was now to be completely cancelled. The two of them began flicking through the pages and oohing over fabric samples and pictures of the venue. My stomach churned, and my eyes began to well with unshed tears. I wasn't numb anymore. I was angry.

"Will you both just shut the hell up? No bridesmaids, no flowers, no potpourri, and no wedding! Okay?" I was screaming so loud, I was convinced the entire town had probably heard about my non-existent nuptials.

The whole room fell deadly silent as all eyes stared at me. I gulped a breath and tried to calm my anger. My mother smiled and shook her head as she began to collect plates and tidy the table. "It's just cold feet. You'll be fine on the big day. Now, Nadine, you were saying about seasonal flowers?" Standing abruptly, I slammed my fist on the table.

"No! Did you not hear me? There will be no wedding! It's cancelled, over, vetoed, and done."

My mother's jaw dropped as she gently and slowly placed the stack of plates she was holding down on the table. She stared at me, and I could feel the tears slowly sliding down my face.

"You called it off? I can't believe this. Less than three weeks until the big day, and you decide to have a breakdown and selfishly call off your wedding! Brad must be devastated, the poor man. Charlene, how could you be so cruel? Don't you have any care or consideration for anyone but yourself? This is so typical of you!"

Adam opened his mouth to interject, but I quickly placed my hand on his arm and shook my head. This was my battle.

"I didn't call it off, Mother! He did!"

Across the table, Nadine gasped and held her hand over her mouth. "You mean you're a jilted bride?"

I could see the smirk on her face even with her boney, thin, witch fingers covering her big collagen-filled mouth. I was about to shoot her a sarcastic remark or venom-filled insult, but Adam quickly jumped in before me.

"No, she's dodged a bullet. She's a survivor."

My mother glared at me. "What on Earth did you do, Charlene? Why would he call off the wedding like this? Don't give me that hurt expression, young lady. I demand to know what it was you did to make that poor man have to call off his wedding."

His wedding? *His* wedding! Was she serious right now? Not only had my mother completely missed the point, but she was also actually blaming me for it! Tears were now streaming down my face, and I heaved a breath. Then came the sobs.

"Are you freaking kidding me? You think I caused this? You really are a royal bitch sometimes, Mother. I didn't do anything. He's having an affair! He's been fucking someone else for weeks, probably months! That's why he called it off. Because he chose her instead!"

My gran cleared her throat beside me and shook her head. "Well, I warned you that if you gave the merchandise away so freely, no one would buy the store. Once again, no one listens to the rambling old woman."

My mother glared at her. "Oh, do shut up, Mother! This is none of your concern!"

Cool, calm, and as straight as a ruler, Gran gave my mother a large dose of her own medicine. "When it comes to marriage, men, and keeping one, you, my dear daughter, have no opinion or advice worth hearing. Pregnant by a married man who decided his thirty-year-old wife was preferable to his twenty-year-old fling. First husband up and died on you, and the second decided you really weren't worth the trouble. Tell me, where do you feel you earned the right to weigh in on anyone's relationship?"

My mother's mouth pressed into a hard line, and she shifted uncomfortably in her seat. Nadine leaned over and whispered something in Gareth's ear. Gran caught her, and I couldn't help but feel a sense of glee as her poison took aim at Miss Perfect. "And you, Miss Boobs-Bigger-Than-Her-Brain, just because you found a husband stupid enough to put up with your shit, doesn't mean that Charlene should settle for anything less than what she deserves. Gareth certainly deserves *you*. I do sometimes wonder if his brains are buried somewhere in those unsightly, and quite frankly, unnaturally large arms of his. He's as thick as two large tree trunks and is about as much use as a chocolate teapot. You're for decoration and ornamental purposes, and don't ever imagine you're anything more. You'd be terribly disappointed in the big scheme of things. Dress it up however you want dear, but you look like Barbie and Ken on steroids."

Adam tried to muffle his laughter as Gran winked at him. Turning her attention to me, she pulled out a handkerchief and handed it to me. "Now, clean yourself up, hold your head high, and move on. You've had a lucky escape. Imagine actually marrying that slimy waste of oxygen. I never did like that toad of a man. He was all mouth and not enough cock and balls. Girl needs a man who will fight for her and fuck her into the ground."

"Mother!" My mother's jaw almost hit the table as she gawped at my gran who simply shrugged.

"What? You all think that just because I'm old, I don't know a thing or two about sex? Good Lord. You'd think your generation invented the stuff. I hate to break it to you, but while you were learning to walk, young lady, *I* was crawling around on all fours. Your father had a cock like a battering ram and more energy than a Duracell bunny."

Adam blushed a deep shade of red while Gareth and Nadine gawped in horror at the eighty-two-year-old woman currently giving me visions that I would, no doubt, end up describing to a therapist later. I held my hands over my face and shook my head in disbelief.

"Charlene, you'll be just fine. And, if all else fails, you can always marry the doctor." She patted Adam's arm and gave him another quick wink. Running my hands over my red, blotchy, and tear-stained face, I groaned. "Well, this has been wonderful as usual. It's always nice to see you all. Thank God we only do it once a year. Thank you, once again, for the support during this awful time. Now, if you'll excuse me, I have an oven begging me to stick my head inside it. Goodbye and Merry Christmas."

Grabbing my coat and the small bag of gifts I had been presented with, I made my way to the door and fisted my hand on my hip. "Adam? Are you coming, or should I drive myself back?"

Quickly getting to his feet, he gave my family an awkward smile. "This was nice. Thanks for dinner, Mrs Winters. I guess I'll see you around." He looked a mixture of embarrassed, awkward, and sympathetic. But mostly, he looked relieved. I was simply angry. Angry for believing they could be anything but awful to me. Angry for allowing myself to be verbally pulverised. But most of all, I was angry with Brad. That arsehole had screwed me over in every way possible, and now I had to pick up the pieces of my broken heart, life, and dreams.

Adam rummaged around in his pocket for his keys as we walked down the driveway to the car. Opening the passenger door, I was about to slide in when my mother came totting down the path in her kitten-heeled slippers.

"Charlene! Charlene!"

Rolling my eyes, I turned around and leaned against the open car door. "What is it, Mother? Come to remind me what a tremendous fuck up I am? How I've ruined your mother of the bride experience? Please, tell me, I'm dying to know."

Biting her lip, she stood in front of me and shifted awkwardly. I groaned loudly and went to climb into the car, but she caught my shoulder and stopped me. Turning me to face her, she wrapped her arms around me tightly. I froze. My mother never ever hugged me. It just didn't happen. But for some bizarre reason, which to this day I still cannot fathom, she hugged me. I cast my eyes over at Adam who was resting his arms on the car roof and grinning at me. My eyes narrowed at him as I patted my mother gently on the back. Releasing me, she brushed herself down and straightened up. "Well, safe journey back. Call when you're home and well. Adam, lovely to see you, as always." He gave her a gentle nod, and we both watched, staring in amazement as she clip-clopped her way back to the house and closed the door. I turned and stared at Adam who gave me a bewildered look and ducked inside the car.

Sitting inside, I was still in shock. "What the hell was that?"

Adam chuckled as he turned the key, and the engine of his car roared to life. "Maybe she genuinely cares. Maybe she feels bad for you."

We both paused for a moment, pondering what had just taken place. I shook my head. "I don't know. What I do know is that I will never look at my gran the same ever again."

He laughed. "Me neither. Jeez, she's something else, but at least she had your back. And she's right you know. You should never settle for anything less than you deserve. And you deserve the world."

I gave him a weak smile before leaning my elbow on the door rest and gazing out of the window. Pulling out of the driveway, I took a deep breath as my stomach churned and flipped inside me. They knew. I was fairly certain that Nadine would take great delight in informing my close relatives about the cancelled wedding, and though I hated her, I was actually glad for her big, boasting mouth for a change. With her spreading it around, it meant I didn't have to. Reliving the horrible ordeal over and over again to every guest was not something I was looking forward to. Thank God for Ness and Dana. I was pretty confident that if I asked them, they'd handle all the gut-wrenching phone calls for me.

The silence inside the car was eerie. It wasn't awkward, just … quiet. I got the feeling that Adam was unsure of how to act or what to say. I mean, I'd been through breakups during our friendship, but nothing quite like this. Leaning forward I turned on the radio. Big mistake. As Harry Nilsson sweetly and loudly channelled my pain into words through his immortal lyrics from the song "Without You," my heart sank deep into my twisting stomach. Tears pooled in my eyes, and I couldn't help but feel completely and utterly exhausted. My journey would be a long one, and the hardest part was yet to come. I was headed back to an empty apartment, empty bed, and my inevitable heartache.

<u>Chapter 4</u>

Lying on the couch, I clutched my almost empty bag of pretzels in one hand while my family sized tub of Ben and Jerry's cookie dough ice cream gently melted as it sat in the crook of my arm. The spoon had long since been discarded, and I was now more in favour of the chocolate-covered digestives, which were sprawled across the coffee table, yet within my arms reach. They were ideal. Biscuit, chocolate, and big enough to scoop an entire mouthful of ice cream. Heaven. All it needed was a squirt of the whipped cream that lay pitifully beside the sofa, and I had the perfect diabetic coma.

Gripping the remote, I mindlessly flicked through the channels. It seemed that every television network had clearly heard of my plight and was torturing me by showing every sweet, romantic, happily ever after movie known to man. It could also have been my cynical and bitter misery of course. Turning it off and hurtling the remote across the room and out of my grasp, I stared up at the ceiling and sighed deeply. I was growing accustomed to the dull ache in my chest and even the sting of my cheeks from all the tears I had cried and yet, I was still unable to peel myself from the couch and leave the apartment. There was a distinct possibility that they would be removing my lifeless, three hundred tonne body from this apartment via a crane and the destruction of my living room wall. I was just pondering how much a coffin that size might cost when the intercom buzzed loudly from across the room.

I groaned and ignored it, choosing instead to turn over and reach for the whipped cream. I gave it a good shake and held it over my open mouth before squirting a large helping right in.

"Charlene Winters, open the damn door. It's fucking freezing, snowing, and I'm wearing suede boots! In the name of fashion, I demand that you let me in!"

Vanessa's desperate voice was wailing through my double glazed window. Even three floors up, I could hear the high-pitched shriek of a woman in a near-ruined pair of Pied A Terre boots! Grunting, I hauled myself from the sofa and pressed the door release button on the intercom. Opening the door a crack, I sauntered back over and flopped myself down onto my couch.

Pushing the door open, Ness gasped as her eyes took in the mess that covered my lounge floor, coffee table, and well, me.

"Charlene, this is ridiculous. You realise that you're a step away from me calling in the men in white jackets, right? I mean, look at this place." Picking up my Ben and Jerry's, she cringed at what was now a cookie dough flavoured soup shake with a few biscuit crumbs floating on top. "Urgh. When was the last time you actually saw daylight?"

In my depressed and deeply dark mood, I had decided to leave every curtain in my apartment closed. The sun was for happy people, and I was no longer a member of that society. Reaching for the whipped cream, I aimed it over my mouth and shrugged. "What day is it?"

"January seventh."

Squirting a large helping into my mouth, I gulped the delicious, sweet, and calorific cream down. "Then I'd say about two weeks."

"Two weeks! That's it. Enough is enough."

Pulling out her mobile, Ness hit the keypad and began dialling. "It's worse than we thought. I know I promised, but this is ridiculous. There's grieving, and then there's wallowing in your own cookie induced coma. She's a tub of ice cream away from an appearance on that hoarder's TV show. Just call Adam, and get your arse over here!"

I rolled my eyes and pulled a cushion from behind me to bury my face in. I could hear Ness pottering around, and as I peeked from beneath the cushion, sure enough, she was cleaning. Well, holding everything at arm's length, but clearing it into a black sack nonetheless. "You don't have to do that, Ness."

Prying the can of whipped cream from my fingers forcefully, she grinned in triumph. "Ha! Well, clearly you can't take care of yourself! Honestly, Charlene. You were dumped, not told you have an incurable disease. It's time to get up, pull yourself together, and get your arse in a bathtub."

I groaned loudly, but was interrupted by a towel being pulled from the dryer and flung at my head. "Now, Charlie. Don't make me drag you into that bathroom myself!"

I would have argued with her, had it not been for my desperate lack of energy or enthusiasm, and also the fact that even I could no longer stand the sticky patches in my hair. That's what you get for laying around and randomly dropping food into your mouth I suppose.

Leaving Ness to her mission of making my home once again hospitable, I sank myself into a hot, steamy bath and tried to soak away the tense and achy tightness that had set in throughout my entire body. Reaching for the shampoo, a lump formed in my throat as I spotted Brads ultra-sensitive body scrub on the shelf. After Adam had dropped me home on Christmas day, I'd packed all of Brad's things into black sacks and dumped them in the entrance of the apartment building. I called, but he wouldn't answer, so I simply left him a message informing him that he could pick up his things whenever he wanted. After I hung up, I realised that leaving them downstairs would give him a clean getaway, so I frantically dragged the bags back upstairs and waited for three days for him to collect it all. I wanted to see him, yell at him, and kick him in the nuts! But the bastard deprived me of the chance. He must have been watching the place because the one time I left the apartment in days, I returned to find everything gone and a note on my coffee table. I'd only been gone ten minutes, and the dirty little rat had snuck in and squirrelled everything away before I even got back! I felt utterly cheated and robbed.

Picking up the bottle of expensive soap, I hurled it at the wall. Okay, so I was still a little bitter and maybe even slightly vengeful, but surely he deserved it? The buzz of the intercom signalled that it was my cue to get out of the tub. I had been in there almost half an hour and was beginning to look like a prune. Drying myself off, I listened as my friends discussed my home, my personal life, and me.

"I told you to give her time, Ness! How does this help anyone? You swan in, throw your weight around and make her even more upset than she was. Urgh, I despise you sometimes."

Once again, Dana had jumped to my defence, but there really wasn't a need. Ness was right. I had been wallowing in my cesspit of despair for over two weeks. Maybe it was time to get up and face the world again. I did miss my job, and I even missed my plastic-stitched boss.

Emerging from the bathroom with my robe firmly around me, I waltzed into the lounge with my head high.

"Okay, stop. Just stop. Dana, be my friend and not my mother today, please?"

"I was just—"Dana began, but Ness quickly cut her off.

"You were just assuming you know best as always."

Rolling my eyes, I stood between them as they continued to bicker. The intercom buzzed again, and I actually breathed a sigh of relief. Pressing the button, I let Adam in. I knew it would be Adam. He was the only one who always pressed the buzzer three times in short bursts. He'd always been the same. When we were kids, he'd knock three times, and whenever I called him, he'd let it ring three times before answering. His mother called it obsessive compulsive. I called it a quirk.

Pushing through the door, he gave me a quick smile. "Are you okay? I've been worried. You won't return calls; you won't answer my texts. If it weren't for the fact that I come past this place every day and see your milk taken inside, I'd be worried you were dead." I was about to respond when Ness yelled loudly at Dana to keep her large nose out of other people's business. Something that for one, was rich coming from Miss Busy Body herself and two, Dana's nose was perfectly average. Turning his attention to our screeching friends, Adam pushed his way between them and gave them a dressing down. Which isn't as dirty as it sounds.

"Hey! Hey! Enough. I don't know what this is about, but when you call me at seven in the evening and say Charlie needs us, all kinds of stuff goes through my head. So, does someone want to explain what the hell is happening?"

Throwing myself onto the couch, I answered before either of them could. "Apparently, I require an intervention!"

"You do!" Dana and Ness yelled back at me. It was the first time they'd agreed since they'd arrived.

"Charlene, we get it. It hurts. You got dumped, but it happens. You're not the first, and you won't be the last. But you cannot sit around and eat yourself to death. What exactly would it achieve?"

I snorted a laugh. "I could try and claim the world record for death by dumping."

"See, you can't even be serious. You're so boring and sad all the time. I feel like I need a Prozac just to be in the room with you!"

Ness wasn't the most comforting of people, but she was usually right. Not that we ever told her that.

Holding my hands in the air, I groaned loudly. "Okay, fine. Tell me, oh great all-knowing ones, what exactly am I supposed to do?"

Adam blushed and pointed at my robe, which had loosened, and I was now sporting some side boob. "You could start with tightening your belt." Diverting his eyes, he shifted uncomfortably.

Taking my hand, Dana smiled. "You need to get out of here and start functioning as a human being again. You're turning into a bitter old woman."

Ness nodded enthusiastically, agreeing with Dana for a second time. Wonders never cease evidently! "You're a bleach blonde bob away from being your mother! And we know exactly how to remedy it."

With an uncomfortable knot in my stomach, I gave them all a confused look.

"Well, you know that wonderful honeymoon you had booked?" Ness had an expression of triumph, and I knew that wherever this was going; it was probably going to be troublesome.

"The one I should be on next week? Yes, believe it or not, I do remember that," I snapped back at her. But she simply brushed off my tone and continued.

"Well, I couldn't get a refund. But, what I did get was an exchange. Two tickets to Australia were exchanged for four tickets to Paris! We're still going to Disneyland, baby!"

I almost choked. "What?"

Adam, first checking I was adequately covered up, put his arm around me and grinned.

"You need some fun back in your life, and where else can you go for that than the place where fun is born? You remember when we were kids and we went there? It was the best time of our lives, and this time, we have these two as well. It'll be amazing, Charlie."

I gave Dana a pleading look, but she rebuffed me. "Not a chance, Charlene. I really want to go, and besides, we never got to do the hen party, and you were all for that idea before. Do you really want to be here when the twelfth rolls around? Holed up in your apartment and crying along to the radio—"

"And the afghan across the street," I interrupted.

They gave me a puzzled look.

"Long story. Really?"

Ness stamped her foot and fisted her hands on her hips. "Okay, fine, it's not ideal, but you had no problems with a trip to the magical kingdom when I planned your big send-off."

"That was before I was dumped and had my heart broken into a thousand pieces! If Disney taught me anything, it was that fairy tales, princes, and happily ever after were a way of life! I was cheated and lied to by them *and* Brad! There's no frog ready to be a prince, just toads who like a good licking. No wonderful fairy to make my dreams come true, just old women with cafes who make addictive cream cakes and treats for the depressed. And I imagine Pinocchio makes a great living as the biggest, lying, oral sexpert in the world! I'll pass."

Dana cringed. "Well, I'll never read that story in the same way again …"

Vanessa scowled at me. "This wallowing has gone on long enough. I bit my tongue when you holed yourself up in this pit and decided to eat your weight in chocolate, and I even kept my mouth shut when you declined an invite to my amazing New Year's Eve party so that you could spend it with your cat! But this, Charlene, is the last straw. Now, get your arse in that bedroom and pack a case or else I'll drag you to Paris in that robe and force you to buy your entire vacation wardrobe! Got it?"

Wide-eyed and feeling like a scolded child, I nodded and shuffled down the hall to my room. Opening the wardrobe, I rolled my eyes at the section I had affectionately called *the honeymooner's outfits*. It was mostly kaftans, swimsuits, and lingerie, but now it all looked repulsive. Closing it quickly, I opened the *fat girl* wardrobe and began flinging frumpy and unflattering outfits into my case. I had no idea what I actually packed as I had been so upset at having to actually wear them, that I simply couldn't bear to look. I threw on some jeans and a sweater before heading out the door.

Dragging the case behind me, I trudged back into the living room. Jacob had, as usual, snuggled down next to Adam and was giving him pleading looks for some affection. Adam wasn't really a cat person, but he and Jacob had an understanding. They'd reached this after I had gone out of town for a few days on business. Adam had promised to take care of Jacob for me and make sure the little guy was fed every day. I was relieved to find someone so willing considering Jacob's temperament and downright disrespectful attitude toward anyone but me. I'd only been gone two days when Adam let himself into the apartment, and as he had done before, he laid food out and called for my bad-tempered kitty. He knew Jacob must have been eating as the dish was always empty, but he hadn't yet seen him. Anyway, he was just about to leave when a blood-curdling scream echoed through the apartment. Naturally, Adam searched the entire place but found absolutely nothing. It wasn't until he sat down on the sofa to calm his nerves that he discovered where the noise had come from.

Sitting at Adam's feet, looking smug and extremely pleased with himself was Jacob. And in Jacobs's mouth was an enormous toad. The poor thing was screeching for its life, and as Adam pulled it from Jacobs's mouth, the cat then decided to try and climb his leg to retrieve his prize. In the craziness, Adam dropped the toad, and it scrambled beneath the sofa. So there they were—the toad, hiding under the settee, and Adam holding up said sofa with one hand and trying desperately to hold Jacob back from it. He managed to save the poor thing but not before enduring a scratching session from Jacob. What Adam described next was something akin to a Mexican standoff: Jacob on one side of the room, and Adam on the other, with the toad in the centre of this showdown. It was cat reflexes versus Doctor Dolittle. Leaping on the creature, Adam scooped the toad up in his hands, and tossed it from the floor out of the open window. Jacob chased after it, but sitting on the window ledge, he decided the jump wasn't worth the prize. Glaring at Adam, the two of them formed a mutual respect. I assumed Jacob felt any human that was that dedicated to saving a toad deserved a little slack. And I think Adam was just impressed at Jacobs's determination for eating it. Either way, it made my life a lot easier.

Walking over, I gave the little guy a tickle behind the ear. Jacob, not Adam. Though I'm sure, Adam wouldn't have minded the attention.

"Who's going to look after Jacob while I'm gone?"

Adam looked up and smiled at me. "I've got it covered. Your gran is going to stay here while we're gone and cat sit."

I gawped at him. "My gran? Are you nuts? I have to go hide some things!"

Catching my elbow, Ness shook her head. "No time. The cab is on its way. Say goodbye to Jacob, and let's go!"

Flinging open the front door, she marched merrily down the stairs. I glanced back at Dana who simply shrugged, gave Jacob a quick fuss, and followed Ness out.

"Adam, please don't make me do this."

He smiled and stood beside me, throwing his arm around my shoulder, and taking my case in his free hand.

"It's going to be fine. You'll see. I'll take this down and meet you at the car." Giving me a quick wink and a peck on the forehead, he left. I sat on the sofa next to my bewildered cat.

"There's no easy way to tell you this. We've been dumped, ditched, and now we're being subjected to hell on Earth. I have to admit, yours is worse. Just stay out of her way, and try not to bring home any nasty surprises. I'll only end up blamed for them, and you'll end up neutered. I think we can agree that you like your balls as much as I like my peace and quiet. Do we have a deal?"

He gave me a look that suggested he had somewhat understood my predicament, but with a sigh and a snuggle, he simply turned over and began cleaning his crotch. Great. Even the males in the *feline* world were neglecting me for their genitals! Maybe I needed this holiday more than I thought.

Chapter 5

The taxi ride from the airport to the park seemed to take forever. Dana and Ness had spent the entire flight and now the short drive to the hotel, pouring over the itinerary for the next four days. Yes, four days with two princesses bigger than any that Disneyland had to offer. Adam gave me a sympathetic smile from across the table. Rolling my eyes, I fumbled mindlessly with the styrofoam cup, which had contained a bitter espresso that promised to 'perk me up,' but was so far falling flat. It's not as though I wasn't grateful to them, but this really wasn't the trip to the Magic Kingdom I had originally been planning on taking.

Ness and Dana had booked us an amazing long weekend for my hen party. They'd each arranged specific challenges and had even bought us princess outfits. I wasn't thrilled at the idea of wearing an enormous ball gown on a rollercoaster, but it did sound like a good bit of fun. And now, I'm going to spend my time there wallowing over my broken engagement and suffering the high-pitched squeals of my two twenty-six, going on twelve-year-old, friends.

"Oh, Oh! I can see the castle from here! This is going to rock," Dana squeaked while bouncing animatedly up and down in her seat.

"Will you act your age for five minutes? God, it's like travelling with a ten year … Oh my God, look at that hotel!"

Ness's attempt to seem sophisticated and unaffected by the lure of the fantasy world was not as convincing as she'd hoped. As we approached the New York-themed hotel, even I had to admit it was a little awesome.

Ness and Dana practically leapt from their seats and hurried into the hotel, leaving Adam and I to pay the taxi and collect our bags. Typical.

Hauling the bags from the trunk, Adam raised an eyebrow at me.

"Well, this is going to be an interesting break. With the Tinkerbell twins acting like children and with you making a face like you just got kicked in the gut, I'd say an all-round successful trip so far."

I raked my fingers through my mass of red hair.

"This is not what I had in mind to help me get over being ditched."

He gave a throaty laugh. "I'm sure it's not. And ice cream, cookies, whipped cream, and stagnating on your couch was working so much better. There aren't any rules or instructions on how to break up, Charlie. You just have to roll with the punches."

Bustling out of the entrance door, Ness held an array of maps in her hands.

"Okay, so here's how this is going to work. Rule number one: no one is to even utter that shit streak Brad's name from this point onward. Rule number two: wallowing in self-pity is strictly prohibited. Rule number three: you will dump every pair of yoga pants and fat girl t-shirts the moment we unpack.

This has got to stop. And the final rule: you will spend the next four days doing exactly as you are told by the three of us." She glanced at Adam who was shaking his head at her.

"Well, me and Dana then. Any questions?"

I wanted to slap her around the face and scream that she was nuts if she thought I was spending the next four days under her reign of terror. But, I decided a vow of silence was going to be far less trouble. Throwing her a simple 'whatever,' I grabbed my case and dragged it behind me into the hotel.

* * * *

The room Ness had booked for us was enormous, and I didn't even want to hazard a guess at the cost. The entire suite was decorated in a 1920s New York style. Ness had already begun hanging her clothes in every possible wardrobe, which left a small chest of draws and very slim closet for Dana and me to share. Lucky for Dana, she was as thin as a broom handle, and therefore, her clothes took up very little space. This thankfully left more room for my tents, pool covers, and bed sheets that I called outfits. But, what Ness pulled out of her case next was anything but frumpy. Holding her hand above her head, she displayed a pale blue and white ball gown.

"Oh my God. You didn't? Please, tell me that you did not bring those horrific costumes!" Dana begged with a look of sheer terror on her face, but it was no use. Tossing the ball gown on the bed, Ness produced a Little Mermaid outfit and a Snow White quickly followed. I held my hand over my eyes, as though not looking would make the horrible things disappear.

"You don't honestly still expect us to wear those do you, Vanessa?" I asked knowing full well what the answer would be.

"Of course we're wearing them! And don't full name me. You only get to full name me when I've broken a girl code rule. No rule was broken here and no way either of you are crawling out of this."

I snickered mockingly. "Crawl out of it? Ness, when we bought those, I was at least three sizes smaller! I'll be interested to know how I can possibly cram my grande sized arse *into* it!"

Dana picked up the Snow White outfit with a coat hanger and held it at arm's length. "Oh, this is just hideous."

Ness fisted her hands on her hips. "Well, I like that gratitude. I paid an extra forty pounds to get that through customs. That ball gown alone weighs a tonne!"

Dana gave me a sympathetic look, and I knew right away that she was swaying in Ness's favour. Shaking my head fiercely, I held my hands up. "Not a chance. I am not playing Cinderella, and I am not wearing that dress! I should have been sliding into my wedding dress this week, not an itchy, nylon outfit that looks as though an eight-year-old dreamed it up! No, no, no!"

The two of them stared at me, and a game of 'who will crack first' began. I had been jilted, cheated, and dragged across the pond. There was no way I was going to humiliate myself any further. No chance at all!

* * * *

Sitting in the most disgustingly happy bar I had ever seen, I gripped my martini and groaned. Ness, suitably dressed as the Little Mermaid and currently on her third blue lagoon, chatted animatedly to the 'Wild West' themed bartender. Dana had managed to wedge herself between the two of us, and with a red bow in her hair, she scoured the drinks menu which she had been clasping for the past half an hour. So there we were, three girls from London dressed as princesses and each of us prince-less. Drowning my sorrows, I looked around at the packed restaurant area and wondered if we would ever get to eat this evening. I was just about to flag down the maître d when a small and over-excited child bowled into my stool and caused my entire drink to spill all over my pale blue ball gown.

The damn thing already made me look like a sausage about to burst its skin, and now damp, it was not looking any better. The parents gave me a quick smile before hurrying to the restaurant, where they were immediately seated! Irritated and hungry, I stood and began wiping myself down with some of the napkins from the bar. Dana looked up from her menu and gave me a confused look.

"Child. Drink. Wet dress. Not only do I feel pathetic, but now, I look it as well. This is a disaster! I was supposed to be on my hen weekend. It was supposed to be sparkly dresses, tiaras, and happily ever after! And now look at me. My dress is soaked. My tiara is with my discarded wedding dress in a cold and dark closet in London, and my happily ever after is never ever after since the man in my life up and left me for the frog princess! When is my handsome Prince Charming ever going to show up? Because I'm beginning to lose my patience."

Ness, who was now glaring at me since I had interrupted her flirtations with the bartender, was about to respond when the door behind us flew open, and Adam coughed loudly. Dana smiled and tried to hide a giggle as I turned around to find him standing behind me in a dapper white and gold prince's outfit. His dark hair was parted at one side, and for some reason, he looked … taller and even broader than usual. Maybe it was those shoulder pads. Biting my bottom lip, I blushed.

"Prince Charming at your service, Cinderella. Well, for tonight anyway. Besides, looks as though you only have 'til midnight."

He laughed sweetly, and I couldn't help but soften. Adam had a way of making everything seem better somehow. He was my security blanket and comforter, and I really needed it right now.

"Where's your drink?" He pointed to my empty glass.

I was about to answer, but Dana interrupted me. "A kid knocked it all over her."

I rolled my eyes. "I'd love a martini." I knew that's what he was really asking, and we knew each other well enough to leave out the middle conversation.

"Ness, considering the bartender is more interested in your lack of clothes than me waving my cash around, ask him for a martini and a beer, will you?"

Ness glanced down at her bright purple shell bra and grinned. "Jealous, Adam? And stop ogling my goodies."

Groaning, he handed her the cash and gave me a quick smile. "So, when do we get to eat?"

I sniggered. "In this place? Let's just say I think we may have stepped into Never-Neverland."

He laughed and gave me a wink before heading into the restaurant. Dana, again, gave me a confused look, but I simply shrugged. Returning minutes later with the maître d in tow, Adam held out his hand for me. "If anyone asks, you are a soap legend from Hollywood, and we just wrapped up a great episode. So, you know, don't open your mouth if anyone comes over."

I feigned offence.

"I love you, Charlie, but if you utter a word, that broad London cockney girl accent of yours will blow our cover. Awl right luv?"

I almost choked on my drink as I laughed at him. Adam was my hero. Prince Charming was a fantasy, and I needed a real life, breathing dream man. But for now, Adam would do just fine.

* * * *

After gorging myself on steak, potatoes, and a mountain of vegetables, I pushed my practically licked-clean plate away and slumped heavily in my seat. Ness had been picking at her vegetable grill platter for at least half an hour and had managed to nibble on a carrot before also pushing the plate away.

"Well, that was a waste of time. It's cold and totally unappetising."

Adam pulled Ness's plate toward him and stabbed a large grilled pepper with his fork before shoving it into his mouth.

"Seems okay to me. You're just too fussy."

Dana and I exchanged glances. This was about to get heated ... again.

"I am not fussy!" Ness spat back.

Adam nodded enthusiastically at her from across the wheel and spoke dining table. "You are so! You're fussy over food, restaurants, cars, fashion shops, men—"

"I am not fussy about cars!"

I held my hand over my mouth and snorted a laugh, and suddenly, the attention fell on me. Giving her a sarcastic smile, I placed a hand gently on Vanessa's.

"Remember when I bought that mini? You know, the one that looked like it was out of *The Italian Job*? You refused to even get in it! You said it was tacky, outdated, and cheap."

Biting her lip anxiously, she looked to Dana for support, which she was clearly not going to get.

"You are fussy, Ness. Remember my twentieth birthday? I invited you to my favourite little restaurant. You were there ten minutes and started yelling that your soup was cold!"

Ness gasped in horror. "It was cold!"

"It was gazpacho! It was supposed to be cold!" Dana snapped back.

"And what's more, you kicked up such a stink about the whole thing that I was told that if I returned, it had to be without you! You were banned!"

Adam slammed his fist on the table and laughed loudly. People began staring at us, but even I couldn't contain my own laughter.

"You're all just mean. Here I am trying to cheer up our Charlie, and you two start calling me names. Well, I like that." Her sarcasm was no match for a heartwarming embrace from the man in our lives. Wrapping his arm around her shoulders, Adam pressed a firm kiss to her cheek.

"And yet, with all of your faults, and there are a lot of them, we still love you Ness-Monster."

He gave her a quick wink, and a sliver of a smile appeared on her lips. Poking her tongue out at us all, she giggled.

"Well, maybe a little. But, what you call fussy I call high standards. Speaking of which, has anyone else noticed that the guy at the table behind us has been checking Dana out all evening?"

Simultaneously, we all rubber-necked around at the table directly behind ours.

"Very subtle guys." Rolling her eyes, Ness took a big gulp of her drink.

The man looked very young and was dressed in a black sweater and faded blue jeans. Catching Dana glancing at him, he gave her a beaming smile. Naturally, she blushed a deep shade of coral. Even dressed in her Snow White get up, Dana was a knockout.

"Go say hi," I whispered.

"Are you nuts? She can't approach him! He has to send her a drink or something. Make his move first," Ness stated, as though she was the authority on picking up a guy in a bar. Well, she probably was. Ness had never been short of a lover and had no time for dating. So, Mr. Right was never an option as far as she was concerned. No, Mr. Right Now was all Ness wanted.

Bickering amongst ourselves, it wasn't until Dana let out a small squeak that we glanced over, and to our horror, found Adam sitting at the guy's table, pointing to us!

"Oh my God. Oh, my God. Oh my God! What is he doing?" Dana was frantic. For a stunning girl, she really lacked the confidence she ought to have had.

I wanted to reassure her that it would be fine, but giving the guy a nod, Adam grinned and headed back to our table. Sitting back down, he took a large swig of beer. We all sat there, waiting expectedly.

"What?" he asked.

"What do you mean *what*? What did he say?" Ness demanded.

"Oh, his name's Gareth. He's twenty-three, and he's an estate agent. Oh, and he's coming over to meet you." Moving over to the next chair, Adam gestured for Gareth to join us.

Dana stared at the table, while Ness and I were glued to Gareth. You see, for twenty-three, Gareth was certainly handsome. He was blonde with chiselled good looks and a dimple in his chin but … he was short. Now, when I say short, I mean short. This guy was easily two feet shorter than Dana.

Dana gave me a puzzled look, but I simply smiled and gave her a thumbs up. *A thumbs up.* What on Earth was I thinking? Suspicious, she immediately swivelled 'round in her seat and gawped in horror. Turning back sharply, her eyes widened, and she stared at me.

"He's tiny!" she mouthed.

Reaching our table, he sat beside her and took her hand in his.

"Bonjour. Dana is it?"

He was French. Okay, that was at least one point in his favour.

"Uh, yes and you're Gareth, right?"

Dana looked utterly terrified. Desperate to put her out of her misery, I held out my own hand.

"Hi, I'm Charlene, this is Ness, and Adam you already know."

Taking my outstretched hand, he shook it politely while smiling and nodding at Ness and Adam.

"So, what brings you to Paris, Dana? Holiday? Fun? Or looking for that special romance?"

Ness held her glass to her lips and grinned. "I think you definitely could do with a *little* romance, Dana. Don't you think so, Charlie?"

I pressed my lips together tightly and tried not to laugh.

"Oh, I think Dana has never been *short* of admirers."

"OUCH!" Ness and I yelled as Adam kicked the two of us beneath the table and glared at us both.

Dana shifted uncomfortably. "Can't say I've really thought about romance, but actually, we're here for fun. You see, Charlene recently broke up with her fiancé, and we thought she could do with a break."

Closing my eyes and shaking my head, I wished the ground would swallow me whole. But it didn't. Gareth gave me a confused look.

"I'm sorry, I thought you and Adam were ..."

"No, no, no, no, no, no," we both chanted.

"Sorry, I didn't mean to offend. It's just ... I saw you in the bar, and the way you were together over dinner just seemed so ... familiar. Comfortable even."

Adam gave me a broad smile.

"We've been together a long time, but purely in a platonic sense. Don't worry, you're not the only one to ever make that assumption."

Dana gave me an apologetic look.

"Sorry," she mouthed. I threw her a quick smile before pushing my chair away from the table, sighing loudly.

"On that note, I'm going to find a bar, sit in it, and drink 'til I either ferment or fall down. Who's joining me?"

Getting to their feet, Ness and Adam both accepted my invitation while Dana stood staring down at Gareth who, yes, was also standing. I was right. At least two feet between them. Giving her a sweet smile, he offered his arm, which she awkwardly accepted, and the two of them led the way out of the restaurant.

"Come, I know just the place for us!" Gareth shouted back. Dana glanced behind her at the three of us and pleaded with her eyes for some help, but all we could do was smile encouragingly and try extremely hard, not to laugh. This evening was beginning to look up. Just like Gareth to Dana.

* * * *

Three bars later, I was done. Dana had been trying desperately to give poor, love-struck Gareth the brush off for hours. Ness had drunk her weight in vodka tonic, and the weight of my fourteen stone body was beginning to wreak havoc on my feet. Ness had ensured that I had the complete Cinderella outfit, which included a pair of ridiculously high and fragile re-enforced glass slippers. They were so fragile, in fact, that as we left the last bar, Ness had staggered into me, caught my elbow, swung me around and almost off of my feet. Thankfully, Adam had caught us both, but not before I had clipped my shoe on a protruding piece of concrete. The heel, naturally, shattered into pieces, and I was left hobbling for the rest of the evening. Teetering and tottering across the street toward our hotel, I was forced to grip Adam's arm for support.

He had obviously realised the pain I was in because as we approached the harbour, yes, a man-made harbour for theme purposes, he suggested we have a little rest.

Dangling my legs over the edge of the jetty, I moaned loudly as I pulled off my one remaining slipper. My feet throbbed. And not that little ache you get after dancing in stilettoes all night—oh no. I'm talking pulsating, red hot, walked over hot coals kind of pain! If I had dipped a toe in the water, it would have sizzled like a steak into a hot pan.

Adam chuckled beside me. "Well, this is certainly an interesting evening."

I gave him a puzzled and slightly irritated look. I found nothing interesting about it at all. I was in perky, colourful hell!

"Well, first you lose your glass slipper, Cinders. Dana has been hounded all evening by quite possibly the tiniest twenty-three-year old I have ever seen. I mean, under four foot, does he count as a dwarf or a midget? And then there's Vanessa. Drinking like a fish, dressed like one, and now totally legless and swimming around in the giant fountain. Proper fish out of water, that girl."

I turned around and caught sight of my red wig-wearing friend splashing around in the large and elegant water fountain. Apparently, she had sat down to remove her flippers and had fallen backwards into the damn thing. It wasn't that she was swimming as such, but more that she just couldn't get back up again. As long as her head was above water, I wasn't concerned. Dana, on the other hand, was trying to wish little Gareth good night, but he insisted on walking her to the hotel. He was a little full on, and the last straw had come while we were sipping cocktails in a tiki-themed bar. Leaning across the table, one hand in hers while the other tried casually to slide up her yellow, puffy, nylon dress, he professed his undying lust for her! The air was blue with the filthy things that horny little dwarf wanted to do to my friend. It took all my strength not to punch him and all of Ness's to stop Adam from doing it. Dana merely blushed, shook her head and said, "That all sounds … different, but I think I'll pass." But he clearly saw this as a challenge. Poor Dana never stood a chance. He followed us to every bar we went to and tried endlessly to serenade her.

Holding my head in my hands, I groaned. "This is a nightmare. When did my life come to this? I mean, where did I go wrong?"

Draping an arm around my shoulder, Adam shrugged.

"I don't think it was you who did anything wrong, Charlie. It was that arse-hat Brad. You were way out of his league. There's punching above your weight, and then there's bringing a ping-pong racket to a boxing match. You know you're likely to get it shoved up your arse."

I giggled a little at the thought. "Yeah, well, I still said yes when he proposed. I thought I knew him. I thought he loved me and that we'd spend the rest of our lives together, but it turns out I was just a wench to cook, clean, and wait for him to come home while he fucked his entire office. And here I am. Sitting in a fake harbour, in a ridiculous dress, minus one shoe, looking like the world's worst princess and what's more, totally prince-less."

"You just feel bad *now*. It will pass. But you have to admit; wallowing in your apartment for two weeks wasn't the smartest move to help you get through this. I mean, did you even see in the New Year?"

I nodded. "Of course I did. Lying on the sofa, cat beside me for company, and a mini heart attack in the form of my meal of a burger and fries. I passed out right before the bell struck the final time at midnight."

Adam rolled his eyes. "Pitiful. You really are determined to let him win, aren't you? Well, I'm not. Where is my Charlie? The no shit, no mess, and never give up girl who I met in a school gymnasium all those years ago? I miss her. That fuckwit has dragged every last piece of her out, and I've spent the entire time picking them up and holding on to them 'til you're ready to put yourself back together. Now, are you still the same Charlie that kicked the crap outta James Hill or not?"

I thought for a moment about the person I had become since meeting Brad—weak, easily led, good little mouse-wife in training. Who the hell was I? Cleaning, ironing, and starching his pants was not the way I had envisioned living my life, and yet, somehow, that's exactly where I had ended up. And while I was losing myself, he was finding Aneska! Growling, I got to my feet and stomped loudly. I was going to have a tantrum, and I didn't care how ridiculous I looked. I yelled, roared, and stamped around like a five-year-old.

"That dickwad ruined my life! He swans in, turns my world on its head, and I let him do it! Argh! That's it!"

Unzipping my extremely uncomfortable dress, I pulled it down, kicked it off and flung it into the water below. Standing in my underwear, I suddenly realised how cold it was, and Adam must have, too. I don't know if it was the goose pimples on my skin or the fact that my nipples were so hard they could have cut bricks, but he immediately removed his jacket and wrapped me in it.

"You're nuts. But I love you. So, what's the plan, Wonder Woman?"

Smiling for the first time in a long while, I began reeling off the list of self-help steps I had mentally noted.

"Number one, lose some damn weight! I don't even recognise myself in the mirror anymore. Number two, go on lots of dates and have lots of hot, dirty, and raunchy sex. I'm sick of sterile, boring, missionary Brad sex! And number three, have some damn fun! When did I become so boring? I'm Charlene Winters! I'm the girl that won an All-You-Can-Eat contest in L.A. I'm the girl who bungee jumped with her best friend for his birthday. I'm the girl who wing-walked at the local air display! No, it's about time I did some dumping myself. Goodbye boring, Brad-beaten, frumpy Charlene. Hello, Charlie!"

Swinging me around, Adam squeezed me tightly. "There's my girl! God, I've fucking missed you!"

Giggling, I hugged him back. "I love you, Adam. What would I do without you?"

Putting me back on my feet, he nodded across the way at Dana and Ness.

"Probably end up like them."

I laughed and shook my head. "We should probably go and rescue them. You take Snow White and her horndog dwarf, and I'll take the Little Mermaid over there."

Nodding, he took my hand and led me away from the harbour, away from the disgusting floating dress, and away from the old Charlene. Adam wasn't the Prince Charming I was searching for, but he was the one I needed right now.

<u>Chapter 6</u>

Walking back into my apartment, I winced at the thought of what might be waiting for me. Almost immediately darting for the door, through my feet and down the stairs, Jacob had clearly had a rough few days. I glanced around the apartment, and my stomach churned. Sleeping on the couch, her glasses at the tip of her nose, and the 'hot guys for mature ladies' channel playing, Gran snored loudly.

Making a beeline for the TV, I quickly switched it off and breathed a sigh of relief before the next instalment of *Granny Humpers* started. I shivered at the thought of what the hell may have gone on while I was gone. With the bottles of Bailey's and dozens of empty chocolate wrappers on the floor, it looked like a bombsite.

I tried desperately to creep past, but as I rolled my case through my littered lounge, it hit a rogue bottle, and the old woman sharply grunted and woke up.

"Oh, you're back."

I gave her a smile. "Yep. How was … everything?" I nudged an empty box of chocolate creams on the floor with my foot, and I was almost certain I heard something squeak.

"How was what? It's only a cat, Charlene. Give a stroke, stuff it now and again, and it purrs for hours just like any other pussy."

I cringed. My Gran was the crassest creature you could ever meet, but she was usually right on the ball. I used to tell my friends that she behaved this way because she was senile, 'til she overheard me one day and decided to call my bluff. She waltzed down our living room stairs in her knickers and began loudly singing show tunes. My mother almost had a heart attack when she started a chorus of "I'm too sexy."

"I see Jacob was keen to get out. You were letting him out, weren't you, Gran?" I asked, knowing the answer.

"Letting him out? Do I look like his concierge? I left the window open, and if he's too lazy to jump, that's his problem. Pushy, posh, pompous, pissed off pussy."

I rolled my eyes and began gathering up the debris that was scattered across the apartment.

"Well, thanks anyway."

Hoisting her arse from the sofa, she waddled over to my phone.

"Thank you nothing. Four days, cable TV, food, drink, and a vibrator—I never had to leave the house! Bliss."

A little vomit made its way up my throat, and I had to force myself not to be violently sick. A vibrator? Surely she …

I stared at my couch in horror. Yes, she probably did, and I would now be sterilising my entire apartment as though Brad and I had been having sex all over it. He really was a freak of nature with his severe germ phobia.

"Well, that's my cab ordered. I take it you had an enlightening break?" Pulling her cardigan around her, she gave me an inquisitive smile.

"It was eye-opening. I spent a lot of time with Adam, and that was definitely what I needed."

She grinned wildly. "Ah, so the doctor finally gave you that physical you've been needing, eh? Did he show you his equipment? Good, was it? I bet he's a right horny little bugger. The quiet ones are usually the best. They don't say much, but they screw you so hard that you feel like you've been hit by a bus right between your thighs."

"Gran! No, he didn't. God, for the last time, Adam is my best friend, and that's as far as it will ever go."

Huffing, she shook her head at me. "You poor, naive, under-sexed, and overly cautious girl. You really are as blind as a beggar. There's a perfectly good specimen of a man hanging around you like a puppy, and there's you acting like a bitch in heat and ignoring the dog that's been dry humping your leg for years. And they say I'm senile."

I sighed and ran my hands over my face. Gran had always been convinced that I should end up with Adam. The truth was, she had always liked him, and as he got older, she would often comment on his striking good looks. Though I struggled to see what it was she saw in him, it became her mission to get the two of us shacked up and shagging. I had come to the conclusion that the old bag was living vicariously through me. But Adam was my friend, and no force on Earth was going to change that. Boyfriends, girlfriends, and a fiancé had passed between us, but our bond was the strongest relationship either of us had ever had.

After seeing her downstairs and safely into her cab, I returned to my empty apartment and threw a sheet over my sofa before slumping down onto it. Jacob had snuck in while I was cramming Gran into the car and was now snuggled happily beside me. Lifting him up and onto my lap, I groaned.

"Seems I'm not the only one who needs a diet, fat boy. I hope you're ready for this. We, my little munchkin, are going to get fit, healthy, and laid. Well, I'm sure you have no trouble with the ladies, stud—if that God awful screeching outside my window every evening is any indication. Just don't expect me to be happy when some little queen turns up with ten kittens. I'm not feeding your mistakes."

Looking up at me, he sighed and quickly made himself comfortable before falling asleep. Turning on the TV, I grabbed a notepad from beside the sofa and began jotting down some ideas to help me achieve my new goals. By the time I had finished, three things were clear. First, I really didn't know much about dieting at all, considering I'd spent most of my life the size of a bean pole. Second, Jacob had clearly been at Gran's bottles or else had befriended a nice Irish man. And third, this was going to be a long process.

* * * *

"You want me to do what?" Dana squeaked down the phone.

"Fitness classes. Oh, come on, Dana. It'll be fun. Remember when we were in college? We used to work out together all the time."

"We did that to meet guys. Who the hell are we going to meet going to those things you suggested? It's a room full of middle-aged women jiggling their muffins around. I think I'll pass."

Pouting, I began pleading. "Oh, please, Dana. You know I'd do it for you. Besides, you owe me one."

She gasped. "I do not! When, what for?"

"Danny Bowman. You wanted to dump him to go out with Matthew Giles and couldn't bear to see the poor bastard cry. So who took him out, sweetened him up, and then broke the awful news to him?"

"That was six years ago! And you had sex with him!"

I cleared my throat and shifted uncomfortably in my seat. Admittedly, sleeping with him hadn't been part of the plan, but it got her off the hook. Poor Danny was so guilt-ridden the next day that he confessed the whole thing to Dana, who I had already told, and she got to dump him for cheating. Totally guilt free break-up.

"At the same time, you were knocking boots with his roommate! Don't get high and mighty with me. I took one for the team. We both know Danny wasn't the greatest lover. I was sore for days. I'm sure he thought oral sex meant actually eating me!"

She chuckled a little, and I knew I had won.

"Oh, all right. Fine, I'll go, but if I see so much as one flabby arse cheek burst out of its tight shorts, I'm out."

"I'll wear something baggier," I offered.

"Very funny. You're really serious about this, aren't you?"

Glancing at myself in the mirror, I rolled my eyes at my dumpling reflection. "Like a heart attack."

Which is what I was probably a doughnut away from if I didn't get my arse into gear and into a gym.

"When do you go back to work?" she asked, knowing well enough that I was trying desperately not to think about it. Walking into the office would be the biggest challenge I had faced yet. Everyone had been invited to my now-cancelled wedding, and they would all know why I had taken a leave of absence. The morning catwalk down the hall would be filled with whispers, sympathetic looks, and comforting hands on my shoulder. Not to mention the mail clerk Henry trying desperately to *accidentally* feel me up. Twenty-seven years old, and built like a brick house, you'd think he was getting more action than a gigolo, but yet he insisted on squeezing past me in corridors, leaning across me at tables and inevitably, brushing my boobs as he did so. I'd have filed a complaint against him, except recently, it was the only form of sexual contact I was getting on a regular basis.

"Tomorrow. Urgh, don't make me go," I begged. Yes, begged. I was that desperate and let's be honest, I wasn't exactly at the top of my game. Cut me some slack.

"I think it will be good for you. Some … normality back in your life. You've got a golden opportunity to re-invent yourself. New look, a new man, and new promotion? You said it yourself, your boss loves you, and she's always giving you great artists to work with. Aim high and snag the next big act that walks into that office. You'll be made partner before you know it!"

I pondered for a moment. I was the best we had. And acts were even beginning to request that I be their publicist and all-around go-to girl. Maybe I could ask for a promotion or at least hint at it.

"You might be on to something there."

"Of course I am! You, Charlene, are the most ambitious, hardworking, and glamorous woman I know. You are gonna bounce back from this stronger, fitter, hotter, and more amazing than ever. I know it. Brad is going to rue the day he let you slip through his fingers. His scrotum will hit the floor when he sees you. That cock-sucking, dick-riding, cowgirl, Aneska, has nothing on you."

I gave a small chuckle. "Okay, Tonto. I gotta go. I'll see you on Friday? Three o'clock."

She groaned. "Yes. I'll be there."

Hanging up, I hugged myself. I truly had the best friends in the world. Who needed Brad when I had people like Dana in my life, and a perfectly good … cringing, I made a mental note … buy a new vibrator.

Chapter 7

Hauling my gym bag beside me, I pushed my way into the gym. The smell of sweat immediately wafted up my nostrils, and I gagged loudly. Dana cringed beside me.

"Oh my God. Charlene, it smells like crotch in here!"

Snorting a laugh, I held my hand over my mouth and nose. She wasn't wrong. It wreaked, but the need to lose weight was overruling my need for fresh—or at least less clammy—air. Holding our breath, we made our way through the reception to the large aerobics hall at the far end. If there was ever a fear of us being blinded by old women and their cellulite … we were wrong. A sea of slim, fit, toned, and tall beauties turned and began scanning us up and down.

"I feel naked. Let's go. We clearly don't belong here."

Spinning around, I moved toward the exit, but Dana blocked my path.

"Nope. You wanted to do this, and I bet they didn't always look like that. Maybe this class really works!"

I furrowed my brow at her "Do you ever drop that optimistic glass you carry around?"

Dumping her bag on a bench, which was pushed against the white-washed wall, she smiled brightly. "Nope."

Well, of course, she was feeling good! As she slipped off her coat, I stared at her wide-eyed. Wearing a pair of tight leggings, a sports top that showed off far too much of her toned midriff, Dana was right at home amongst these women. I groaned in displeasure.

"Are you kidding me? Where did you get that body, and how much did you pay for it?"

She tilted her head to the side and tutted. "You had one, too, 'til Brad started steamrolling your fitness regime. Remember?"

Did she *always* have to be right?

A loud clapping pulled me from my jealous glare at Dana, and my attention was now focused on the petite, short blonde-haired, and clearly never-ate-a-cake in her life, fitness instructor at the front of the room.

"Hello everyone! It's nice to see so many familiar faces, and I notice some new ones. Come up!"

I gawped at Dana who shrugged, grabbed my hand, and began dragging me to the front of the class.

"Hi, hello! It's always nice to have new blood in our class. I'm the instructor, Francesca. Is this your first time at Zumba?"

I stood awkwardly as dozens of eyes stared at me. That's right, ladies, I'm the fat girl. Every fitness class has one. And you all suddenly feel so much better about yourselves. That carrot you scoffed for breakfast doesn't look so bad now. Does it?

"No, it's our first class," Dana answered.

Oh no. Didn't she know that she had just committed the cardinal sin of fitness class?

"Well, you ladies stay right here up front and follow the routine, you'll be just fine."

I was in hell. Not only was I the only chubby girl in the room, but I was also now the entertainment at the front of the class! Clapping her perfectly manicured hands again, *Francesca* encouraged people to move into a space as she hit the play button on the CD player. The Brazilian sounds of the lambada filled the room, and I felt sick.

Swaying her disgustingly tiny hips back and forth, Francesca began a routine that looked like it belonged on the stage; not a hall in one of the smelliest gyms in London. Dana, of course, was a natural. Swaying, bouncing, and shaking her pert little arse around the room like a pro, she put the rest of us to shame. Well, I say the rest of us, but I mean me.

I bounced, jiggled, and wobbled myself around that mat as though I had a feather tickler shoved up my arse. I wasn't sure how this would help me lose a few pounds, but with the flailing of my limbs and sporadic movements of my hips, there was a good chance we'd have rain.

By the time we were done, I felt as flat as a pancake and as wobbly as jelly. My legs ached, and my whole body was screaming for a long soak in the bath. A year ought to do it. Draping my broken body onto the bench, I guzzled the bottle of water I had brought with me, as Dana sipped hers lightly and beamed at me.

"That was fun! It wasn't nearly as intense as I thought it would be."

Panting, I raised an eyebrow at her and squirted the remains of my drink in her perky little face.

"Hey! What was that for?"

Wiping herself off with her towel, she scowled at me.

"You." *Pant.* "Suck." *Pant.* "I'm dying, and my heart is about to explode." *Pant.*

Rolling her eyes, she gathered our things and held out her hand for me. Taking it, she pulled me up and flung my arm around her shoulder as I limped, lifelessly, beside her to the exit.

"I'm never coming back here again. The smell, the women, Francesca … makes me sick."

And as we pushed through the doors and the cold wind hit me, that's exactly what happened. I hurled. Bent over like a porn star, I threw my guts up. Grabbing the potted plant beside the door, I heaved loudly and emptied my breakfast into it. Scrambled egg wasn't so nice when tasting it a second time. Pulling my hair from my face, Dana gagged.

"That's disgusting, Charlene. Maybe you overdid it today. You should probably find something with a slightly slower pace to start with."

Lifting my head, I wiped my mouth and glared at her.

"Really? You think?"

When I finally got back to my apartment, I was exhausted. Lying on the sofa, I drifted in and out of sleep. I would have been more committed to a nap, but I was worried they'd be crashing down my door in fear that the smell seeping from every pore of my body was, in fact, my rotting corpse. Though, to be honest, I really don't think my neighbour cared enough to notice. No, I would be found half eaten by my cat and dressed in sweatpants. A truly dignified way to go. Death by Zumba.

Pouring us cups of coffee, Dana sat on the floor in front of me.

"So, how was work?"

Damn it. Wincing, I tried to turn my head and look away. I'd had every intention of going back on Monday, truly I had, but as I'd pulled the door open onto the busy street, I just couldn't face it. The looks, the whispers, and the sympathy was too much. I needed more time. I would be stronger in a week, and maybe it wouldn't bother me so much.

"Charlene, don't tell me you postponed it."

"Okay, I won't tell you."

"Charlene! What happened to getting back to normal?"

I laughed at myself mockingly. "Dana, look at me. There is nothing normal about my life right now. I think I deserve a little credit for even being able to drag my arse out of bed every morning. Saturday should have been my wedding day, and instead, I spent it in a nylon dress sipping cocktails and almost getting banned from the Magic Kingdom! Define normal."

Pressing her lips together, she gave me a disapproving look.

"Fine, but you have to go back next week. Promise me."

Feeling as though my mother was lecturing me, I nodded. After an hour of being scolded on the need for me to take better care of myself and the state of my fiery locks, my friend and hairdresser decided to give me the peace I'd been craving since I'd vomited my Zumba routine into a fern.

Just as I began to relax and forget the awful hour I had spent dancing my weight away, the phone beside me rang loudly, and I almost cried as I lifted my limp arm and reached for the receiver.

"Go away."

"Well, I like that. I called to say I heard about the Zumba thing. I told you that stuff was ridiculous. You need something fun, sexy, and private. Not a room full of shaking, wobbling, and sweating bodies."

Attempting to raise my head from the cushion, I groaned.

"You don't say. And I suppose you have the answer, Ness."

I could almost hear her smug and satisfied smile through the line.

"Abso-freaking-lutely, I do! Be ready on Tuesday at five. Wear shorts."

Fearing what she had in store for me, but deciding it was best not to argue, I agreed. After all, I'd lived through Zumba, so what could she possibly throw at me that was any worse than this? I may live to regret that question. Well, provided I make it through the next twenty-four hours without needing resuscitation.

Rolling over, I pulled the throw that was strewn across the back of the couch, over me and wrapped myself tightly in it before falling asleep. Maybe I'd be an inch smaller when I woke. Now I really was dreaming!

<u>Chapter 8</u>

Walking from the train station to the office on Monday, I groaned. I hadn't even reached the main door yet, and my stomach was in knots. My brow was damp with sweat, and my hands were clammy. I was going to have to face everyone sometime, but the endless questions and glances over the shoulder were going to be torture. When getting dressed that morning, I'd been tempted to wear my running shoes just in case I needed to make a dash for freedom. It would be the most activity they had seen in a long time. Sitting in the back of my wardrobe, they were practically new.

As I approached the large double glass doors of R.J. Littman's Record Company, I could feel my breakfast trying desperately to remain in my stomach. Taking a deep breath and swallowing hard, I pushed my way inside and prepared myself for the day. The main reception area was clean, quiet and painted a crisp white. A black and chrome desk was situated in the middle and sitting behind it was Jenny. Jenny had been the receptionist there for almost a year and was the epitome of cute. Her long, dark hair, brown eyes and perfect tan, made her the most attractive part of the team. No wonder she had been put in place as the welcome committee. She was only twenty-one, but Jenny had met and dazzled many of our biggest clients. Her perky personality and equally perky breasts were vital assets to the company.

Whipping off her headset and hurrying around from behind the desk, she threw her arms around me and squeezed tightly.

"Oh, Charlene," she sobbed. "I couldn't believe it when I heard. My heart broke for you. I couldn't sleep or eat knowing how awful you must have been feeling! You poor thing."

Rolling my eyes, I mentally shook my head at her. I was the girl who'd been jilted by a cheating arsehole, and here she was, blubbering all over my neck!

"I'm fine. Honest," I reassured her.

Her grip tightened. "What a jerk. I cannot believe he did that to you. You deserve so much better. Honestly, I don't know anyone who deserves to be happy more than you do."

Finally releasing me, she gave me a sympathetic look. There it was—that, 'you poor, broken, and shelved old maid' look. I should probably become accustomed to it, considering I would be seeing it a lot today.

"Thanks, Jenny. His loss right? Better I know about it all now, rather than once we were married."

She nodded and offered me a small smile. I needed to get away from this. As tears began welling in her eyes, I looked around for an escape. Glancing at the clock, I gasped in feigned horror.

"Gosh! Is that the time? I better get upstairs. I've probably got a mountain of paperwork to sort through, and I'm sure Regina will want to get me up to speed on everything I've missed."

Nodding, Jenny wiped at her heavily mascaraed eyes.

"Sure. We'll do lunch? My treat?" Charity. Great. Well, if I was going to be the office gossip, maybe a little TLC wasn't the worst idea. Nodding back at her enthusiastically, I totted across the room and swiped my ID card through the security check by the door.

"Absolutely, I'll meet you here at one."

I didn't wait for a reply. Hurrying through the doors, I breathed a sigh of relief to find the hallway completely empty. Taking my chances, I walked briskly toward my office at the end of the narrow and usually cluttered hallway. The various cubicles that surrounded my door were bustling with people, and as I rounded the corner, every pair of eyes turned to me. Silence fell on the entire room. I wanted the ground to swallow me whole. Closing my eyes, I reached for the handle and rushed through the door to my secluded little room, closing the blinds as soon as I entered.

With my back to the door, I sank to the floor in a heap. This was hell. I looked around my office, and as my eyes fell on the pile of paperwork, envelopes of unopened mail and stacks of CDs, I felt an enormous sense of relief. At least I had an excuse to hole myself up in there all day. I was just thinking about how to possibly get out of lunch with Jenny when the door to the left of my office swung open. Regina's own space was adjacent to mine, and the connecting door had come in handy. We usually left it open and discussed clients, office gossip, and threw random snacks at one another via the damn thing. Today, I wished it were bolted.

Dropping yet more work on my desk, the tall and mostly plastic woman, spun around.

"Oh, Charlene, good; you're here. I have a tonne of work waiting for you to sift through. Six bands have their demos on your desk, and I have a large coffee waiting for you in my office. Come on, quick, quick. We don't have all day for you to finally pull yourself together and out of that heap on the carpet. I just had it cleaned after all."

Smiling, I lifted myself up, dumped my bag beside my desk and headed into Regina's office. The pink and dazzling silver furniture was a reflection of her eccentric taste and also of her third husband's excessive bank account. My own office was simplistic with three magnolia walls and the back wall, papered in a bright purple floral design. The sofa was black leather, and a coffee table separated the conversational area from the work area around my desk. Regina's office was essentially for celebration. I would sign the acts and then send them through to her office for the fun stuff.

Handing me a large cup of coffee, she perched on the edge of her desk and gestured for me to sit on her plush white sofa.

"I'll spare you the sympathetic crap. You don't need it, and you don't need that arsehole either. Look at me. I'm fifty-three, have been married three times, and I couldn't be happier. I'm independent, run my own company, and still have an arse you could bounce pennies off of. My countless boy-toys can vouch for that. So, why did it take you so bloody long to get back here?"

Placing my cup on the glass table in front of me, I held my head in my hands, and heaved a sigh, exasperatedly.

"I couldn't face all the looks of concern, gossip, whispering, and damn eyes staring at me. It was bad enough just walking through to the office today."

Raising an eyebrow, she nodded at the door. "Out there? That's what's bothering you? And I suppose you'll be hiding in your office for the remainder of the day?"

Blushing, I nodded.

"And tomorrow? Next week? The week after?"

I groaned. "I don't know. I just hate it."

"Well, you have to face it some time. But, until you're ready, I have a project for you."

Skirting around her desk, she sat at her computer and gestured for me to join her.

"Look at this."

Pulling up a picture of three men, she swooned at the screen.

"Aren't they gorgeous?"

I studied the image. They all seemed to be fairly young. Maybe twenty at best. A tall, dark-haired, and cocky looking guy holding drumsticks was on the far left. On the right, a blonde, spiky-haired, baby-faced bass player, and in the centre, was a stunning, pierced, gorgeous, rock god. Grasping a guitar, his lip ring had clearly caught the light from the flash of the camera as he smiled. He was certainly a heartbreaker.

"I saw them while I was in L.A. last week. They were playing at some bar. My friend had dragged me there to celebrate another contract signed at our California office, and there they were. I can't for the life of me remember their names, but I do have their details. I also managed to record some of their material on my phone. I've mailed everything to your inbox, and I need you to track down as much information on them as possible. Not only are they stunning and knickers-droppingly hot, but they're also amazing musicians. I want them signed with our L.A team immediately!"

I gave her a surprised look. "Me? You want *me* to head this up?"

She seemed confused at my question. "Of course. No one knows this business better than you. You're my protégé, and I need you on this."

I bit my lip and grinned. "I'll start working on it today!"

"There's the girl I hired! You're fine. And as for the lemmings and sheep out there, if you don't want to be the office discussion topic, remind them they're here to do a job and who the boss is."

Giving me a wink, she gave a wave of her hand and ushered me out of the room. "Now, go get me those hotties!"

I couldn't help but laugh at her. My very own project! This band wasn't just being signed by me, oh no. I was scouting, hunting, and would make it my mission to make them a part of the R.J. Littman family. Settling behind my desk, I switched on my laptop and began my search.

* * * *

I'd been scouring the internet for hours, and so far, I could find nothing about this band. It was as if they were fictional or a figment of the imagination. There were musings, Twitter mentioned them frequently, and endless reams of women claimed to have bedded them, but their names, contact details, and private lives were a total mystery. Groaning, I folded my arms on the desk and banged my head heavily onto them in frustration.

"Ahem, Charlie?"

Lifting my head, I tried to see who had spoken, but unfortunately, my sticky forehead had glued a piece of paper to it and was now blocking my line of sight. Pulling it away, I smiled as Adam's large frame stood in my doorway. Holding a beautiful bouquet of flowers, he tilted his head to the side and beamed at me. I'd never noticed before, but his eyes seemed to sparkle and soften when he smiled.

"I thought these might cheer you up. Dana told me you were heading back in today and I figured, I was in the area so …"

Pushing away from my desk, I hurried over and wrapped my arms around him. Pecking him on the cheek, I took the flowers in one hand and inhaled the sweet aromas. The stunning spray of lilies, roses, and daisies were breathtaking.

"You, Doctor, are the best."

Placing the flowers on my coffee table, I slumped onto the sofa. Adam sat beside me and draped an arm over the back.

"What's wrong? Tough day?"

I nodded. "I have a project that is proving impossible. Regina wants this band signed, and I cannot trace them anywhere. This is a big opportunity for me, and I'm doomed to fail. And then there's that!"

Pointing at the open door, I growled at the sound of people whispering my name.

Rising from his seat, Adam walked over and slammed the damn thing shut.

"Don't let it get to you, Charlie. You're a huge success, and you don't need to worry about the idle gossip of the office teenagers."

I grunted. "I feel as though everyone is talking about the jilted bride and her arsehole ex-fiancé! It's exhausting."

He smiled at me. "Come here."

Walking over to the desk, he brushed the contents onto the floor, which made an almighty crash. I held my hand over my mouth and stifled a laugh. What he did next was surreal. Well, for me at least. Groaning, grunting, and growling, Adam began calling my name and banging his fist on the desk.

"Oh, Charlene! Oh, God yes! Oh, that's so good!"

Gesturing at me to join him, he continued to make his loud expressions of pleasure.

"Right there. Mmm. Oh, baby!"

Trying desperately not to laugh, I moaned, groaned, and called his name.

"Oh, Adam! Yes, harder. No one makes me feel as good as you do!"

I heard the distinct click of Regina's office door locking, blushed deeply, and almost lost my composure. Watching as I played the role of office sex kitten, Adam stared wide-eyed and amazed at me. Pressing his finger to my lips, he banged three times on the desk, groaned, and gave his triumphant finishing yell.

"Oh, Charlene! Fuck! Yes!"

Losing control, I fell on the floor and laughed. My hands held firmly over my mouth, I rolled around and panted, trying to catch my breath. Finally calm enough to see straight, I looked up to find Adam standing over me with a gleam in his eyes.

Holding out his hand, he took mine, yanked me from the floor and stood me in front of him. He scanned me from head to toe and grinned. Grabbing my clip, he released my long, red hair and tousled it a little. His other hand hastily unbuttoned my shirt, revealing the top of my ample cleavage and the white lace of my bra. I stared at him in horror, but was frozen in astonishment.

"Perfect."

Pulling me to the door, he swung it open. Walking out backwards, he made damn sure I was visible as he winked, turned, zipped up his trousers, and strolled through the sea of cubicles and gawping faces. Once he was out of their sight, every head spun around at me. Biting my lip, I smiled before brushing myself down, buttoning my shirt and straightening up.

"Back to work! If those reports aren't on my desk by Friday, you'll all be here for the weekend, too! Anyone got a problem with that?" I yelled authoritatively. Bustling and hurrying back to their desks, the lemmings began hurriedly typing, making calls and pretending to be busy.

Closing the door, I began picking up the debris from my office floor with a large grin on my face. The sounds of Adam's primal and very convincing pleasure echoed in my ears. Wow. Who knew? Adam, my Adam, was a total stud! No wonder the girls that went out with him always looked so dopey and love-struck. If his fake performance was anything to go by, I couldn't imagine what his full and no-holds-barred show would be like!

Shaking the thoughts of my best friend's sex life from my mind, I continued to clear up the mess we had made. I had just sat back down at my desk when my phone buzzed beside me. Opening the message, I giggled.

That'll give them something to talk about. Have a good day. ;)

Replying with a simple 'sure will,' I pulled my hair back and tied it in a tight pony. My email was next to ping.

From: Regina
Re: Office Behavior
Message: Charlene Winters. You bad, bad girl. ;)

It seemed our little afternoon matinee had even convinced my boss. Shaking my head and still grinning like a maniac, I continued my search for the mysterious L.A. band. Maybe this day wouldn't be so bad after all.

Chapter 9

Walking into the high-end and swanky gym that Ness had dragged me to, I whistled in admiration at the vast and luxurious reception area. Black leather sofas were lined up against the wall on my left, and a large glass desk was to my right. Pictures of models and fitness trainers were mounted on the wall with motivational notes below them. I was particularly taken by one that read, 'The body is broken, but the spirit is willing.' What the hell did that mean? If my body was broken, which it was, then my spirit had long since run off and reached for the ice cream. It hadn't dragged my fat arse to the gym.

Ness grabbed my arm and began pulling me through the reception and over to the stairs. I gave her a confused look.

"The studio's upstairs. Come on, we'll be late!"

Dressed in her sweatpants and vest, Ness had abs that rivalled a Spartan warrior. The woman was a force to be reckoned with—a fiery temperament, fierce personality, and wonderful loyalty. And as we reached the top of the stairs, I discovered something else about her …

"Welcome to pole dance fitness!" she yelled.

I gazed in horror at the sight before me. A large studio hall, with mirrored walls and an impressive sound system, was the setting for what appeared to be pole-dancing classes for a small group. Five poles were fixed between the floor and the low ceiling. I turned to Ness, speechless. Gripping my shoulders, she steered me inside.

"You said how awful Zumba was, but that was because it was such a large group. This class is very exclusive. Luckily for you, the instructor is a client of mine. Marina is an ex-pole dancer and stripper. Now, she teaches others how to take their clothes off while she gets paid to keep hers on. Once a week, she does a fitness class. It's a great work out for your whole body."

I shook my head in disbelief. Finally finding my voice, I pulled her aside and gave her a hard stare.

"You have got to be kidding me! Ness, I can't climb a pole!"

"Psshh. Nonsense. Of course, you can. Besides, your large thighs will give you a great grip. Just trust me, will you?"

I had a distinct feeling that I really wasn't going to have a choice. Rolling her eyes, she began stripping off her clothes as I watched in horror. Tying her vest into a knot and whipping off her sweats, she stood before me in skin-tight, black hot pants and began to oil up her thighs. Handing me the bottle, she fisted her hands on her hips.

"Well? Come on. Get on with it."

Sitting on the floor, I pulled off my own sweats, leaving my shorts where they were. There was no way I was cramming my arse into hot pants!

"You'll need to oil up, or you'll find it kind of chafes."

Taking a handful of the sweet-smelling liquid, I began rubbing it over my legs and thighs.

I'd just got back to my feet when a tall, toned, dark-haired woman entered the class. Making a beeline for us, she grinned.

"Vanessa! Hi! It's great to see you, and who's this?"

Turning to me, Ness introduced me to the instructor, Marina.

"Well, I can see you're a little nervous. Don't be. It's a friendly class, and I'm here to guide you through. Only attempt the moves that you feel comfortable with, etc."

Shooting me a warm smile, she made her way over to the CD player and hit the play button. The sound of Def Leppard filled the room as Marina began instructing us on a suitable warm up. It seemed simple enough, and I hoped that this level of simplicity would continue throughout the rest of the class. Three other women had joined us, and each was much like Ness and Marina. Skinny. *Great,* another class where I'm the chubby girl.

* * * *

After giving me a crash course in how to sex up a metal pole, Marina beamed at me.

"So, now that you know the basics, it's time to climb that pole!"

I cringed. Gazing up at the ceiling where the pole was nailed in securely, I swallowed hard. I positioned myself in front of it, gripped it tightly between my thighs and began to pull myself up. I couldn't believe it! The small amount of oil on my thighs meant I slipped, slid, and glided my way up! It was almost effortless. I felt triumphant and full of excitement. Flipping my hair about and swirling around the top, I felt like a Spearmint Rhino stripper, or at least a fifty-dollar lap dancer! I was glamour, sex, and sweat. It was invigorating, and I felt amazing. Looking over at Vanessa who was now spinning around the damn thing like a pro, I grinned.

"Great, how about trying a straight drop back down?" Marina called up.

Looking down at her, I nodded. I was easily around seven feet from the ground, but it seemed only a short distance, and I imagined since getting up there had been so straightforward, getting down would be a breeze.

Wrong.

Wrapping my thighs around the cool pole even tighter, I had begun my descent toward the ground confidently, when I let out an almighty cry! You see, when I had applied the damn oil, it seemed my shorts had soaked the majority up, and the tops of my inner thighs were now sliding, chafing, and sticking to the pole as I quickly headed for the ground. My crotch pressed against the bar and was now also feeling the painful effects of a rapid descent. Landing with a thud, I rolled onto my side in agony. Ness ran over and helped Marina get me to a chair where they both watched me with amusement. My legs were spread wider than a hooker's at a stag night.

A quick glance down at my legs, which were akimbo, made me suddenly aware of why they were sniggering. It seemed that with the rapid speed at which I had hurtled toward the floor, and the distinct lack of lubricant, had left me with severely painful red and angry marks between my thighs. They looked as though I'd had a rampant sex session with the human torch, and I had the blisters to prove it! My crotch was on fire!

* * * *

I sat rigidly on my sofa. I'd managed to dig out my inflatable rubber ring from my wardrobe, and it was now being used as a doughnut between my arse and the seat. Every movement made me squirm in pain. The pain reminded me of when I'd lost my virginity. The burning, scraping, and stinging was certainly a familiar feeling. If someone had told me back then that having sex for the first time would be like rubbing the inside of my vagina with sandpaper, I would have been less inclined to accept Daniel Harnet's invitation to 'study' that evening. We'd eaten pizza, sprawled our books across his bed, and then knocked them off to awkwardly and clumsily hump like the horny little teenagers we were.

Sighing heavily to myself, I reached for the remote and began flicking through the endless channels. I was set for an entire evening of being stuck on the sofa when the buzz of the intercom meant I would be forced to remove my sore and raw arse from my seat. Walking like John Wayne, I made my way over—cringing, growling and almost crying from the pain between my thighs. Due to my being a chubby girl, I lacked that gap that naturally occurred between them.

"What do you want?" I groaned.

"To inspect your burns. Now, buzz me in."

"Adam, you have a key, and I have possibly just caused a layer of skin to die between my legs just by answering the damn intercom!"

Pulling the door open, I pressed the release button for the entrance door before waddling back to my seat on the sofa. Adam closed the door behind him and gave me a sympathetic look. He was wearing his black trousers, and a pale blue shirt with the sleeves rolled up to the elbow, and I couldn't help but notice how … thick his arms were as they fought to be released from the restrictive fabric.

"Don't look at me like that. It can't be the first time you've seen this kind of injury."

He laughed and pulled some ointment from his pocket.

"I usually see it on jockeys, those who enjoy straddling mechanical bulls, and some very adventurous sexual types. This is my first stripper pole injury. Now, spread your legs, baby."

Winking at me, he knelt down, pushed my knees a little farther apart and shook his head. I scowled down at him.

"I'm not sure how comfortable I am with your head down there. You could at least have bought me dinner, wined me, or whispered sweet nothings first."

Glancing up at me over the top of his thick, black-rimmed glasses, he smiled.

"You know I love you. What more do you want?"

I scrunched my nose up and chuckled as he squirted the ointment into his hand before gently rubbing it into my broken skin. The cooling sensation paired with the massage of his hand made me instantly more at ease. The burning had been replaced with a very strange sensation. I wasn't sure if it was the ointment or Adam's hands on my inner thighs, but I felt a sense of … contentment. *Jeez*, it had been a long time since I'd had a man's hands on me. In fact, it had been a long time since I'd even been satisfied in any sense by a man. I stared down at him as he continued to work the gel into my burns. Smiling, he finished, looked up, and placed a soft kiss on my knee. The two top buttons of his shirt were undone, and from my angle, I could see the defined contours of his chest as the fabric pulled taught with the movement of his arms.

Rising to his feet, he gave me a stern stare. "Promise me you won't keep doing these stupid classes? You're going to end up really doing some damage. Your body wasn't made for this stuff, Charlie. If you really want to get in shape, I 'll help you."

I gave him an inquisitive look. "How?"

He made his way over to the kitchen sink and washed his hands.

"Well, we'll start with a diet and nutrition profile, and I'll also give you some exercises to do. Then, when you're ready, you can start running with me. I run three times a week in the evening so it won't interfere with your schedule. What do you say?"

I thought for a moment and then cast my eyes down at my thighs. It wasn't as though I had anything to lose. Sighing with defeat, I nodded.

"Okay, Doc. You win."

He grinned. "Good."

Grabbing two bottles of mineral water from the refrigerator, he strolled over and bounced down onto the sofa beside me.

"For the record, Charlie, you're gorgeous. Brad's a jerk, and your weight has nothing to do with his cheating. He's an arsehole, and he doesn't deserve you anyway. You could be the size of this couch, and you'd still be worth ten of him or his little hussy."

Draping a protective arm around my shoulders, he scooted closer. "I assume our performance at the office caused a bit of a stir."

I laughed. "Oh, yes. It was all everyone could talk about. You don't really sound like that when you … you know …"

Taking a sip of his water, the corner of his mouth curved up into a smile. "Maybe. Do you sound like that when you … you know …" he teased.

I bit my lip. "I guess you'll never know, stud."

He nudged me playfully. "I've heard you, remember?"

I gave him a puzzled look.

"College. There was that party at Dana's? You and some guy from your class. Josh, I think it was. You disappeared, and when I tracked you down, you were both sneaking into the spare room. The whole top floor could hear that."

I blushed and stared at him with my mouth open wide. His head rolled back, and he laughed—hard.

"Well, with a mouth like that, no wonder he was enjoying it so much, Charlie!"

I picked up one of the throw pillows and threw it at his head.

"I cannot believe you were listening. You pervert."

He smirked at me. "Hey, at least one of us was getting some."

I shook my head and pretended to be offended. "Well, at the rate I'm going these days, I think my hymen is almost totally healed over. There are cobwebs in there."

Adam cringed. "Appealing. Well, I'm sure your little dry spell is only temporary. I mean, if it weren't for those damn burns you have, I'd certainly throw you down."

I almost choked on the mouthful of water I had taken. Shaking his head and patting my back gently, Adam grinned wickedly.

"Relax, baby girl. I'm teasing."

Settling back onto the sofa, he began flicking through the channels. I stared at him a while, slightly in shock. He *was* kidding, wasn't he? Giving me a sideways glance, he leaned in and pecked me on the cheek.

Of course, he was kidding. Adam was my friend. And friends don't have sex. It's complicated, ruins entire relationships, and yet the thought of his hands on my thighs, the sounds of his groans and moans, and the intoxicating smell of his designer aftershave ... was making me distinctly horny.

Rolling my eyes, I mentally chastised myself for being so ridiculous. I clearly needed to get laid. Soon.

Chapter 10

Thanks to Adam's diet regime, I had lost fifteen pounds. However, I was beginning to notice a distinct plateau in progress. It always happened to me. I'd lose a hefty amount of weight and then find I became stuck between bell thighs and muffin top. I had been flicking through a copy of my favourite women's magazine at work when I'd stumbled across the latest detox diet. It seemed simple enough. You didn't eat anything solid and lived on speciality soups, smoothies, and juices for a month.

While on my lunch break at work, I'd scoured the internet for all the recipes and information I could find for my new liquid detox. The recipes consisted of fruit, vegetables, natural herbs and some strange ingredients that I'd never even heard of. Luckily, links for online stockists were a click away. I'd now been on the damn thing for two weeks, and to say I was suffering was an understatement. My stomach was churning like a washing machine, and I'd spent so much time in the bathroom, I was considering sending out change of address cards! My insides were akin to a large water slide! I'd been chowing down bottles of prune juice, cucumber and papaya smoothies, and some very questionable soups. I wasn't sure what some of those ingredients had been when I added them, but roughly translated, I believed it meant laxative or peeing out of my behind!

It had been a good thing that I had kept that rubber ring from my pole dancing mishap handy. It was still serving as a doughnut for my poor behind. It felt as though I was passing lava these days. On the plus side, I'd dropped another fourteen pounds. I hadn't yet been running with Adam, and I knew he was beginning to get frustrated. I simply wasn't ready for all that panting, sweating, and straining. I was doing enough of that in the bathroom. I wasn't a runner. It wasn't that I lacked the motivation. It was more the fact that my thighs rubbed together so much that I was sure they'd end up setting my lady bush on fire!

Sitting on my sofa, I inhaled deeply. It had been five months since Brad had dumped me, and it still stung just as bad—almost as bad as my own arsehole right now. I'd managed to rid the entire apartment and my life from any memorabilia of my time with Brad. In fact, Jacob was all that remained, but I wasn't going to hold it against him. His affiliation with the enemy wasn't enough to condemn him. Besides, he was the only male that seemed able to live with me long term. I'd had no inclination to date or 'get back in the game' as Dana had put it, but I had to admit … I was getting a little lonely.

I glanced at the refrigerator. The lure of the Ben and Jerry's was beginning to call to me. I had almost given in to my temptation when, as if by magic intervention, my phone began vibrating beside me. Picking it up, I smiled at the irony of the caller.

"Hi, Adam."

"Hey, Charlie. How's it going?"

I cringed and thought about telling him about my new detox but decided there were some things even your best friend didn't need to know.

"Actually, you just saved me from crashing. I'm a little down, and junk food was looking really good."

He chuckled. "A little now and then is fine. But I'm assuming you were talking a full-on binge."

"As if there's any other way to eat junk? Anyway, what's up, Doc?"

He gave a frustrated and long sigh. "I've gotta get out of my place by the end of the day. The whole building is being fumigated. Apparently, my neighbour died, and they didn't find the body 'til this morning. I just thought he was being lazy and not cleaning his place again. I didn't think the smell was … him."

I gasped. "Oh my God. That's awful. That poor guy."

He hummed in agreement. "C'est la vie. When it's your time to go, it's your time, I guess. Anyway, the reason I called was … well … I was wondering …"

I rolled my eyes. "You know you can stay here. I don't know why you even thought you had to ask. I'll make up the spare room, and you bring the pizza. I'll see you in an hour?"

I could almost hear him smile. "You're the best, Charlie."

Hanging up, I gingerly stood from the sofa and waddled over to the spare room. No one had used it since Gran had stayed, and after scrubbing the entire apartment with disinfectant, I was fairly satisfied that it was fit for Adam to stay in. I placed blue sheets on the double bed and a picture of the four of us on the bedside table. The thought of having my best friend under the same roof as me for the first time in ten years was exciting. I felt like a teenager again. Adam had spent three weeks staying with me when my father had died. He refused to leave my side until he was sure I was able to function or at least eat without him constantly pecking at me. And truth be told, I had missed him when he'd left. This was going to be fun and a chance to spend some quality time with him without Ness and Dana.

* * * *

"You can't possibly be unpacking still! This pizza is going to be stone cold if you don't hurry up!" I yelled through to Adam. He'd arrived quickly and had immediately handed the pizza box over to me before heading to the spare room to unpack the two large suitcases he'd dragged behind him.

"I'm almost done. You don't have to wait for me. You can totally dig in," he shouted back.

I eyed the large box and bit my lip to stop myself from drooling. "No, I need you to stop me from inhaling the entire thing," I confessed.

I heard him laugh and smiled to myself. Adam had a laugh that warmed your insides. A deep, husky, and totally sexy laugh. If I'd never seen him or known him, his laugh would have had my knickers snapping and dropping purely on their own. Running my fingers through my hair, I closed my eyes tightly. What the hell was I doing? Was I that hard up?

The phone rang over on the kitchen counter, and I was grateful for the distraction from my inappropriate thoughts about my friend. Well, that was until I answered.

"Hello?"

"Hello, Chicken."

I groaned and held my hand over the receiver.

"Hi, Gran. How's it going?"

"I'm in my eighties, Charlene. *Everything* goes south."

I cringed at the thought. "Thanks for the insight. I meant to say, what can I do for you?"

"I need to ask that nice Doctor for a favour. Can you get him to call me? I've been trying all day, but I'm not getting anywhere," she complained.

"He's not home. He's … staying elsewhere." I decided to grant Adam at least a little privacy. But that was short lived. Waltzing out of the spare room, he threw a cushion at me and grinned, reaching for the pizza box.

"Are you going to be gassing on that all evening or do you want to eat?" he teased.

I glared at him and gestured for him to be quiet. Making a cut-throat movement, I indicated that one more word and I would be forced to kill him.

"Oh, Charlene. You bad girl. Is that him I hear now?"

I sighed and ran my hand over my face.

"Yes, Gran. He's staying here for a while."

She tittered wickedly. "Finally shacked up with him, eh? About time. I wondered how long it would take you two to give in to your urges."

Grabbing a bottle of water from the refrigerator, I hurled it at Adam who caught it in one hand. He didn't even stop eating.

"Gran, for the last time, he's my friend. He has been for the past twenty years."

She huffed. "Foreplay. He's just been waiting for you to ripen up so that he can give you a good squeeze and suck on that juice!"

I wanted to vomit. My stomach was already a little delicate, and it was now rolling like a hurricane. "Gran, stop," I pleaded.

"Nonsense. Honestly, at your age, your bed should be rocking more than Fred Flintstones! Make like a bunny and hop on him before someone else does."

"I'm going to hang up on you, I mean it."

She tutted, and it irked me. Gran was still insistent that Adam and I hook up. I swear the woman was sex mad and senile.

"Fine, fine. Don't come crying to me when he's found some long-legged bosom pillow. Now, if you'd hand me over to him, I have a favour to ask."

Holding out the phone, I gestured at Adam to get up. "She wants to ask you for something."

He winced. "Oh, I dread to think."

Putting down his slice of pizza, he wiped his hands on his faded denim jeans and took the phone from me.

"Hey, Grammy. How's my best girl?"

I made a vomiting motion and stuck my fingers down my throat in jest. Adam simply winked and smiled.

"Uh huh. Okay … I see. Well, come by on Monday, and I'll get one of the team to take a look for you. Don't worry. It's not a problem. Be there at eight, and I'll get you seen bright and early. Okay, take care. Bye."

Hanging up, he placed the receiver back on the stand and strolled over to resume his spot on the sofa. I folded my arms and tapped my foot impatiently.

"Well? What did she want?"

Looking up from the TV, he shrugged. "Nothing much. Just needs some medical stuff chasing up. Don't worry about it."

I gave him a suspicious look, but he seemed unfazed. Cautiously making my way back over, I continued to eye him carefully. He grabbed my hand and yanked me hard onto the doughnut.

"I told you, it's just some stuff she wants chasing. Probably for her insurance and stuff. Now eat."

Raising an eyebrow, I settled down and began shovelling a slice of ham and mushroom pizza down my throat. It was heaven. I could almost hear my hips crying in defeat, but I didn't care. I knew they said that nothing tasted as good as skinny felt, but holy fuck, this was pretty good.

Adam leaned back and draped his arm around my shoulders.

"This is nice. I like this—me and you, pizza, and the TV. It feels so comfortable and natural. Like we've been doing it forever." He beamed.

I giggled, and a few tiny specks of pizza flew from my mouth.

"We have been doing it forever. Friday nights were pizza and a movie night, remember?"

He shook his head before resting it on his outstretched arm. "Not once you met Brad. You kinda went off the radar for a long time. You changed a lot. I missed you, baby girl."

I let out a long and rueful sigh. "I know. I think I lost myself somewhere between germ-free sex and weekends at swanky bars for cocktails with his colleagues or the boss he was arse kissing. I'm sorry. I promise while you're here, we'll make up for all of that lost time. I swear it on my cat."

Adam chuckled as Jacob climbed lazily through the window and curled up beside his shoulder on the back of the sofa.

"Well, we wouldn't want anything to ruin his cosy little lifestyle. I'll hold you to it."

I nodded and held out my hand. "Shake on it?"

Taking my palm, his held it tightly and leaned in. His lips brushed my cheek gently as he placed a small kiss on my jaw. My body shuddered, and a prickling sensation shot down my spine. I jumped in my seat and then hurried to the bathroom.

Gazing in the mirror, I panted. What the hell was that?

"Charlie, are you all right?" Adam called from the living room.

Opening the door slightly, I yelled back to him. "Yeah, I'm fine, just, you know, when you gotta go … you gotta go."

I tried to sound nonchalant, but inside, I was shaking. What was happening to me? First, his hands on my thighs, then me staring at his chest through his shirt, and now this! I was either going crazy, or I was so desperate to get my coochie filled, that my body was even considering Adam as a perspective plumber! My pipes were getting rusty, and the next part of my self-help plan was going to have to come into effect sooner than I'd thought. Operation: Get Me a Man was in effect immediately.

Chapter 11

"A dating site? Charlene, sweetie, those things are for the desperate, the unattractive and workaholics. You are none of those things."

Still tapping away at my laptop, I ignored Ness's rant about internet match-making.

"I mean, what if you meet a guy and he's a total creep?"

Beside me, Dana smirked over the rim of her coffee cup. "She could meet one of those anywhere, Vanessa. The internet is just a bigger pond."

Rolling my eyes, I placed the machine on the table and slumped back onto the sofa.

"There. Done. I'm now officially fishing for a man. I just hope one bites."

Ness hurried over from the kitchen and grabbed the laptop with a ferocious interest.

"Oh, God. You really are doing this, aren't you?"

I nodded enthusiastically. "Yes, I am. It's time you came crawling into the twenty-first century. Dating sites are not just for creeps, weirdoes, and workaholics. It's for people who want to meet away from the toxic environments."

She eyed me suspiciously. "Toxic environments?"

"Yes, toxic. Bars, clubs—anywhere that serves booze basically. I mean, come on. How many guys have we dated between us that we met in one of those places?"

Dana cringed. "Too many to count."

Turning to her, I placed my hand on her shoulder gently.

"And they all turned out to be total jerks or one night wonders."

Ness fisted a hand on her hip while balancing my fragile laptop on the other.

"I take offence to that. Gary, for instance, was a great guy. He was sweet, handsome, fun, not too clingy, and he spoiled me rotten."

Dana threw her head back and laughed, earning her a stern and irritated glare from Vanessa. Getting to my feet, I made my way to the kitchen and shook my head.

"Vanessa. He was married!" I threw back at her over my shoulder.

She huffed loudly. "That doesn't make him a bad person."

I gawped at her with my mouth open wide. "It makes him a slimeball! He was easily ten years your senior, and you were his little weekend romp when he was on business. How can you think that a guy like that isn't toxic?"

I rolled my eyes in exasperation. Ness was gorgeous, intelligent, and successful, but she truly had the worst taste in men.

"Maybe Charlene has a point. I know that *I* haven't dated anyone in a long time because I'm sick and tired of the same routine. Boy meets girl in a bar. Boy buys several drinks for girl and then makes his move. Girl then wakes up in a stranger's bed, with beer breath on her face and a horrible feeling of self-loathing. If she's lucky, she leaves with his number," Dana stated.

"Because he wants a repeat performance the next time he's drunk and horny. Usually a Saturday night around two in the morning," I interrupted.

Dana gestured over at me with one outstretched palm. "My point exactly. So, she tries a little online bar hopping, but without the loud music, booze, and endless hours of scanning the crowd. These guys come to you. You have all of their vital statistics here, so it makes weeding out the undesirables even easier."

I nodded in agreement as I took a sip of the coffee that had been sitting on the kitchen counter since Ness had made it. I'd been so caught up with making my profile appealing, food, drink, and sustenance was a secondary thought. I'd been as honest as possible while blurring some minor details such as my weight, and I decided to leave out the whole 'works for a major record company' part. The last thing I wanted was rejection based on my career success. When I'd met Brad, I was the office junior. I was pretty sure Regina had taken me on out of pure pity back then. I was a young, ambitious, and overly keen temp. I would run errands like a lunatic and practically became her slave.

One day, she'd made a lunch date with one of her many boy toys. She had been gone for around half an hour when her husband showed up with an enormous bunch of flowers. I was mortified. Regina's diary contained all of her appointments, and when I say all, I mean booty calls, too. I'd been sitting at my desk, stuffing a chicken sandwich in my mouth when I'd spotted him waltzing toward her office. I knew her diary would be wide open on her desk, and if he saw it, he'd know that she was probably in a similar position at that time. Throwing my sandwich in the trash, I bolted across the office, past Mr Littman, and through the office door. He must have thought I was crazy, but as I crammed the contents of Regina's desk into her draw, locked it, and crammed the key into my bra, I looked up to find him raising an eyebrow at me in confusion. I brushed myself down, strolled over to the door and released the breath I'd been holding with relief. He caught me, and in a moment of brilliance, I rolled my eyes and smiled.

"Lunch deadline on a report. She's a slave driver, but I like the challenge."

He smiled back at me and nodded. "Good workers are hard to find."

And somehow, Regina and I both got away with it. She'd been so grateful when she'd arrived back at the office, she promoted me to Assistant Contracts Advisor on the spot. I was thrilled. I'd rushed home in a stupor from pure excitement. I assumed Brad would be thrilled, too, but when I told him, his immediate reaction was to inquire how much money I would be making. Safe to say, my five-figure salary was marginally higher than his, and he was suddenly irked for the rest of the evening. I should have realised even then that he was a good for nothing butt-munch, but I was in love. It's not as though I was the first to be blinded by the stuff. Though on reflection, I wasn't just blinded by it, I'd clearly spent the entire relationship in a loved-up coma!

I began wondering what Brad's online profile might say and sniggered. *Clean freak with a severe germ phobia* might not have attracted many perspective bed harlots. God only knows how he managed to find one to have an affair with. I had been with him for three years before it became an apparent problem so by then, I was already invested. Aneska was a newbie to sterile sex. Or maybe she was just as weird. I shuddered at the thought of their two bodies, lubed up with alcohol cleansing gel and Brad slipping on condoms as thick as tree trunks.

"You've got a message! Oh my goodness! Charlene, you got a bite!"

Pulling me out of my daydream, Dana bounced up and down excitedly on the sofa. I clicked the small envelope icon and cringed. There were five messages in my inbox, and as I began scrolling, it became evident that at least three were definitely not prospective dates. Enlarging the pictures in each, Ness, Dana, and I winced and made disgusted noises.

"That's disgusting. I mean it's wonky, and it's almost at a total right angle. Was he fucking around corners?" Dana snapped. Pulling the laptop toward her, Ness quickly sat between us and opened a message that appeared to be more about conversation than penis exposure and began reading the damn thing aloud.

"Hi there, Charlene. I'm James. I'm twenty-four, live on the outskirts of London, and I work as a mechanic. Urgh, Charlene, he's a grease monkey. Delete ..."

Grabbing the laptop from her hands, I scowled. "No! There's nothing wrong with mechanics."

Dana giggled. "Skilled hands that fiddle with the inner workings of machinery all day? Sounds great. Especially considering Charlene's cogs could do with a good spin."

She shot me a playful wink, and I chuckled.

"I work at my family garage, and when I saw your profile, I just had to get in touch. I'd love to get to know you. Maybe you could send me an email, and we could have a chat?" I continued.

He didn't sound creepy or weird at all. The jury was still out on a workaholic. Clicking on his picture, I bit my lip as I waited for the image to expand on my screen. Dana gasped.

"Wow. He's hot." She drooled.

Ness snorted. "Ha, if that's even him in the photo. It could be an internet image or whatever."

I was sharing her scepticism, but the picture certainly looked genuine. He had spiky blonde hair, and his red t-shirt allowed part of a sleeve tattoo to show on his impressive arms. It made sense that he'd be rather well built considering all the machinery he would be working with day in and day out. I scrunched my nose up and cringed with uncertainty.

"I don't know. Should I write back?"

Dana continued to bounce while Ness simply raised her eyebrow at me as though it were the most ridiculous question she had ever heard. Taking the laptop into my own hands, I balanced it on my knees and sent a reply.

"How does this sound? 'Hi, James. Nice to meet you. As you can tell, I'm Charlene. I'm twenty-six, and I work in London. I think a chat would be great. Here's my email.'"

Ness stood and walked over to the kitchen counter before turning and leaning her back against it.

"And here's how a date with James would go."

She cleared her throat loudly. "Hi, Charlene. I'm James. I know, I know, I look nothing like my picture. I'm actually forty-six, live with my parents, and work as an office clerk. That picture is of my son. Now, where can we go and have sex?"

Dana threw a cushion at her. "You are so pessimistic, and you always believe that people must be inherently bad. Don't you ever get tired of being such a damn buzz kill?"

"No, and here's why. One, it keeps me safe to always be suspicious of everyone. Two, guys like James are looking for a quick bunk up and nothing else. Oh, maybe a free meal and a night on your sofa. And three—"

Abruptly cut off by the door swinging open, Ness looked relieved and immediately made her way over to an exhausted and extremely over-worked looking Adam.

"Thank God! Someone who can talk some sense into you."

Adam dropped his briefcase and marched over to the refrigerator for a bottle of water. He barely even acknowledged the harpie yelling after him.

"And then, she gets a message from a guy who wants to 'chat.' I think we all know what that really means. Tell her she's nuts, Adam. Please, I could use the voice of reason."

Turning to face her, Adam pulled his glasses from his face and raked his hand over his eyes. He looked stressed, and I could see his whole body visibly tense with every word that left Vanessa's mouth.

"Vanessa, I have no idea what you're going on about, but I really don't have the energy for one of your moments. So please, in English, give me the cliff notes."

"Charlene is online dating! And one creep already wants into her underwear."

Pushing them back onto his face and with his head down, he peered at me over the top of his glasses with a raised brow.

"Really? Isn't that a little desperate, Charlie?"

I tilted my head to the side and gave him a concerned look. "Are you okay?"

He nodded. "Tough day. Anyway, don't change the subject. Are you really going to try online dating?"

Now I was the one shrugging. "It's not as though I have a whole lot left to lose, is it? Clearly, the old fashioned way didn't work out so well for me. Maybe I can find my match on the internet. I mean, he has to be out there somewhere, right? My dream guy—the one that I was meant to be with all along. The one that really *is* the other half of me. I'm tired of losers, arseholes and cheaters. I want my Prince Charming, and if I have to trawl through some frogs to get him, I will."

Dana let out a long breath. "That's so romantic."

Adam grunted and stared at me. "Yeah, well, good luck with that. I've been chasing princesses for years waiting for my queen."

He took a large mouthful of water and headed for his room, slamming the door behind him. Ness and Dana shot me a puzzled look.

"I don't know what that was about, but I do know that I'm trying this online dating thing. I'm not saying I'll find my future husband, but I might at least get a good lay out of it! I'm beginning to think by the time I get a hot man on top of me, I'll be too old to remember what to do with him."

Ness laughed. "There's a lot to be said for a little of what you fancy. Fine, if you really want to give it a try, go ahead. But don't say I didn't warn you."

I nodded and gave her a quick salute. "Yes, ma'am."

* * * *

After the girls had left, I quietly made my way to Adam's room. His reaction and mood when he'd come home had me worried. Adam was always so calm and cool; it was never a good sign to see him worked up. Something *had* to be seriously wrong. Pushing the door open gently, I pressed my palm against the wood.

"Adam? What's going on?"

Wearing a white t-shirt and some sweatpants, he was laying on his bed with his forearm resting over his eyes.

"Nothing. I'm fine, honest."

I rested my head against the doorframe and stared at him. Dropping his arm, he held his hand out and gave me a smile. Without hesitation, I hurried over and lay beside him. He pulled me close and held me tightly in a warm embrace. I wasn't sure what was wrong, but he obviously didn't want to discuss it, and I wouldn't press him. With my head on his chest, I listened to Adam's breathing. I could feel the broad and muscular movements beneath me, and it was soothing. His eyes were closed, and after placing a small kiss on my forehead, he quickly drifted off to sleep. I moved to leave, but his arm held me tighter, keeping me in place. I'd never known him to be so clingy. He needed me, and tonight, I was happy to be his comforter. Snuggling in, I breathed deeply and drifted into a comfortable and deep sleep.

Chapter 12

Sitting at my desk, I let out a long and frustrated groan. I'd been searching for the band Regina set me after for almost two months, and I was getting nowhere fast. All I seemed able to find out was that the drummer was a little bit of a player and the bass player was from Michigan. The lead singer and guitarist was a total mystery. The hottest of the whole group, I'd assumed he'd have been their selling point. I trawled social network sites, the media, and endless calls were made to various bars. Regina had failed to note the name of the establishment where she had first seen them, and this meant I now had a list of over three hundred of them in that area. I was coming up blank.

The sound of Regina's heels clicking on the wooden floors pulled me from my hopelessness. Standing in my doorway, she smiled.

"So, tonight's the big date, huh?"

I nodded. "If you can call it big."

"How long have you two been exchanging emails now? Three weeks?"

I smiled back at her. "Something like that. He seems normal, and he has a great sense of humour."

Walking in, she sat on the edge of the sofa and rested her elbows on her knees.

"What's the plan? Dinner? A movie? Hot and rampant sex?"

I chuckled. "Actually I have to go running with Adam first. I promised I would, and I keep procrastinating.

She rolled her eyes. "I never could understand the allure of running. All that sweat, racing pulse, and panting. I can think of at least three other things, or people, I could do to get me into that state. But, for the record, I have noticed how ... healthy you're looking these days. Doctor Dishy must know what he's talking about."

I had to agree. Adam's regime and strict prohibiting of junk food in the apartment had left me on a diet of salad, chicken, and grilled meats. Granted, I was still trying to come up with new ways to make the meals more exciting, but they were certainly having the desired effect so far. I wasn't quite back to my slender self yet, but I was determined to get there. However, there were only so many ways you could cook asparagus.

Furrowing my brow, I gave Regina a regretful look. "I can't find that band, Regina. I've hunted all over, and they're just nowhere. I can't even find their name. I'm so sorry."

She sighed. "Well, shit. I really thought there had to be something about them out there. They were phenomenal. I wish I could remember the name of that damn bar."

Stopping, she gasped and quickly got to her feet before hurrying through to her office. I pushed my chair away from the desk, walked over, and leaned on the doorframe. I watched as she frantically burrowed through stacks of paperwork, rummaged in her handbag, and threw the contents of her draw on the floor.

"Aha! There it is."

Holding up her hand in triumph, she was clutching a crumpled and somewhat dirty napkin. I stared at her in confusion. Waltzing over, she beamed at me, took my hand, and pressed the napkin into my palm.

Unravelling it, I grinned.

"Benny's Bar and Grill?"

Regina nodded enthusiastically. "That's the bar I saw them at. There is an address and phone number on the back of the napkin. Call them and see what you can find out. If they try to be shady, offer them some cash. I'm willing to do whatever it takes to get that band on our books."

Quickly returning to my desk, I set about gathering all of the relevant information. When I finally got through to the bar, they didn't seem too keen to hand over their best act. I had to explain that I wasn't some other venue trying to steal their band away. After a lot of flirting, negotiating, and offering the man on the other end of the phone a considerable amount of gratitude money, he finally gave me the details.

Leaping from my seat with excitement, I squealed with pleasure. Yes, it really was the small things in life that pleased me, but this was my big chance! I had a name, contact number, and even the names of the entire band. The guy was so grateful for that large donation; he even gave me a brief history. Totting in my five-inch heels over to Regina's office, I pulled open the door and grinned at her.

Her floor was still covered in debris. Sitting at her desk, she looked up and mirrored my expression.

"You found them?"

I nodded. "Yes! Quick, pull up that picture again!"

She quickly began typing and clicking on her laptop, and as the photo enlarged on the screen, I began introducing Regina to our possible new addition.

"Regina Littman, meet D.O.A. The drummer, from what I could find out, is called Nick. The bass player is Eric, and that hot, sexy little piece of man meat at the front there, is Oliver Green. The guy on the phone said they're his best act. I had to sweeten him up with a large payment, but I managed to get a phone number."

Holding out my hand, I showed her the scribbled black pen on my palm. She quickly placed a big kiss on top of it; leaving me with red lipstick marks.

"You are a genius! Now, get on the phone and call the L.A office. I want Denise and Nicola on this immediately! The two of them appear to have a talent for making these hot rock boys stars. I'm sure once you show them who they're working with, they'll bite your hand off."

I laughed. Denise and Nicola were the biggest, dirtiest flirts in the company. There had yet to be an act for them to meet where one of them didn't end up in bed with. But they knew the business better than anyone else, and their results spoke for themselves.

* * * *

The commute back to my apartment seemed to be the quickest it had ever been. Maybe it was the impending dread of my run with Adam or the buzz of excitement of tracking down my first official project at R.J. Littman. Either way, I now felt as though I could take on the world.

Within fifteen minutes of entering my apartment, I had changed into my sweats, eaten an apple for energy, and was now sitting down to check my mail. As I opened my inbox, I held my breath. There was only one message, and it was from James. Great, he must be writing to cancel.

Opening it, I smiled.

> **From**: James
> **Re**: Tonight
> **Message**: Hi, Charlene. Just wanted to say that I can't wait to meet you later. I've booked us a table at Bistro Valentino for seven o'clock. I'll be in jeans and a black shirt with a rose on the table. Looking forward to it."

Relieved that I wasn't getting stood up, I smiled. Pushing the laptop away from me, I made my way to my bedroom and began rummaging through my wardrobe for my trainers. When I pulled them out, I couldn't help but roll my eyes. They'd really never been used. I'd paid a fortune for them back in my gym-going and fitness freaking days, but when I met Brad, my time became so consumed with being in love, that I just ... stopped going. People tell you that you put on a little weight when you're in a relationship, but I had blown up like a balloon and been completely oblivious. I'd gone from a svelte and sexy size twelve to a size eighteen! How could I not have seen it? Blinded by love maybe, but the rapid expansion of my arse should have been a sure fire sign that something was up—my cholesterol, heart rate, and weight being the top three!

* * * *

Adam had texted me and told me to meet him at the park. I'd hardly seen him since that night I'd fallen asleep next to him. If I were the paranoid type, I would have said he was avoiding me, but considering he was still living in my apartment, I figured it was just a busy work schedule keeping him away. Either way, this was a great opportunity to talk and do a little exercise.

Walking over the small hill that led to the running track that ran through the park, I smiled as Adam's tall and muscular physique came into view. He was jogging in place while stretching his arms above his head. His white vest was already damp with sweat around the neck, and his black shorts revealed toned and very thick legs. I'd never noticed how … fit … Adam was. I knew he took care of himself, but damn! I should have been training with him sooner. If I had, maybe I wouldn't have gotten so squidgy!

Looking around, Adam spotted me and grinned. Waving, I made my way over to him. His brow was dotted with beads of sweat, and for the first time in a long time, he was wearing contacts! I gasped and held my hands against his cheeks, forcing his face forward and down toward me. He gave me an odd look, and I think he presumed I was going to kiss him because he immediately turned and pecked me on the cheek. I giggled. Staring into his deep blue eyes, I smiled.

"You're wearing contacts! You never wear contacts. What's up with that?"

Pulling my hands away, he shrugged. "Just trying them out. Don't they suit me?"

I nodded. "They look great. I'm just not used to seeing you without your frames, that's all."

He ran his fingers through his hair and glanced around.

"Well, shall we get started?"

I winced. "Be gentle with me."

He grinned, draped his arm around my shoulder, and began propelling me forward. "Go hard or go home, Charlie. You want to get into shape, you have to work for it."

I groaned and began jogging beside him, trying to keep up.

"I haven't seen you around much lately. Is work okay?" I asked, trying to speak through the heaviness of my breathing.

He nodded. "It's fine. Busy, but fine. What about you?"

I smiled and began telling him all about my triumph in locating the band Regina had been so eager to sign. He mirrored my enthusiasm.

"That's great!"

He began to pick up a little speed, and our light jog was now a gentle run. I could feel myself getting out of breath already. My neck was beginning to sweat, and my pulse was picking up rapidly. I took a quick peek at my watch. Catching me, Adam gave me a puzzled look.

"You late for something?"

I shook my head. "Not yet. I have a date tonight."

Speeding up again, he looked down at the pavement where our feet were now pounding at a brisk pace.

"With that guy from the internet?" he asked.

I nodded; unable to form words, I continued to try and keep up with him.

"I think you're crazy. You're young, attractive, intelligent, successful, and you could do so much better than some loser online! Jeeze, Charlie. You're driving me nuts with your damn self-esteem crap. You're just not willing to try. Always taking the easy option. Like this — running. You're only doing it because you're hoping it will get you the fastest results. Some things are worth waiting for. They're worth all the work, effort, time, and patience. You've always been the damn same."

I stared at him in shock. He was running so fast that I was sprinting just to keep up. My breathing was laboured, my pulse was racing, and my legs were turning to jelly beneath me. Unable to focus, I began to feel dizzy. Halting my steps, I put my hands on my knees, bent forward and threw up. Adam stopped a few feet from me and jogged over.

"God, Charlene! Did you eat today?"

I nodded, and as I tried to regulate my breathing, I gasped and panted for air.

"When? What did you eat?"

I couldn't form words. I was too busy trying not to die from exhaustion.

"Here, there's a bench over there."

Steering me to the grassy area across the track, he pushed me gently onto the wooden bench and sat beside me.

"I had a yoghurt for breakfast and a sandwich at lunch," I panted.

He rolled his eyes. "That's not enough. I told you to eat a proper meal."

I groaned. "Got a habit of telling me what to do lately. Don't you?"

His brow furrowed, and he stood abruptly. "Only when you don't have the common sense to figure things out for yourself. I feel like I have to babysit you! And you know what, it's always been that way. The Charlene Show has been a re-run in my life for the past twenty years! But it's all the same shit. I've been taking care of you and watching you make mistake after mistake for too long. It actually occurred to me today that you are the only significant relationship I have ever had with a woman!"

Getting to my feet, I squared up to him. "That's crazy! You've had girlfriends and hook-ups."

He shook his head fiercely. "Hardly! Every time I get close to it, something happens in your life, and I just drop everything to stop you from falling apart. Well, you know what? I'm done. You clearly don't want or need my advice so I won't give it to you anymore."

I stomped my foot and glared at him. "Don't try and put your shit on me! It's not my fault you strike out so much. You don't even try. Every relationship you've ever had, you've found some fault in the girl and ended it. And you're the one with self-esteem issues. Always hiding behind your shirt, tie, and stethoscope. You blush when you see sex on TV for crying out loud!"

Turning, he began to walk away from me.

"That's right, walk away! I don't need a father, Adam. I wanted a friend, and you see me as a project. Well, thanks so much for wasting my time for twenty years!"

He stopped, turned, and stormed back to me. Pointing his finger in my face, I could see the fury in his eyes, and the trembling tone of his voice told me he was also close to tears.

"You are so selfish, and I am done being your keeper, Charlene. And for your information, you have never been a project. You were then, are now, and always will be the best friend I have ever had."

I could feel tears welling in my eyes, and Adam must have seen them too. His hand fell to his side, and his face was filled with remorse.

"I have to go. You should get ready for your date."

I sniffed a little, hurt by his callous tone and confused as to what had happened between us that could cause such a rift.

"What's happening to us?" I tearfully asked.

He shook his head ruefully. "I don't know. Growing up and growing apart maybe? You said you wanted to change, and I guess I just thought I'd get the old Charlie back. Instead, you started acting so differently. You wallow a lot, you let what others think affect you, and now you're going on dates with guys you met on the internet."

I placed my hand gently on his shoulder. "I'm still me. I don't understand what's going on."

He sighed deeply and rubbed his forehead with his finger and thumb. "I'm scared, Charlie. I'm scared that I'm going to lose you; that *you're* losing you."

And there it was. Fear. I'd been changing so much about my life and myself; I'd forgotten to take care of the one thing that had always been my constant—Adam. I'd neglected our friendship.

"I'm sorry, Adam. I really am. But you are not going to lose me. You're stuck with me for life. I might try crazy weight loss classes and diets, but I will always be your friend. And as your friend, I can tell when you're holding out on me."

He stared at the ground in silence.

"Adam, what's going on? You've been acting strange since that night you came home from work all riled. You didn't want to talk then, but you have to talk to me sometime. What is it?"

He slumped back against the bench. "I got a promotion at work."

I held my hand to my mouth and grinned. "That's amazing! Why didn't you tell me?"

He shrugged. "It's not a big deal, and besides, I'm turning it down."

I gave him a confused look.

"Why the hell would you do that?"

He groaned. "The boss is a bitch. She makes my life hell! My workload has tripled, and she is giving me the most awful cases. Half of my patients are terminal and a quarter are children. Charlie, do you know how heartbreaking it is to see the same kids, parents, and people walk into my office every week and know that there is almost nothing I can do to help them? It's killing me. I'm not ready for this shit. I've only been a doctor for two years, and I'm still finding my feet. This has been like diving into a shark-infested tank."

I moved closer to him and rested my head against his shoulder. "That sucks. But if you weren't good at your job, you wouldn't have been promoted. Maybe she's trying to challenge you—"

He cut me off and scoffed at my comment. "No. She fucking hates me. She changes my work schedule, which means I work mostly in the evenings, and she is always on my case! She even stays at the office to watch me and make sure I get her damn paperwork done."

She changes his schedule, stays at the office and makes his life hell. I forced myself not to giggle. Adam's problem was simple. His boss was crushing on him. Needing more information, I began questioning him.

"Is she married? Surely she has a husband to harass?"

He shook his head. "No. She's the same age as me, but she got her doctorate a year before so she's already worked her way up. You'd think it would make her a little more understanding. I mean, she was a newbie not long ago."

I nodded. "And I suppose she's the really pretty type who probably flirted her way up?"

He shook his head again. "I doubt it. Don't get me wrong, she's attractive, but she's clearly got a good work ethic. Yesterday, one of the interns asked her out, and she immediately began giving him the rundown on dating your superior and how unethical it is."

And the fact that she would rather be in your pants, I thought.

"Well, I'm sure it will all straighten out. Maybe you could ask her to lunch one day and discuss it. If she's the professional you say, she'll be willing to hear you out," I suggested.

He raised a brow at me. "You think so?"

I nodded enthusiastically. "Absolutely. What have you got to lose?"

Wrapping his arm around me, he pulled me close and kissed my forehead.

"I'll give it a try." He glanced at his watch. "You better get going. You have a date, remember?"

Smiling, I jumped to my feet and immediately regretted it. My legs still hadn't quite recovered, and as I began hobbling back over the hill, I had to lean on Adam to stop myself from falling over. I only hoped a long soak in the bath, and some heat gel might relieve my aching body before my date. I'd have hated for him to think he already had the upper hand when I stand before him and my knees literally weaken. This time, I would be cautious. My heart had been broken, and I wasn't ready to allow another man to play with it just yet.

Chapter 13

Walking into the crowded restaurant, I clutched my purse
in my hand tightly and bit my lip. Adam's tirade about my
search for romance was playing on my mind all afternoon.
Didn't he want me to find anyone? I mean, here I was, about
to meet a drop-dead gorgeous hunk, and all I could think
about was Adam and his tongue-lashing! And I mean what he
said, you filthy creature. Mentally reprimanding myself for
allowing Adam's words to get to me so much, my eyes
scanned the entire room until they fell on a tall, blonde,
knickers-dropping, tongue-unravelling hunk! James's picture
did not do him justice! He was way hotter in person! His hair
had a just fucked look about it, and a little gel had clearly been
used to keep it that way. He was standing beside our table a
few feet away, waving me over with an enormous grin on his
face.

Trying to maintain my composure and not seem like an
awkward teenager, I slowly walked over. I couldn't stop
staring at him. He was like the sun. You know you're not
supposed to look directly at it, but you enjoy the warmth of it
on your skin so much that you risk the burning of your
retinas. And clearly, he was blinding me. As I approached the

table, I didn't see the handbag strap that was strewn across the floor. It belonged to the woman at the table beside ours. My six-inch stiletto heel immediately tangled itself in the damn thing, and I was sent hurtling, head first, into my date.

Reaching out with both hands, I caught the thighs of his jeans, and as I fell to the ground … so did his trousers. I was mortified. There I was, in the middle of a crowded restaurant, on a first date with a man who only knew me by what he had read in my emails, and I had just stripped him down to his boxer shorts! Perfect.

With my eyes tightly closed, I cringed. I was still gripping his trousers when he abruptly grabbed at them and began hurriedly pulling them up. Pushing up onto my knees, I glanced up at him, still unable to lift my head. People around us were staring, giggling, and murmuring to one another. I wanted the ground to open up and swallow me whole.

But it didn't. Deciding to simply take the opportunity to make a quick getaway, I scrambled to my feet and turned to leave. A hand reached out and caught my wrist, spinning me around in the process.

"You're leaving? Were my shorts that horrendous?"

I lifted my head and found myself gazing into two gorgeous eyes. When I say gorgeous, I don't mean the, 'I want to marry you, fall deep into your eyes, and make lots of babies with you' type. Oh no. I mean the, 'Come to bed, and I will fuck you seven ways to Sunday and then back again' type of eyes. They practically screamed it, and my body was more than willing to accept the invitation!

Shaking my head, I bit my lip anxiously.

"Not at all. They're very nice. I've always been a Calvin Klein fan."

He gave a deep and throaty chuckle. "Well, glad all the awkwardness is out of the way. Feel like staying for dinner? Or did you get enough to eat when you landed in my crotch?"

I almost died. My mouth agape, I stuttered and stammered. I didn't have an answer for that. I wasn't a prude, and I was certainly no virgin, but he was so … brash. It excited me. Tilting my head, I smiled. "I have a big appetite, I think I could manage a little more."

Laughing, he pulled out my chair for me and gestured for me to sit. Placing my purse on the table, I carefully held my little black dress in place and slid myself in. James leaned into my ear. "I'm glad you have a big appetite. I have a lot worth eating."

My eyes widened, but I tried to hide my obvious embarrassment. I was sure I must have been blushing because my cheeks were on fire. Sitting opposite me, James grinned, and I realised he was enjoying making me feel so flustered. Straightening myself out, I smiled back.

He reached a hand across the table and took mine. His thumb brushed the back of my knuckles gently. "I'd ask you all about your job, family, and all the boring shit people talk about on a first date, but after all those emails, I feel like I already know you. So, why don't you take a little time to ask me things?"

I gave him a surprised look. A guy who actually *wanted* to talk about himself? Was he gay?

"And no, I'm not gay if that's what you were thinking."

I cleared my throat. How did he do that? This man had to be the slickest, hottest, smoothest guy I had ever met. His crisp white shirt was slightly unbuttoned and also a little tight. It was clearly intentional as I could see every curve and flex of his muscular chest. His sleeves were rolled up to the elbows, but the dark lines of his tattoo were visible through the sheer cotton. I squirmed in my seat. I hadn't had sex in months, and the sex with Brad wasn't exactly thrilling. I had a feeling that James was a wildcat in the sack.

The waiter brought over a bottle of red, and James quickly poured me a glass. Picking his up, he raised it in the air and encouraged me to do the same.

"To first dates with gorgeous redheads."

I grinned. "And to burying my face in a hot guy's crotch."

He laughed lightly and took a long sip of his drink. I set my glass down and smiled sweetly. Deciding to play my hand and make my intentions known, I got a little flirty and dirty.

"So, how big *is* your ego, exactly?" I teased.

He gave me a playful smile and set his glass down, stroking the stem. "Huge. Some might say I'm cocky and a little hard to be around. But, I haven't had any complaints so far."

Well played.

"I see. Well, personally, I think there's nothing wrong with a woman stroking a man's ego now and then. It can really deepen a relationship."

His smile widened. "Yes, it can. I certainly like it deep. I mean, you don't want it to choke you, but you want it to be meaningful and ultimately fulfilling. Happy endings for all is my belief."

I was beginning to squirm. "Agreed. And who doesn't enjoy the thrill of a brand spanking new adventure with a new partner?"

Now *James* was blushing. Clearing his throat, he shifted in his seat. Bingo.

"I'm suddenly extremely ravenous, Charlene. Are you hungry?"

I nodded and bit my lip. Reaching across the table, I gripped his collar. "I want another taste of the appetiser I sampled at the beginning of this evening."

Grabbing my hand, he stood and pulled me toward the door, never saying a word. He quickly handed the hostess a fifty before pulling the door open and leading me to a nearby taxi. I giggled uncontrollably. I hadn't been this excited, turned on, or overwhelmingly horny in such a long time. Sliding into the taxi, James tugged on my hand to urge me inside. The moment the door closed behind us, his hands were all over me. Clawing at the back of my dress, palming my breast, his lips hungrily took my own in a deep and sensual kiss. Holy hell! This was hot!

Murmuring into my mouth, he grabbed my hand and pressed it to his bulging crotch.

"Where? Your place or mine?"

I thought for a moment. Adam would be working all night, and the apartment was only two blocks from where we were. Leaning forward and tearing myself away from James, I knocked on the partition glass.

"Where to, lovebirds?" the driver sarcastically threw back over his shoulder.

"West Street. Just opposite the Carpenter's Arms."

Nodding, the driver set off and began to run the meter.

James pulled me back into his arms and slid his hand sleekly up my thigh. I was glad I'd decided on suspenders and stockings over my big girl tights after all. This was going better than I could have ever imagined. His fingers played with the lace at the top of my stocking, and a grin spread across his face as his tongue darted into my mouth. God, I was hot! I was practically convulsing with lust!

As we pulled up outside my apartment, I fumbled for my keys as James tossed a twenty to the driver. I pushed the car door open and totted over to my front porch, hurriedly opening the door as James pressed his body against mine behind me. His solid erection was pressed against my behind, and I was desperate to put it to some good use. We tripped, giggled, and fondled our way up the stairs and finally into my place. Gripping him by the shirt, I kicked off my shoes and pulled him toward the bedroom. He unbuttoned his shirt en route and quickly cast it aside as we entered my room. It was dark, and only the small amount of light from the street lamp outside my window lit the room. I stood back and gazed at James. He was Adonis!

Rushing at me, he spun me around and unzipped my dress, before pushing it over my shoulders and hips in a frenzy. I stood before him, in my black lacy underwear, and I was glad for the darkness. Darkness hid all the unsightly wobbly bits. Okay, so he would feel them soon enough, but I figured he'd be too wrapped up in his ecstasy by then to care. His hand grasped my ass, and he smacked it gently. I let out a small yelp and turned abruptly, unbuttoning his jeans as my lips explored his muscular and perfectly toned chest. He let out a soft moan, and I melted. Pushing him onto the bed, I whipped off his jeans and straddled him. All that remained between us were his shorts and my knickers, and I was sure he'd be taking them off soon. His thumbs hooked inside the elastic at my waist as his hands urged me to rock against him. I was coming undone with how much I needed my orgasm. I couldn't remember the last time I had experienced a truly mind-blowing, toe-curling, breathtaking, and heart-pounding orgasm.

Breathing heavily, he panted into my ear.

"Where's the bathroom?"

I gave him a puzzled look but quickly pointed toward my en-suite. Shifting me from his lap, he disappeared into the bathroom. I quickly adjusted myself and tried to look … alluring … for when he returned. When he did, he had a small tube and a condom in his hand. Grinning, he made his way over to me and pressed me against the mattress. His hands slid down my body to my underwear, and slowly, he pulled them off. If I hadn't been cloaked in darkness, James would have seen the deep shade of crimson I was now sporting across my face. I couldn't see what he was doing as I was now staring at the ceiling, but I was sure I heard his shorts drop followed by the sound of foil tearing. What came after was surprising. A squirting sound and I began to wonder what that tube was. My wonderings soon disappeared as suddenly, James thrust inside me. I gasped. He was huge, and I was in shock. I'd forgotten how good sex could feel. It didn't have to be robotic or rehearsed. It could be spontaneous, sensual, passionate, and downright rampant!

Rocking his hips back and forth, James moaned, groaned, and panted in my ear. My hands gripped his back. I could feel every part of me tightening. Tightening and … opening my eyes, I furrowed my brow. James continued to plunge in and out, but his thrusts were becoming slower, more forceful and … sticky!

"Uh, James?"

He groaned slightly as though trying desperately to continue his movements, but he soon halted and not out of choice.

"Charlene, I think … I think I'm stuck!"

Trying desperately to scoot myself up the bed and push him away from me, I gasped. "What kind of condom are you using?" I yelled.

He shook his head and yelped as I kicked against his thighs trying to separate us. He just wouldn't budge!

"Just your average store bought box-of-three type. They're a little bit dry sometimes, but I found some lube in your cabinet."

I shook my head in confusion. "What lube? I don't have any lube."

He groaned loudly as he tried to pull out of me, but it didn't get us anywhere. I was beginning to feel the burn of chafing, and I assumed he must have been, too.

"Sure you do. It was in your cabinet next to your birth control in that half circle case thing."

I shook my head. "I don't use birth contr—"

I gasped loudly and held my hand over my mouth in horror.

"Oh my, God, no! James, that's denture glue! Those are my grans' dentures! Not the fucking pill! Jesus Christ, you just shoved a shit load of dental-fix into my hoo-ha!"

Now he panicked. "It's what? Well, how do I get it off? It's all over the place! I can't even get the condom off because the damn stuff is all tangled in my undergrowth!"

I grimaced and tried again to free myself. "Haven't you ever heard of man-scaping, and why the hell did you go in my cabinet in the first place!?"

He grunted. "I was looking for lube!"

"Well, clearly you didn't find it!"

He was almost crying by now as he tried frantically to get away. If the denture fixer hadn't done it, his current emotional state had now certainly killed my buzz.

"Oh God! What are we going to do? Do something, Charlene!"

I placed my hands on his shoulders and pulled myself up.

"You're going to have to carry me over to the phone. It's on the table beside the bed. Nodding, James made a heaving sound as he carried me over, and we both fell onto the bed. Grabbing the phone, I dialled the only person I could think of who might be able to help.

"Doctor Fitz, how can I help you?"

I rolled my eyes and took a deep breath.

"Hi, Adam. It's me."

"Charlie? I thought you were on a date?"

I sighed deeply and cast my eyes at James who was hovering over me.

"Yeah, well, things got complicated and don't say I told you so. Anyway, the reason I called is … I wondered, do you know what un-fixes denture glue?"

He let out a soft chuckle.

"Why on Earth would you need to do that?"

I thought quickly.

"Jacob managed to get it all over his paws. Gran left some here."

He laughed loudly. "Serves him right. Curiosity killed the cat and all that."

I was beginning to lose my patience. I was sticky, frustrated, and glued to a man who was crying over the current ripping out of his pubic hairs.

"Adam, the cure, please?"

He coughed and cleared his throat. "Sorry. Only one thing for it, I suppose. A warm bath. He won't like it, but it'll loosen the glue, and then some good old soap and water will do the rest."

I breathed a sigh of relief. Visions of James and me strolling into the hospital with the old 'I slipped and fell' excuse was not high on my list of things to do before I die.

"Thank you. Thank you so much! I'll see you later, bye!"

Hanging up before he had a chance to question me further, I turned my attention to James. "We have to have a bath. Quick, carry me to the bathroom."

He groaned. "Seriously? Do you realise how heavy you are?"

I immediately began wriggling and writhing around, forcing a few more of his precious hairs to become instantly plucked from his forest.

"Ouch! Okay, okay. I'm sorry."

Picking me up, he carried me to the bathroom where I awkwardly ran us a bath, and we both climbed in with great difficulty.

So, there we were. Two people who met online, spent three weeks exchanging pleasantries, had an impromptu strip show in a restaurant and were now glued together in a bathtub. I sat, straddling his thighs, and we waited for the glue to begin to dissolve. Neither of us spoke. I'd managed to grab a towel that had been hanging on the bathroom door, and now had it firmly wrapped around myself to hide the rolls and tyres. Not that it made much difference now. I was fairly certain James had little desire to continue our little session. I know I definitely wasn't looking for a repeat performance.

After about an hour, we were finally able to pry ourselves apart. James hurried to the bedroom to pull on his clothes while I finished cleaning the bathtub and myself. He didn't say goodbye, but I heard the front door slam as he left. I wasn't offended or hurt. I was glad to see him go. If this was what I had to look forward to by dipping my toes into the dating pond, I was severely out of my depth already!

Chapter 14

There's something to be said about London in the spring …
it's busy. Tourists flock to the centre of the capital to take in
the sights, and the shops and boutiques suddenly become
flush with bright, summery colours and patterns. I hated it. As
a fiery redhead, it was nearly impossible for me to find any
colour that didn't instantly make me look as though I was
slapped in the face with some white wash paint and had my
head set on fire. The Irish blood running through my veins
ensured that I had the complexion and skin tone of a china
doll.

Wearing a pair of jeans that I hadn't been able to cram my
arse into for almost a year and a green shirt, I watched the
people passing by. I was sitting outside a charming little café.
When I had moved to London six years ago, I was in awe of
the place. The people, the hustle and bustle of the everyday
commute, and the endless streets that were lined with shops.
Now, I found it overcrowded, the people seemed rude, and
the shops were too expensive. My mother had once suggested
that I had outgrown London, but I was pretty sure that it had
been her roundabout way of trying to lure me back home.

144

Emerging from the café, Vanessa and Dana were animatedly chatting to one another. Handing me a cup of tea, Dana sat opposite me while Ness sat between us.

"So …" Taking a large sip of her scalding hot coffee, Dana gasped and pressed her lips together before returning her attention to me. "How did your date go?"

I hadn't seen the girls in almost a week, and let's face it, my disastrous date with James wasn't exactly the type of conversation I wanted to have over the phone.

Resting my elbow on the table, I leaned my cheek against my fist and ran my finger around the rim of my cup.

"It didn't quite go to plan."

Ness gave me a quizzical look.

"What do you mean?"

I sighed. "Just … we didn't … connect."

That was a lie! We were so connected that evening that we were literally inseparable!

Dana shrugged. "No spark, huh?"

I nodded. "Something like that."

Ness giggled a little and took a sip of her coffee.

"That's not what I heard."

I immediately turned my attention to her, curious as to where she could have obtained any information.

"I heard you two didn't even make it through dinner."

My mouth dropped open in surprise.

"Where the hell did you get that information from?"

Dana leaned in closer, clearly eager to hear more.

"I have my sources. I heard that the two of you spent around fifteen minutes in the restaurant after you'd tripped and landed in his crotch, that is."

I stuttered.

"I … you … oh dear, God."

Hiding my red and embarrassed face in my hands, I shook my head.

"So, I guess it wasn't the chemistry that was a problem." Dana giggled.

"Was it the biology? Was he tiny? Couldn't get it up? Too slow with the quick draw, and then too fast with the shooting? Tell us!"

She was practically bouncing up and down in her seat.

"It wasn't like that. He was great. Sexy, hot, he had a great body, and he was a good lover."

Ness furrowed her brow.

"Then what was it?"

I took a deep breath and lifted my head from my hands.

"Promise not to laugh?"

Dana and Ness both shook their heads.

"Absolutely not," they chimed.

I rolled my eyes and began regaling them with my horror story. I didn't leave out a single detail. From the trip to the denture glue, they listened with looks of sheer hilarity on their faces. When I finally stopped and took a breath, the two of them stared at me in silence as my face heated with embarrassment. The silence didn't last long as they both immediately burst into fits of laughter. It was loud, belly laughing, and I was utterly mortified as people around us began to stare.

"Will you two please try to control yourselves?"

But my plea went unanswered. Dana rocked in her seat while Ness hammered her fist on the table as the two of them convulsed and cried with laughter.

"Oh my God, Charlene. That's hilarious."

I stifled a giggle. Their own laughter was infectious, and in hindsight, it was slightly humorous.

"You guys, it was awful. He had to carry me to the phone, and I had to call Adam for advice!"

This prompted yet more hilarity.

"Adam? You called Adam!" Ness asked through the tears rolling down her face.

"I told him Jacob had gotten it all over his paws. I couldn't confess what really happened!"

Dana held her hand to her chest and took several deep breaths.

"Did he at least apologise for pumping your vagina with Fixodent?"

I shook my head. "No. I stayed in the bathroom to clean up, and he made a quick getaway. I haven't heard from him since, and I don't want to."

"What a jerk! He could at least have said something before he bailed." Dana had now regained her composure while Ness was wiping the streaks of mascara from her cheeks.

"Yeah," Ness interrupted, "he had the nerve to stick his dick in you, but not the courage to face you afterwards. Sounds like a lucky escape."

I scoffed a laugh. "Ness, I was lucky to get detached from him, let alone escape."

Dana laughed lightly as she took another mouthful of her coffee.

Folding my arms onto the table, I rested my forehead against them and stared at the ground.

"I am a walking, talking calamity. I'm the unluckiest woman I know—doomed to roam the Earth alone, orgasm-less. It didn't help that Adam gave me a lecture on internet dating. I swear he'd have me stay celibate for the rest of my life. What is his problem? Every time I get close to a guy, Adam always has to do or say something to fuck it up. Like when I got engaged to Brad. He hardly spoke to me for weeks.

He even started scanning every episode of *Crime Watch*, convinced that Brad was a con-man looking to bankrupt me. The male black widow."

Dana patted the back of my head and tutted. "I'm sure he has his reasons."

Ness snorted. "Yeah, and we all know what they are."

Dana gave her warning glare, but Ness ignored her and rolled her eyes. I eyed them with suspicion but decided it just wasn't worth pursuing.

I slammed my head back down onto my arms as Ness began rummaging in her purse. As I lifted my head to see what she was doing, she pulled out a small business card.

"Aha! I knew it was here somewhere. Charlene, what exactly is it you're looking for? Mr Right? Or Mr Right Now? Because in my hand, I might just hold the answer to your problems."

I eyed her curiously. "I'm listening."

Dana peered over at the card and raised her eyebrows. Catching her, Ness tutted disapprovingly.

"This is a very special card. It will get you into the most exclusive, high-class, swanky and filled to the brim with hot males, bar in London."

I reached out my hand to take the card, but she quickly snapped it away and pressed it against her chest.

"This isn't the place you go to meet your future husband. *This* is where you go to find your orgasm."

Dana made a grab for the card, but Ness batted her hand away.

"You kept that place quiet! No wonder you seem to always have a hot, successful, stallion of a man on your arm! You've found their hunting ground!" Dana fumed.

"Ness, I'm not looking for a gigolo."

She chuckled and shook her head. "They're not for hire, Charlene. They're men who have little time or desire to go chasing after a relationship. They will, however, give you the most memorable night of your life. It's kind of an invitation-only type of thing. But this card guarantees you entry."

"And a sexually transmitted disease, too, by the sounds of it." Slumped back in her chair and cradling her drink, Dana sulked.

"Dana, you complain all the time about one-night stands, and casual sex making you feel cheap. If I actually thought you'd have an interest in going there, I would have invited you a long time ago."

Dana opened her mouth to respond, but shrugging, she closed it again.

"So, what do you say, Charlene?"

Ness held the card between her fingers and rubbed it provocatively with her thumb as she offered it to me.

I thought for a moment. Did I really want to go to a club, pick up a random guy, have him drag me back to his place and have pornstar-worthy sex all night and then a walk of shame in the morning? The answer was simple: hell yes I did! Swiping the card from Ness's fingers, I bit my lip as I read it.

Bar 69. *Original*, I thought.

Picking up her cup, Ness grinned. "You won't regret it, sweetie. The best sex of my life. We'll go this weekend."

Dana sat bolt upright and beamed at Ness.

Rolling her eyes, Ness smiled. "Yes, Dana. You, Charlene and I will *all* go together. It'll be fun. Three lionesses out on the prowl."

I wasn't sure that I classed myself as a lioness, but I was certainly interested in obtaining some juicy piece of meat to play with! My sex drive was going into overload, and I was losing control of the wheel. I needed some satisfaction, and after my sticky situation with James, I was eager to find myself a man with a little less pubic hair and a lot more experience. Maybe Ness's club wasn't where I'd find my knight in shining armour, but I could at least ride a few stallions while I waited for his arse to hurry up and sweep me off my feet.

Besides, I'd been flogging the same dead horse for five years, and Brad was certainly nothing to shout about. He was of average build, ruggedly handsome, and had dark brown hair. For a guy with a need for extreme hygiene and germ precautions, he was also less than attractively hairy. It was a good thing he was opposed to oral sex. When we were first dating, I had gone down on him several times, and on each occasion, I had found myself almost choking on a rogue hair or coughing up a fur ball! Honestly, guys, man-scaping. It's a girl's best friend, and what's more, it makes your junk look bigger and a lot more appealing to us. No pluck, no suck!

Smiling, I dropped the card into my bag, picked up my cup, and took a long gulp. Ness and Dana both grinned at me.

"Okay, I'll go. Who knows, maybe I'll find myself a real sexpert who can clear my cobwebs for good."

Dana cringed while Ness giggled. Internet dating hadn't panned out too well, and I knew how I preached on about toxic environments, but I was looking for a little bit of toxic right now. Mr Right was taking too long, and my desire to fulfil my orgasmic needs was outweighing my need for a relationship. It didn't guarantee you great sex anyhow. The best boyfriend in the world could still be an awful lover, and the biggest arsehole could be the stud you always dreamed of. I was sure it was the reason, so many intelligent, successful, and beautiful women ended up with some real losers. I figured they must be totally comatose from the mind-blowing sex. I had never personally been one of these women, though.

Sex had never been about the actual pleasure. It was about the relationship or the amount of alcohol I had consumed. One-night stands weren't really my thing. But there again, neither was being jilted by my fiancé. The new Charlene was changing in many ways. Maybe, this was just one of them, and I hoped it was a change for the better. Either way, I needed to get some action, and I needed it soon ... minus the denture glue, of course!

Chapter 15

Dressed in my jeans, black halter-top, and a pair of kitten heels, I checked and re-checked my reflection in the mirror. Adam, who had installed three around my apartment, had forcibly lifted my ban on the damn things: one in my bedroom behind the door; one in the bathroom beside the tub; and another on the wall between the kitchen and his room. It was hell. I couldn't walk freely around the place without the constant reminder of my weight, and I was tempted to tear them down, except I was slightly reluctant to endure twenty-one years of bad luck. I had enough bad luck already; I didn't need anything else to up the ante.

Clip-clopping my way into the lounge, I groaned. Dieting, exercise, and that awful detox had only managed to rid me of one dress size. Surely, I was doing something wrong! I wasn't hoping to be a size eight or even a ten. No, I wanted to be a curvy, cuddly, and sexy size twelve Charlie again. I loved her. She had a great arse, perky boobs, and cleavage you could get lost in. I'd lost her somewhere when I was busy wrapping tyres of jelly around my waist.

I made my way to the fridge and pulled out a bottle of mineral water and some leftover chicken salad. If I were going to end up drowning my sorrows tonight, I would rather do it on a full stomach. A strawberry daiquiri is not as much fun when it's coming back up. I learned that the hard way on my twenty-first birthday. I was just about to stab my fork into a chunk of chicken when Adam breezed in, threw his briefcase on the floor, and slumped down onto the sofa. Jacob, who was curled up at the other end, lifted his head and gave Adam a deathly stare. He was naturally incensed at being woken by this invader.

Resting my arms on the counter, I lifted my fork and pointed it at him.

"What's wrong with you?" I asked, shoving a fork load of lettuce into my mouth.

He sighed and rubbed his brow. He was still choosing to wear his glasses to work but would frequently ditch them in the evenings for contacts. He said he was trying to allow his eyes the time to adjust before going all in.

"I hate my job. I hate it."

I giggled. "No you don't, you liar. You love your job."

He shrugged. "Not today. I have a shit load of paperwork that still needs doing, so it seems my weekend just filled up, and my boss made me stay an extra three hours so that she could go over some inventory with me! That's the intern's job. Why did I have to make the damn lists?"

Poor Adam. He really was blind, even with those thick-rimmed glasses. An idiot could have seen that his boss was crushing on him.

"So, have it out with her," I suggested.

He shook his head. "It's not worth it. She's a senior, and I haven't been in the department long enough to throw my weight around."

I nodded in understanding.

Finishing my salad, I dumped the plate in the sink and skirted around the counter into the lounge. Sitting up and placing his elbows on his knees, Adam gave me a curious look. His brow furrowed as his eyes moved up and down my body.

"What are you all dressed up for? Got another hot date with that internet guy?"

"Ha! Yeah, right. I won't be seeing him again. Our date didn't exactly end well."

Adam smiled. "I assumed something had gone wrong when you were home and calling me about denture fix."

I almost choked on the water I had sipped. "What do you mean?"

He laughed. "Well, if it had gone well, you wouldn't have been home, alone, cleaning your cat."

I physically relaxed. The thought of Adam knowing about my sexual mishap with James was less than appealing. Bending to take off his shoes, he glanced up at me over the rim of his glasses and smiled.

"Well, his loss, Charlie. You're the catch of a lifetime."

I scoffed. "Yeah, like a sexually transmitted disease."

Adam shook his head and neatly lined his shoes up beside the sofa. "There you go again, putting yourself down. How do you expect to find the man of your dreams when you don't even love who *you* are?"

I exhaled slowly. "I thought I *had* found him. Until he ran off with some home-wrecking harlot."

"Maybe a little time getting to know yourself again would be a better idea than searching for your next big romance, Charlie."

It was good advice, but surely I could meet myself *and* have mind-blowing sex, too?

"Maybe. But for now, I'll settle for hot, sexy, and willing to fuck my brains out."

Adam's eyes widened at me, and he blushed, adjusting his tie.

"If that's what you're looking for. I'm assuming that's why you're dressed up and wearing your best heels?"

I glanced down at my feet. "Naturally. Guys hate a girl who is too tall. Kitten heels get me laid, and there's less chance of me falling on my arse."

Or my face … I thought back to my date with James.

"I just think you could do so much better, and you deserve better. I'm going to have a bath and relax with a beer while I plough through that heap of paperwork in my case."

Rising from the sofa, he walked over and placed a light kiss on my cheek. "Try not to get into too much trouble, and if tonight does turn into your lucky night, try to keep it down."

Heading toward the bathroom, he turned and winked at me. My insides did a tiny loop-de-loop, and I found myself grinning like a maniac. Adam always knew just what to say to boost my confidence. He was everything a girl could want, but yet he continued to be single. No woman ever seemed to measure up to his standards. I had wondered if they felt intimidated by his relationship with me, but most of them had embraced our friendship and those who found it harder, I would try hard to win over—usually with a pretty high success rate. Adam was fussy, picky, and was clearly holding out on these women. They were usually gorgeous, successful, and totally head over heels for him, but he was always so oblivious or reluctant to actually maintain the relationship. Hell, I couldn't even remember the last time he'd had a girl at all. Was he practising abstinence? I cringed and shook my head. I knew all too well how hard it was to be in a sexual desert, and it had to be even harder for a man. At least we ladies have endless options of battery-operated boyfriends, sex buddies, one-night stands and meaningless fumbles behind a bar. I knew for a fact that for women, finding a willing male for a quick bunk up and fast exit was relatively simple. Finding a woman who was also looking for the same … nearly impossible. However, I realise that this is a little hypocritical considering what I'm telling you about my prowling for some stallion sex beast to make mine for the night. Don't judge me. You know you've all been there. Passion, rampant, hungry, and horny sexual appetite raging, we've all wanted to tear Matt Bomer or Ian Somerhalder's clothes off at some point. If not them, someone at least. And yes, I know I should seek help for that Somerhalder obsession, but we've all got that list … you know, the 'It's not cheating if he's a celebrity,' list.

Lost in my lustful thoughts of celebrities, I jumped a little as the sound of a horn honking downstairs echoed around the quiet street. Peering out of the window, I saw Ness and Dana waving up at me beside a waiting taxi. Grabbing my purse and quickly checking myself in the mirror, I shrugged.

"Yep, as good as it's gonna get I'm afraid." I cast my eye back at Jacob who glanced up, but with a long stretch, simply turned around on the sofa and settled with his back to me. Hopefully, the males at the bar would be a little more attentive. Otherwise, my *own* battery operated boyfriend, and my Ian Somerhalder calendar were getting a serious work out tonight!

* * * *

Walking into the bar, I felt like a fish out of water. The décor was incredibly decadent. It reminded me of a 1920s gentlemen's lounge. Tall, golden columns with vine detailing made up a large portion of the room, and the rest was made up of the three, elegant, and dark wooden bars. Behind each was an array of expensive-looking spirits, wines, ales, and the bartenders were dressed in black ties and white shirts. The seating was also very luxurious. Red velvet chairs with golden trim similar to that of the pillars, sat in pairs around small, round wooden tables, which matched the bars. It was like stepping out of Kansas into Oz. The music was playing softly from large speakers, and the people that were already beginning to crowd the bars were equally as classy as the place itself. When Ness said this place was exclusive, she wasn't kidding!

You could practically smell the pheromones in the air. Men and women all on the hunt for that perfect hook up. I gave Dana and Ness a worried look. The women in the bar could only be described as sleek, sexy, and confident lionesses. And I was a plump little bunny caught in headlights. Ness was swaying a little to the music and grinning.

"Why do you look so worried? You wanted Mr Right Now, and here is where you'll find him. There's everything you could possibly be shopping for in one place: blondes, brunettes, redheads, and some from the 'other' pile, such as the guys with typically modern rocker styles. You know, all dip-dyed with blue and stuff. But one thing they all have in common—"

"They've all shagged you?" Dana interrupted. Ness glared at her and gave a sarcastic laugh.

"Funny. No, they're all looking for a quick hook up with no strings. And, they're all dynamite in the sack."

Dana giggled. "So you have slept with them all then. I assume you're speaking from experience."

Giving her a gentle shove, Ness pointed toward the bar. "You are such a bitch sometimes. Come on, let's get a drink and mingle."

I rolled my eyes and shifted uncomfortably. "I'm going to need *a lot* to drink before I even think about trying to mingle with these people."

Dana nodded at a couple in the corner. The two of them were getting a little carried away considering we were in a public place. It was turning from PG-13 to soft porn in mere seconds.

"Is that the norm in here?" Dana asked with a look of pure terror.

Ness nodded. "Oh yeah. To be honest, that's mild compared to how heated it can get in here. That's why the bar hires out rooms upstairs. You can go in a couple, threesome, foursome, anything goes."

I almost choked on a breath. A foursome! Was she serious? I came to get laid, not to take part in a group activity.

"And you've … indulged?" Dana's interest was piqued by now, and Ness wasn't getting away without divulging intimate details of her experience in this bar.

"Once or twice. I'm a firm believer in trying everything once before you decide it's not for you. Besides, sometimes it was just two of us, and someone who likes to … you know … watch."

I burst out laughing, and Ness quickly nudged me and shook her head.

"Will you pipe down? I'm known here, and you're embarrassing me!"

I covered my mouth and tried to breathe through my laughter.

"Watch? Ness, sex isn't a spectators' sport!"

She giggled a little. "Don't knock it until you've tried it. Anyway, this isn't about me. Tonight is about you finding a hot guy to play with."

I rolled my eyes. "Yeah, like that's going to happen. Look at these women." I gestured around the room.

"So? You know the only difference between you and them?"

I scoffed. "You mean aside from at least three dress sizes?"

"They have confidence, and they go after what they want. Guy's don't actually care that much about your dress size. If you have confidence and you flaunt your best assets, they're putty in your hands."

Pulling me to stand in front of her, she yanked on my halter-top hard and forced my cleavage to pop right out of the low-cut neckline. She then removed the clip from my hair, and my thick, red mass of locks cascaded down and over my shoulders. Taking a step back, she looked me up and down and squinted.

"Something's missing. Oh, I know! Dana, give me your purse."

Snatching it from Dana's outstretched hand, Ness began digging through 'til she found what she was looking for—a bright red lipstick. I shook my head fiercely.

"No. No way. I'll look like a china doll or a Geisha girl!"

Ness folded her arms and tapped her foot. Giving me an irritated and impatient look, she raised an eyebrow at me.

"Will you just, for once, have some faith in my styling? It is my job after all!"

She had a valid point. I always found it hard with Ness. I'd known her for so long, and though I knew damn well that she was a professional stylist with excellent taste, it was difficult not to think of her as that crazy, party girl I had met in college. That stiletto, short back dress, way too much make up wearing girl was still buried beneath Ness's now cool, sophisticated, and classy exterior. Conceding defeat, I allowed her to 'make me up,' and I had to admit that as she pulled out a small, round compact mirror from her purse and aimed at me, I looked … hot! Sultry, sexy and vixen-like.

Handing Dana her purse, Ness grinned. "Now, let's go and get a damn drink!"

Dana and I nodded in agreement and followed as Ness led us over to the bar on the far side of the club. It was a tactical move. By walking our way across, we were literally on display to the entire room. Eyes followed us, and Dana blushed as a tall, blonde, and muscular guy winked at her. I rolled my eyes. Her and her damn insecurities! It frustrated me that not only was she so stunning, you could go blind just looking at her, but Dana also had the sweetest, most caring, wonderful personality, and yet she was completely oblivious to it! Men would gaze at her wherever we went, and it seemed that Ness and I were the only ones to notice.

Ness was happy with her string of men, but Dana had always been the monogamous and long-term kind of girl. Her ex had been her great love. Everyone had that great and all-consuming love at some point in his or her life. I had thought Brad was mine … clearly, we were not on the same page of that romance novel. But for Dana, Kieran Sawyer was hers. Considering I was very overprotective and sometimes critical when it came to my friends and their partners, Kieran had passed every possible standard I could have set. He doted on Dana, and I had never seen a couple so in love. I was convinced they would end up married with a whole brood of stunning babies, but when Kieran was offered a job in the states, it seemed to spell the end for the lovebirds. He'd begged Dana to go with him, but she'd refused, saying her job and her family was too important to leave. When he left, Dana just sort of … gave up. They never called, wrote, or contacted each other again. She claimed she preferred it that way, but I wasn't convinced. I still wasn't. I don't think she ever got over losing him, and every man since had fallen flat because he wasn't and couldn't be Kieran.

Standing beside Dana at the bar, I decided to broach the subject.

"So, I was thinking the other day—"

She giggled. "That's dangerous."

I gave her a playful nudge. "I know. But seriously, I was just wondering the other day if you ever hear from Kieran?"

Dana's smile immediately dropped. "Why would you be wondering about that?"

I shrugged. "Oh, I was just messing with my computer, and I came across some old pictures," I lied.

She glanced over at Ness who was currently being chatted up by a broad, dark-haired guy with a full sleeve tattoo.

"No. I haven't heard from him or tried to contact him since he left."

I placed my hand gently on her arm. "Dana, you can tell me to mind my own business, but why not? It wasn't as though you parted on bad terms, and I know for a fact that you still keep his picture in the top drawer beside your bed."

Her eyes widened, and she quickly pressed her hand over my mouth, checking that Ness hadn't heard me.

"Shhh! It's not that I'm still terribly in love with him. It's been over a year for God's sake. I just …"

She hesitated and removed her hand from my mouth. I shook my head at her.

"You just can't get over him. You can deny it all you want, but you still love him."

She scoffed and took a long sip of the cocktail Ness had ordered for each of us.

"Dana, you've barely dated since he left. And the guys you have dated never measure up to the man you're trying to replace."

Her eyes cast down at the floor, she bit her lip. "What am I supposed to do? I've tried to get over it, and I know you all think I'm just fussy, but … I don't know. I guess, in the end, he wasn't just my boyfriend. He was my best friend. Can you imagine ever being without Adam?"

I thought for a moment, and she was right; my heart wouldn't just break, it would shatter. I suddenly had a little understanding of how she must be feeling. It would take me a lifetime to get over losing Adam.

Wrapping my arm around her waist, I pulled her to my side and rested my head on her shoulder.

"You're right. I'm sorry I brought it up. Hey, maybe tonight will change both of our lives!"

She gave me a halfhearted smile and guilt consumed me. I really did know how to pick my moments. I was beginning to think that the night was officially ruined until, out of nowhere, two large and very handsome guys appeared at the bar beside us. They were easily six feet tall with dark hair and caramel-coloured skin. I almost melted. Nudging Dana, I nodded over toward them. Turning around and being completely obvious, she stared at them. One of them caught her eye and gave her a beaming smile. He was wearing a white shirt and a pair of black, tailored trousers. He looked as though he'd come there straight from the office and if Ness's description of the calibre of men in the bar was anything to go by, he may well have.

Dana blushed ferociously and gnawed on her lip. Tapping his friend on the shoulder, the hottie picked up his drink and turned to face us.

"Hi. I'm Sam, and this is Anton. Can we get you ladies a drink?"

Dana appeared speechless as Sam's big green eyes sparkled down at her. Rolling my eyes, I smiled.

"Thanks. I'll have a vodka and cranberry, and she'll have a rum and coke."

Stepping out from behind Sam, Anton beamed at me. His teeth were so white, you needed sunglasses just to look at him directly, and his eyes were a dazzling blue. He was wearing jeans and a black shirt which was unbuttoned just enough to show off a little of his broad chest. Sam ordered our drinks from the bartender as Anton's eyes dragged up and down my body. I suddenly felt exposed, naked, and under a spotlight. Was it hot in here?

"I feel at a disadvantage. You know my name, and I've yet to find out yours," he purred. Yes, purred. His voice was delicious! It was silky yet manly all at once. It had my knickers twitching already.

"Charlene," I stated, trying desperately not to sound as though my underwear was about to slide down my thighs. He nodded and smiled down at his drink.

"That's nice. I've not seen you here before."

"It's my first time. My friend is a regular though." I pointed over at Vanessa who was sitting in a large velvet chair beside the beefcake she had been chatting with at the bar. Anton smirked.

"Ah, Vanessa. Yeah, she's certainly a regular in here."

I frowned. Great, it would seem every guy in the room probably knew my friend intimately, and the idea of mounting the same horse as her, made my stomach churn. I was nowhere near in the same league as Ness. If he was hoping to find a girl as adventurous, sexually or otherwise, he would be severely disappointed. Anton caught my glum expression and laughed.

"I don't know her personally, but I've seen her around. Don't look so bummed."

I mentally did a backflip.

"So what brings you here?"

It was a loaded question, and even as he asked it, I was sure he already knew the answer.

"I'm single again for the first time in a few years, and I'm … looking to play the field a little."

Anton grinned and swirled his drink in his glass a little.

"Play the field? Is that what you call it?"

Leaning in, he whispered into my ear. His breath warmed my skin, and he smelled of my favourite aftershave.

"I come here to find a hot girl, take her to my place or the nearest wall, and fuck her senseless."

My breath caught in my lungs, forcing my huge knockers to press against his chest. He noticed them immediately.

"And you, Charlene, are incredibly sexy."

Was he serious? Had he lost his glasses? It had been a long time since anyone had called me sexy and even longer since I had actually considered myself to be.

His brow furrowed as he stood back and gazed down at me.

"You don't think you're sexy?"

I shook my head gently as my face heated with the intense embarrassment.

"Wow. That ex of yours must have really done a number on you. What do you think it means to be sexy? I'm curious."

He had a ghost of a smile on his lips, and it was slightly irritating. It wasn't smug, but it was certainly cocky.

"Let's be honest, Anton, I'm not exactly the most slender of women in this room. I'm a size fourteen with bright red hair and a huge arse. I don't consider that to ooze sex appeal."

Throwing his head back, he laughed. I crossed my arms over my chest and glared at him. I didn't need him to physically mock me!

"You know what, I knew tonight was a bad idea."

Grabbing my purse from the bar and quickly throwing back the vodka and cranberry Sam had bought for me, I made a move toward the door. Dana was engrossed in conversation with Sam who had dragged her into a corner where an array of cushions lay on plush velvet sofas. I was on my own. This night was clearly a huge mistake. Well, at least that's what I thought.

Catching my elbow and spinning me around on the spot, Anton's mouth closed over mine hungrily. His tongue darted inside, and I moaned deeply as his hand slid from my back and down to my behind. Palming it firmly, he grinned against my lips. I was in shock. Panting and breathless, I was totally speechless.

"Now this," he grasped my arse tightly, "is sexy."

I gasped and stared at him wide-eyed. *Oh my God!*

Chapter 16

I felt like a teenager again! After dragging me into a dark corner, Anton's hands were roaming all over my body. His lips caressed my neck, cleavage, and earlobe, while his hands greedily palmed my flesh. Sliding them down my back, he pushed his way down and into my jeans. I was thankful that I'd decided to wear my best lingerie because as his fingertips brushed against the black lace of my knickers, he groaned deeply into my ear.

"Oh, fuck. I love French lace underwear. On your curves, I bet it looks even more tempting."

I grinned against his shoulder. I could feel the hard length of him as it pressed firmly against my hip. Slipping my own hand into *his* jeans, I rubbed gently at his bulging boxer shorts.

"Mmmm. Charlene, you have two choices. I'm either going to fuck you right here against this wall, or we can go to my place. But either way, I am going to fuck you."

Grabbing his hands, I practically dragged him toward the door. Dana caught my eye as I hurried past her, and seeing the man I was currently gripping hold of, she grinned and gave me a thumbs up. I wasn't looking for approval, but as my eyes wandered around the room, I could see some of the other women staring at me with a knowing smile on their lips. I wondered how many of them had sampled Anton's goodies too. Not that it mattered. Tonight, he was my cookie jar, ice cream cone and everything bad for my health in, oh, so many wonderful ways!

* * * *

Anton's place was only a short drive from the bar and was located in the high end of London. When I say high end, I mean swanky apartments that girls my age got via a rich daddy or sugar daddy. For men, it was usually a case of working too many hours and living the party boy lifestyle. Neither was overly appealing to me, but as we stumbled, fumbled, and groped our way up to his suite in the elevator, I really didn't care if he lived in a swamp! I was getting laid tonight, and there wasn't a tube of denture glue in sight.

Pinning me against the wall of the elevator with his hips, he caged me in as his palms pressed against the wall on either side of my head. His lips trailed kisses from my jaw to just behind my ear. My knees were weakening, and if he hadn't skillfully slipped his hand quickly onto my behind, I was sure I would have been a crumpled mess on the floor. His mouth worked slowly from my ear down my throat before arriving at my cleavage. His other hand grabbed, groped, and fondled my right breast as his lips sought out my nipple. Before I knew it, he'd pulled my halter aside and fully exposed my waiting flesh. His mouth closed over my nipple, and he sucked gently before nibbling on it and grinning as he did so. I was in ecstasy!

As the doors opened, he quickly released me, took my hand and led me down the long whitewashed wall hallway. I began stuffing myself back into my halter top as we walked, but I'd only managed to push my breast halfway into my bra when we stopped outside apartment twenty. Pressing my back against the cool wood, Anton began pulling at the zip on my jeans. My own hands made quick work of his shirt buttons as he opened the door and backed me into a large, dark room, lit only by the moonlight streaming in through the vast window. I kicked off my heels as I pulled his shirt over his muscular shoulders and tore it away from his body. My jeans were now completely undone and sliding his hand into them, he rubbed my swollen clit through my underwear.

"Oh, Charlene, you are so fucking hot!"

His voice was a low growl, and it was totally intoxicating. His lips caressed my neck as his free hand pushed my jeans down, causing them to fall to the floor around my ankles. I stepped out of them carefully. In this strange room, in the dark, I was blind, but as Anton urged me backwards, the backs of my knees buckled as they hit the cool leather of what appeared to be a sofa. Laying me down gently, he continued to palm, massage, and stroke my pussy. Yes, I called it a pussy. I have an intense dislike for that *other* word.

I groaned with pleasure as his leaned forward and took my wet, lacey knickers between his teeth. Glancing up at me, he grinned wickedly. Releasing the delicate fabric, he began trailing kisses up to my belly button. I could feel my lack of confidence beginning to wither away as this man continued to worship and attend to my body. His tongue glided over my stomach and pushing up my top, he smiled.

"These are the most succulent, gorgeous, delicious tits I have ever tasted."

I bit my lip and blushed. Dipping his fingers into the cups of my bra, he gently pulled them downward, exposing both of my large and full breasts. His hands massaged them firmly as his mouth, tongue and teeth unleashed a heavenly attack on my nipples. I could feel the sensations pulling like a direct line through my stomach to my pussy. It wouldn't take me much to reclaim that long lost orgasm, and I prayed Anton would lead the way soon.

His body was tangled with mine. His jeans hung loosely around his behind, and I could feel the stretch of his boxer shorts as his solid, hard erection pressed against my leg. He was writhing on top of me, the friction against my clit was heavenly, but I needed more.

His teeth caught my earlobe, and he breathed heavily in my ear.

"Talk dirty to me, Charlene. Tell me what you want me to do to you."

Huh? Was he for real? It's not that I am opposed to dirty talk, it's just that, well, I'm not very good at it. Trying desperately to think of what to say, I tried to relax and let my body do the thinking for me.

"I want you to fuck me. I want you so deep that I can hardly stand it. I want to feel you fill me up and pound into me until I almost break in half."

Wow. I guess I'm not so bad at it after all. He let out a long hiss.

"Oh, baby. Yeah. I wanna fuck you so hard. I'm gonna bang you like a drum then bend you over and give it to you in a way that you only see in nature films."

His cock was rubbing fiercely against my thigh. Reaching between us, I slipped my hand inside his shorts and gripped him, hard. My hand moved back and forth with every grind of his hips. He was so hard I could barely stand it! Urging his jeans down farther, I unleashed him and continued to pump, stroke, and tease his cock. He groaned loudly.

"Oh, yeah. Oh, you make me so hard. Do you like that, baby? You like seeing me get hard for you."

Is that a trick question? Of course, I like it! I want it!

"Mmmm. You're so big and hot for me. I love to feel you throbbing between my fingers."

His mouth opened, and his eyes closed tightly. I loved the effect my naughty little mouth was having on him.

"I bet you taste incredible—your thick, silky smooth cock in my mouth. My tongue teasing you 'til you can't take anymore."

He gasped and bit his lip. His thrusts into my hand were getting stronger.

"You want to fuck me, Anton?"

He nodded but seemed unable to speak. His forehead pressed against my shoulder as his lips kissed and sucked my breast. I moaned with enjoyment, and as I slid my free hand into my underwear to remove them, Anton groaned.

"Oh, Charlene, you feel so good."

I do? My hand was now doing none of the work, and as he moved back and forth heavily against my fingers, I quickly foresaw a problem.

"Anton."

He moaned. "Oh, Charlene."

"Uh, Anton?" I said a little more impatiently.

"Oh, Charlene. Oh, baby, I think I'm gonna…"

My eyes widened, and I shook my head fiercely!

"Oh, God! No!"

Grimacing and moaning so loud that his voice echoed through the entire room, Anton sat up and began pumping at himself.

"Oh, yes!"

No! No, no, no, no, no! Oh, this wasn't happening!

Aiming his weapon at my face, he moaned and hissed. You should know that a penis could shoot semen up to eleven inches at a speed of around twenty-eight miles per hour. In one, quick blur of a motion … I discovered this very fact firsthand as Anton's climax found its way from its vessel, across the sofa, and straight into my left eye!

My eyes closed so tightly, I couldn't even speak. You should also know that when that stuff gets you right in the eye, it stings! It burns and glues your lids together in a flash! As I tried to wipe it off with a throw pillow that had fallen to the floor in our frenzied fumble, my orgasm sobbed heavily in the corner of the room, discarded and forgotten while his danced a fucking jig! Not only was I completely and utterly sexually frustrated, but I had also just had my leg dry humped like a damn dog and been blinded by a premature ejaculation!

Collapsing on top of me, Anton breathed heavily against my chest. It was lucky for him that he couldn't see my expression because I wasn't angry, oh no, I was seething.

"Mmmm. That was amazing. You're a dirty girl, Charlene."

I didn't reply but simply continued to try and remove the sticky mess from my eye. He lifted his head and furrowed his brow.

"What's wrong?"

My mouth opened wide in astonishment, and I began yelling. I don't mean a little; I mean the full-on screeching of a harpie.

"What's wrong? *What's wrong?* Are you kidding me? You give me the green light and rev my engine with a whole host of foreplay, then you throw me on the sofa, whisper dirty little thoughts in my ear, and when I reciprocate, you start humping my leg like a dog, and *I* end up turning into a howling, frustrated, and incredibly infuriated bitch! Urgh!"

Standing, he quickly pulled up his shorts and jeans. Running his fingers through his hair, he blushed a deep shade of crimson.

"There's no need to scream about it. Jeez. I can't help it if you turn me on so much."

Swinging my legs from the sofa, I squinted up at him. "You fucking blinded me!"

Wincing, Anton handed me a tissue to wipe myself clean. Snatching it from his hand, I growled with anger. *Great.* Frustrated, dry humped, and covered in semen. I wanted to die.

Handing me my jeans, he gave me an apologetic smile.

"I think maybe you should go. You're obviously not the kinda girl I thought you were."

I huffed loudly, and standing abruptly, I sniped at him.

"You mean I'm not made of plastic? Wipe-able? Or maybe you prefer your women a little more two-dimensional. Like a porno magazine! You can come over them all day! You should come with a health warning and a pair of fucking goggles!"

Pulling on my clothes, I held the tissue against my eye and mumbled to myself. I was beyond pissed; I was furious.

"Where's the bathroom? I need to try and clean this gunk out of my eye before I attempt the journey home!"

He pointed toward a door on the far side of the room.

Pushing my way inside, I located the light switch, and as I caught my reflection, I wanted to cry. My hair was a tangled, mass of red. My eye was swollen and almost as red as the lipstick smeared across my face. My breasts were still hanging over my bra, and as I pushed them back inside to straighten up, I noticed the hickey on my neck. That was the last straw. Washing my eye out as best I could, I stormed back into the lounge, grabbed my purse and shoes, and headed for the door. Grabbing the handle, I turned back to Anton who stood in the middle of the room looking extremely humiliated.

"I'd say thank you, but considering I'm leaving here a Cyclops with a sexual hunger that is once again going unfed, I think I'll pass! Goodbye!"

Slamming the door behind me, I made my way to the elevator, stepped in, and slumped against the back wall. This was a disaster. My love life, sex life, and well, my whole life, was a total train wreck. And now, there was only one person who could help my poor, sexually abused eye and me. This would be the most awkward conversation of my entire existence, and it would be with my best friend. Great. Could my life get any worse?

Chapter 17

Remember when I asked if my life could get any worse? Well, apparently it can. Never tempt the universe or call it out to challenge you because it would seem that it has a habit of biting you in the arse or kicking you hard in the crotch. I was feeling a little of each right now.

Walking into the apartment with my hand over my eye, I scanned the room. Adam wasn't in the lounge, which I was thankful for, but I could hear music coming from his room, and the light was streaming through the gap of his slightly opened door. Maybe I could just clean it up myself, and it would be fine. I could give it a good scrub, and no one would have to know!

Marching across the lounge, I hurried toward my room, but as I passed the sofa, I didn't notice the snoozing feline on the floor beside it and promptly stepped on his tail. Screeching and darting into Adam's bedroom, Jacob hissed and growled in outrage.

"Charlie?" Adam called from the bedroom.

Closing my eyes tightly, I threw myself onto the sofa.

"I'm in here."

His door opened, and light began to fill the room.

"Oh, please close the door. Darkness is very much my friend right now."

Adam's tall, broad frame cast a large shadow over me as he stood in the doorway. My hand still covering my eye, I sniffed a little as tears slid down my cheek.

"Charlie? What's wrong? Why are you covering your face?"

Marching over to me, he tried desperately to remove my hand from my eye.

"Charlie, stop it! Did someone hit you? Let me look!"

He was panicked and furious.

"No, I'm fine. No one attacked me."

He furrowed his brow and kneeled in front of me.

"Then why are you hiding?"

I took a deep breath and slowly, embarrassedly, and with trepidation, lowered my hand. Lifting my chin, Adam examined me.

"I need to turn the light on to look at you. You look sore and a little red. Did you get something in there?"

Oh, boy did I. Getting to his feet he walked over and turned on the main light. As it filled the room, I squinted.

"Holy shit, Charlene. What the hell did you get in there?"

I groaned and picked up one of the throw pillows to bury my face in. I mumbled into the pillow.

"Charlene, I can't hear you. What is in your eye?"

I mumbled louder. Grabbing the pillow from me, he snatched it away and scowled down at me.

"It's cum!" I shouted.

He raised a brow.

"You mean ..."

I nodded and turned beetroot red. "Yes. Spunk, semen, cum, love juice, jizz, or whatever you want to call it; it's in my eye. I *really* don't want to talk about."

A smile played across his lips, and I could tell he was trying desperately not to burst into laughter.

"I see. Well, I'll just … get some gloves."

As he left the room, I could hear him chuckling. *Arsehole.* When he returned, he was wearing a pair of medical gloves and carrying a small bottle of clear liquid and some swabs.

"I won't ask how it happened, but looking at that fuck me badge on your neck, I'm assuming you had a good night?"

I snorted loudly.

"Hardly. You'd think, considering my current state that I at least got some enjoyment. But, no. Can we *please* not talk about it?" I was getting desperate.

Adam poured some of the liquid onto gauze and dabbed at my eye. The sting was instantly soothed, and the stickiness was now also subsiding. Able to fully open my eyelids again, I blinked several times. Adam smiled at me and shook his head.

"Close your eye. I need to clean it."

I nodded and resting my head back against the sofa cushion, I breathed deeply as Adam dabbed the swabs on my face. Tears were still dripping down my cheeks.

"There, all done."

He was quiet, and as I lifted my head to look down at him, he gave me a rueful smile.

"I shouldn't have laughed. Sorry." He handed me a tissue, and as I took it, I scoffed.

"Why? My whole life is a joke. Look at me."

Lifting my chin with his knuckle, he shook his head lightly.

"I *am* looking at you. I'm always looking at you, and do you know what I see?"

I shook my head.

"I see a fun, gorgeous, sexy, and incredibly amazing woman."

I sniffed into my tissue and gazed at him through my tears.

"Really?"

He nodded.

"Well, if everyone thinks I'm so damn hot and sexy, why can't I see it, and why the hell am I still yet to get laid?"

He chuckled. "You *are* hot, sexy, and incredible. I have no idea why you don't see it. As for why you haven't gotten laid, the guys you're choosing clearly have no idea what they've got in their hands."

I gave a halfhearted smile. "I don't know about that. Maybe I'm just doomed to be sexless and alone forever. I mean, who wants someone who is riddled with self-esteem and body confidence issues? I know *I* wouldn' — "

Cutting me off, Adam lunged forward and pressed his lips firmly against mine. I blinked rapidly at him in total shock. *Oh, my God!* His hand slid up my thigh as the other slid behind my neck, pulling me closer. My mouth opened instinctively to allow his tongue to slide inside. *Is this actually happening?* Adam, my Adam, is kissing me and … I'm letting him. I closed my eyes as my body gave in to the wonderful sensations. His touch was gentle, attentive, and the feeling of his hands on my flesh was so foreign yet thrilling. It was forbidden fruit, and I tasted it with every stroke of his tongue.

Pulling away from me sharply, he ran his fingers through his hair and winced.

"I'm sorry. I shouldn't have done that. It's just that you're so …"

I didn't let him finish. My insides were on fire, and my sexual desire was burning like the sun. I needed him; I wanted him. Hell, I just wanted a man to touch me, caress my body, and drive me crazily to orgasm! Reaching out, I grasped a fistful of his shirt and dragged him onto the sofa. He gawped at me as I quickly pushed him down and climbed on top of him. Straddling his hips, I hurriedly unbuttoned his shirt as his own hands glided up and down my thighs before reaching around and grasping my behind. Tearing his shirt from his body, I stared at him. Adam was ... gorgeous! When did he get a body like that? Why the hell had he been hiding it, and how the hell did I not notice it 'til now? His broad shoulders, thick muscular arms, and perfect abs had me salivating. The deep Apollo's belt that led temptingly into his trousers was simply begging to be licked!

Lifting himself up, he wrapped his arms around me and gently tugged at my halter-top. I immediately took it off, and as my flesh slid out from beneath it, Adam's hands cupped over my bra and massaged my breasts. I moaned deeply. His lips trailed sweet and gentle kisses from my cleavage to my neck, up my throat, before resting on my lips again. My head was spinning with everything that was happening. I was turned on, hot, and completely aroused, but I was also scared, worried, and my brain screamed at me that we had to stop. But my body was on a mission. My hips were grinding, and I slid my hands over his chest, down his body to his trousers. He smiled against my lips as I unzipped them.

His fingers fumbled nervously with my own zipper and buttons. Everything I was doing was purely based on instinct. I couldn't think; if I did, then I might come to my senses and put a stop to this, but every inch of me was screaming that this was right.

Adam's tongue brushed against my collarbone, and I moaned, biting my lip. I could feel myself becoming wetter as his erection pressed against my clit. I was a starving woman at a buffet of hot, sexy, muscular man meat! I wanted to grab him with both hands and tear him apart with my teeth! Pushing me backwards, he laid me on the sofa with my back resting on the plush cushions. He gazed down at me, his eyes sparkling, and an intensity in them made me catch my breath.

He reminded me of a predator stalking its prey. His fingers dipped inside my jeans, and he pulled them off with achingly slow care. The fabric glided over my hips and lowering himself, Adam's lips kissed down my thighs, following my jeans inch by inch as they slipped from my body.

Tossing them away from us, Adam sat back on his heels and stared at me. His eyes dragged from my feet all the way up 'til he met my own gaze. I wrapped my arms around myself and closed my eyes. My embarrassment and insecurity over how I must look consumed me. I didn't feel comfortable in my own skin, and even Adam's gentle hands on my own brought me no relief from my hatred of my body. His fingers entwined with mine and he lifted my hands gently to his lips.

"You're beautiful," he whispered.

I opened my eyes and looked up at him. He was beaming at me. I'd never seen him this way. But then, I'd never felt so exposed to him. Oh, I'd been semi-naked with him before, but this was different. I wasn't just opening my legs and body to him; I was giving him a piece of me that for twenty years had been the one thing in our relationship that was missing. I wondered if he also felt this as I watched him slide down his jeans and shorts. He swallowed hard and took my hands in his one again. Pushing them up above my head, his grip tightened. He was nervous. But it didn't last long. Trailing his fingertips down my pale skin, he hooked his thumb on the crotch of my underwear and pulled them aside.

I hitched a breath, and my head fell back as Adam's full, thick, and solid length slipped inside of me. It was beyond anything I could describe. All you need to know is that it was good. His hands explored every curve of my body before tangling in my hair. My eyes stayed closed as his hips ground, rolled, and he thrust inside me. I could feel my orgasm teasing, coming closer and closer with every touch of his lips on mine. His scent was intoxicating, and I could hardly control myself. I moaned, groaned, growled, and purred like a kitten who had desperately wanted the cream. The low, deep, and erotic tones of Adam's own sexual satisfaction were filling the room, and as he dropped his hand between us, his thumb rubbed against my clit. My nails gripped his back, my legs tightened, and my entire body shook as my orgasm came rumbling through me. I cried out, loudly, and was joined by the Afghan hound across the street. It felt as though I was soaring. My eyes flew open, and with my mouth open, panting, I watched as Adam bit down on his lip. He was close.

"Charlie, I need to come."

We hadn't used a condom. Holding him by the shoulders, I stilled him and pushed him away. Sitting up, I lunged forward and took him in my mouth. I don't usually indulge in oral sex, but there was something so tempting about Adam's delicious cock that called to me. His hands grasped at my thick red hair, and he began to pant, hard. I could feel him getting closer. Rolling my tongue over the tip of his cock, I sucked, licked, and teased him. His head fell back and breathing erratically, he came. The salty liquid slid down my throat, and as my hands gripped his thighs, I felt him shudder.

When he opened his eyes again, I couldn't take mine off of him. What would we do now? What happened next? Sliding downward to lie flat, he grinned down at me.

"I've never done that with *you* before."

I nodded and smiled up at him with my chin resting on his stomach. "Mmmm."

He laughed again. "Can't do that again."

I shook my head and giggled. Biting my lip, I gazed up at him with mischief.

"Wanna do it again, stud?" I teased.

Bolting from the sofa, he stood, scooped me into his arms and kissed me.

"Oh, God yes!"

<u>Chapter 18</u>

The hound across the street began his morning song, and as I opened my blurry eyes, light began to filter through partially opened curtains. I hadn't drunk much at the bar, but it had been enough to leave me with a slightly dull headache. The type of headache that settles right between your eyes and requires some painkillers, total darkness, and an entire reservoir of water. My mouth was so dry it was akin to Jacob's litter tray. Turning over to face the door, I felt movement behind me. I was suddenly wide-awake. A strong arm was wrapped around my waist. Panic set in as the events of the previous night began flooding back.

Oh God! Oh God! What have I done? What have *we* done? Flailing my arm across my face, I flinched as it brushed against my sore eye. Ah, yes. The friendly fire incident. This wouldn't have happened at all if I had just stayed home in my pyjamas! I could have slipped myself into another sugar-induced coma, but no! Adam sighed in my ear. I stilled, worried he might wake up, and we would both be forced to have a very awkward moment. If I was going to have *that* conversation, I at least wanted to be dressed.

Gently lifting his hand from my waist, I tried to ease it down onto the bed and off of me, but as I turned over and successfully freed myself, he too rolled over and right onto my outstretched arm. I had a habit of shoving one arm beneath a pillow at night to enjoy the coolness of the unused, un-drooled upon, fresh cotton. Now, I was discovering the hazards of sleeping in such a position. Rolling my eyes and groaning under my breath, I contemplated chewing my arm off. I had another one, would I really miss it? I wasn't hoping to be a world champion tennis star or anything, and robotics was coming on in leaps and bounds these days!

Deciding my arm was far too precious to be amputated, I forcefully slid it out from beneath the pillow. Finally free, I grinned in triumph 'til I realised I had yet to get out of the room undetected. Swinging my feet out of bed, I placed them silently on the floor and began tiptoeing my way out of the room. The door was open, and as I reached for the handle, I let out a long breath with pure and utter relief. It was short lived. Springing out from behind the sofa, Jacob came hurtling at my feet with a dead rodent hanging from his jaws. I jumped and held my hand over my mouth to hide the screech that was begging to be released. Jacob quickly placed the dead animal at my feet and paraded around the lounge like a warrior bringing back the spoils of war. I glared at him before casting my eye back at Adam. Silence. Thank God!

Pulling the door behind me, I crept out of the room. All I had to do was close it, and I was home free! Well, for now. The click of the lock echoed through the apartment, and I winced. Hurrying to my bedroom, I closed the door quietly behind me and flopped back against it, sliding all the way down to the floor.

"Morning, Charlie," Adam's voice echoed through the wall. Damn it. So close.

I rested my head in my hands.

"Morning," I yelled back. Smooth, Charlene, very smooth.

I waited for him to say something, but as silence fell on the apartment once more, I took the opportunity to make a dash for my bathroom where I would soak, scrub, and try desperately to wash away my sins of the previous evening. I'm not saying it was bad. Oh, dear heavens no! It was amazing. It was the best sex I had ever had, and that included the intense and mind-blowing orgasm I had experienced the first time I had self-indulged with my battery-operated boyfriend. He had a twisting shaft for optimum pleasure and bunny ears for clit stimulation. It had been bliss, but what Adam had done to me last night was like nothing I had experienced before. It was rainbows, unicorns, and leprechauns. It was the stuff of legends and myth! I'd heard of this kind of sex being had by people, but I figured it was hype to encourage us, women, to keep at it with a guy, give him the chance to improve, and to get men to try harder! Adam didn't need to try harder. He was there with bells on!

I shook my head at myself as I slid into the hot and wonderfully lavender-scented tub. It didn't matter how hot, sexy, erotic, unbelievable, heart-stopping, leg-trembling and body-shaking the sex had been. We shouldn't, couldn't, and wouldn't be doing it again! It was insanity to have done it at all. Not only had we broken the cardinal sin of friendship, but we'd also done so twice! Loudly!

This was a complete mess.

* * * *

Standing in the kitchen, I stirred my freshly brewed coffee. I must have been doing it for a good ten minutes, mindlessly twirling the spoon in my fingers as my brain buzzed and hummed with pain, anxiety, worry, and the stupidity of our actions.

"Morning."

Coming out of my trance, I turned around to find Adam sitting on a stool at the counter. His sweatpants were hanging low on his hips, and the deep V of his pelvis had me instinctively licking my lips. Damn it!

He was shirtless, and his hair was slightly damp from his morning shower. He wasn't wearing his glasses either.

"Morning," I managed to choke out in a half whisper and half cough.

He gave me a small smile.

"Charlie, I ... I mean, we ... wow, this is awkward."

Taking a deep breath, I held my hands over my face and groaned.

"Adam, last night ... I want to apologise" I started, but he immediately interrupted.

"No, no, don't apologise. I mean ... we were both there. And I'm not saying it wasn't—"

"Amazing" I offered.

"Exactly. It's just that I need to tell you that—"

I shook my head and held up my hands, signalling for him to stop.

"It's okay. I don't hold you responsible, Adam. It was the heat of the moment. Fueled by my despair, alcohol, and unsatisfied sexual needs. I just think we should try and put the whole thing behind us. We're friends, and I don't want this to change that. I adore you, and to lose you because we can't get past one night would be a real shame. I'm so sorry that I caused this tension between us, but I promise, it won't happen again."

He stared down at the counter and nodded gently before looking back up at me.

"You really feel that way?"

I bit my lip. Sex with Adam was incredible, but there was no way that we could do it again. It makes things complicated, and my life was complicated enough!

"I do."

Smiling, he stood, ran his fingers through his damp hair, and nodded slowly.

"Okay. I should probably go and get dressed. I have a heap of errands to run before work tomorrow. You have plans today?"

Picking up my coffee, I took a sip and smiled at him. "I'm just gonna go see how Ness and Dana did last night. Catch up on some reading later maybe."

Wow. This was so … unnatural. Talking to him had never felt so forced and uncomfortable. He nodded before holding up his hand in a sort of goodbye wave and walked to his room, closing the door loudly behind him. The sound of Smokey Robinson and The Miracles echoed through the door. Shit. Adam's go-to when he was pissed off or upset was to put his father's old records on. In this case, since all of his stuff was in storage while his place was cleaned, he would make do with CDs and a loud sound system.

Slumping onto the now vacant stool, I folded my arms on the counter and dropped my head onto them. My forehead hit the cool surface, and the dull ache I already had throbbing between my eyes was joined by the sharp pang of the counter. Was I doomed to be just one huge fuck up? In my entire life, I had never been in so much shit. And why? What had I done to deserve it? I'd been faithful, doting, hard-working, and loving to one man for five years, and where had that gotten me? Jilted, dumped, and shelved! Then, I played the sex siren. Cool, sassy, and outwardly confident, and that had resulted in a vagina full of dental glue and an eye full of semen! And now, to top it all off, I had gone right ahead and fucked my best friend. My life, my body, my self-esteem, and my relationships had all inevitably ended up the same way … broken!

Picking up the phone, I dialled Dana.

"Hello?"

She sounded raspy and a little horse.

"Dana?"

"God, I hope so." She yawned. "What time is it?"

"After ten," I groaned.

"What day?"

I chuckled lightly. "Sunday. Are you at home?"

She yawned again.

"Yeah. You?"

I paused a moment before speaking, wondering if I should tell her the events of last night over the phone. I decided it was better left for a face-to-face conversation. "Yeah. Actually, I was wondering if I could come over."

She yawned down the phone, a little louder this time. "As if you needed an invitation. See you in an hour."

Hazarding a glance at Adam's door, I rolled my eyes. Maybe a little space to get our heads back in the right place would help. I grabbed my coat and bag and headed out.

* * * *

For a woman who claimed to have drunk seven vodka and cranberries and at least a dozen shots of tequila, Dana looked astonishingly bright when I arrived. Dressed in a pair of blue sweatpants and a white t-shirt, she pottered around her kitchen making coffee while filling me in on her eventful night.

"He was incredible, Charlie. I knew he was trying to get me wasted, but I honestly think I wouldn't even have needed the booze! He was super cute, very sexy, and an amazing kisser!"

I smiled and nodded as she handed me a steaming hot cappuccino.

"So did you come back here or go to his place?"

Sitting down beside me on the sofa, she let out a long sigh.

"No. I came home alone."

I gave her a puzzled look. "But you said—"

She growled a little and picked up a cushion before burying her face in it and screaming. The muffled sound was that of a woman in sincere pain. Pulling it away from her, I urged her to continue.

"It was your fault, Charlene! All that talk about Kieran got me feeling all lovesick! After that, I couldn't stop thinking about him. Sam was great, but he never stood a chance once Kieran was back in my head."

I furrowed my brow and opened my mouth in feigned shock.

"Oh, please! He's never out of your head! You know the real reason you couldn't be with Sam last night is the same reason you haven't been with any guy since Kieran left! You're still madly in love with him! God, why don't you just admit it? We all know the truth anyhow."

She scowled at me. "Because I can't love him! It hurts to love him because he's not here. I can't do long distance, and I'm too jealous, selfish, and needy to be able to trust he wouldn't stray. I can't do it. I spent too long wallowing over him, and it still hurts. Surely, you of all people understand that."

I scoffed loudly at her. "Seriously? You think I'm the authority on heartache? Dana, I did trust my man. I trusted him so much that I didn't notice the skank he had been banging for weeks. It doesn't matter if you're in the same country, town, or even apartment. If a man is going to cheat on you, he will. He doesn't have to move away to do it."

Flopping back against the sofa, she twirled a finger in her hair mindlessly. It was her tell. Dana could never be a professional poker player.

"I know. I'm just trying to make myself feel better. Anyway, you haven't told me about your night. I saw you and Anton in the bar, and you two were practically ripping each other's clothes off as you left."

I winced at the memories. Dana stared at me, waiting for an explanation and no doubt the juicy details of my sexual encounter. Saved by the bell. Dana's doorbell chimed loudly in the hall and rolling her eyes, she left to answer it.

"Is that the same dress you were wearing last night?" I heard Dana ask with a distinct tone of disapproval.

"Hell yes, it is!" Ness snapped back.

Waltzing into the lounge, Ness paced back and forth like a proud peacock.

"It was amazing! Mind-blowing and awesome!"

Dana and I gave each other a knowing look. Here she goes again.

"His name's Henry. He's a very successful chef, and he recently opened his own restaurant. And oh my God, he knows his food. I spent half of the evening drizzled with something sticky that he could lick off or being fed something utterly delicious while blindfolded. Though I have to say, his very own sausage was a delightful main course."

I cringed. Sausage? Really?

"It was magical. I'm talking sparks flying and Earthmoving."

Dana nudged me. "More like knickers flinging and legs spreading."

I giggled and held my hand over my mouth as Ness continued to gush about her amazing night of passion. Dropping onto the sofa between Dana and I, she sighed with contentment.

"So, how was your night with Anton? I see a hickey, but what the hell happened to your face? You look like you have pink eye."

Ever the tactful one, Ness stared at me expectedly.

"I'd been meaning to ask about that eye actually," Dana added.

Covering my embarrassed face with my hands, I took a deep breath.

"I got semen in it."

Ness and Dana looked confused. "Uh, honey, I'm no expert but—" Ness began.

"Ha! No expert," Dana interrupted earning her a thunderous look from Ness.

"Anyway, like I was saying, I'm pretty sure the penis goes at the other end."

I groaned. "I know."

"I'm confused. You had sex, right?" Dana asked.

I cast my eyes to the ceiling and bit my lip. "Well, not exactly."

"So just oral then? Is he good? Is he skilled? Did you come? Was it multiple? Details, Charlene, I need details." Ness was bouncing up and down like an excited child.

"Not exactly."

I began telling them the whole horrid story and watched as their expressions turned from shock to horror and then finally, they both fell about laughing.

"Oh my God! That's so funny! Friendly fire. Hit in the eye with a sperm shooter!" Ness cackled.

I could feel my cheeks getting red.

"Oh Charlene, how do you get into these situations?" Dana panted.

Hurling cushions at them both, I laughed.

"Guy's, it's not funny. And besides, that wasn't the end of the story."

Stopping, the two of them composed themselves a little and smiled at me.

"Do continue. Because I know for sure you got laid last night. You have that post-orgasmic glow about you. You look like you just walked out of a nuclear waste zone."

Biting my lip so hard that it began to bleed, I winced.

"I did have sex."

Ness and Dana both grinned and giggled.

"I knew it! So Anton managed to get the pole erect again? Did you wave your white flag and reap the spoils?"

I shook my head. "I said I had sex. I never said it was with Anton."

<u>Chapter 19</u>

"You had sex!" Ness's screech almost burst my eardrum, and I was forced to press my hands firmly over my ears.

Dana stared at me with her mouth open wide. She stuttered and stammered before finally shaking her head and collapsing back against the sofa.

"It wasn't like I planned it! It just … happened!"

Ness was pacing up and down with her hands on his hips.

"Just happened? Are you kidding me? This doesn't just happen. I mean, we were wondering how long it would take for you two to finally hop on the good foot and do the bad thing, but this is a disaster."

I furrowed my brow at her. "What do you mean you were wondering when? I didn't even know it was going to happen!"

Dana's jaw fell open, and she stared at me with surprise. "Seriously, Charlene? You two have been tiptoeing around the sexual tension for years. But I figured maybe you'd both come to your senses, become a couple, and *then* hook up."

I couldn't believe what I was hearing. "You're both nuts! We're friends. We don't feel that way about each other. It was just sex. I was upset, feeling low, and painfully sexually frustrated. She who has not fucked out of desperation cast the first stone!"

Ness dropped her hands and muttered under her breath briefly before speaking up. "Okay, fair point, but this is going to make things so much harder. You two won't be able to separate the sex with the friendship, and then we," she gestured to herself and Dana, "end up like the children of divorce. And not the good kind like it was with my parents. Oh, no. There'll be no gifts and grand gestures of love to try and win us over. No, it'll be awkward, you'll fight, and then inevitably the two of you share custody of us, and we see you every other weekend. That's until one of you meets a new squeeze of course. Then it just gets worse."

Dana and I looked at each other before turning our attention back to Ness. Her parents had really done a number on her with their divorce. It was my theory as to why she was such a commitment-phobe. Her father had been a serial womaniser, and her mother was a classic lush. Whenever we'd been over at her place, she was usually found with a younger man wrapped around her and a bottle of wine within arm's reach.

"Ness, it's not going to get weird. It happened once, and it won't be happening again. Will you please relax?"

She exhaled slowly, taking deep breaths. "Fine, if you say so, but don't expect me not to give my biggest *I told you so* when it all goes south."

I rolled my eyes and turned my attention to Dana who was yet to give her view on the situation.

"Well, Dana? What do *you* think?"

"Would it make a difference?"

"I guess it depends on what you have to say."

"I think you're both playing with fire, and one or both of you will end up burnt. Do you honestly think you could be around each other now and have ... no feeling at all? I mean, how was it this morning?"

I rubbed my forehead with my thumb and finger. My tense headache was getting worse.

"Awkward. Uncomfortable and forced."

Ness gave me a self-righteous smirk, and I stuck my tongue out at her.

"Exactly. And ..." I knew she was itching to ask the question on both hers and Ness's lips, but that each was too embarrassed to ask.

"You want to know how it was, don't you." I had a slight smile on my face, and they both stared at me, waiting eagerly for the juicy details. I settled back on the sofa and sipped the fresh coffee Dana had made me.

"Don't keep us in suspense, Charlene! Tell us!" Ness demanded.

"What do you want to know?" I teased.

Dana shifted closer to me and placed her hand on my leg.

"Was it good? Was he hot? Is he hot? I can't imagine Adam as, well, anything but the nerdy doctor that buys me bread-makers and stuff on my birthday. Tell me everything!"

I scrunched my nose up and pretended to think. I didn't need long to remember the events of last night. They were embedded in my brain. They played over and over like a movie.

"He was ... hot. Very hot."

Ness groaned. "Like Ryan Gosling hot or Jude Law hot?"

I gave her a puzzled look as Dana raised an eyebrow in confusion. "What are you talking about?"

Ness rolled her eyes. "Well, Jude Law has that whole gentleman, suave thing going on and that makes him hot. But Ryan Gosling, he has that sexy, smooth voice. That toned, defined body, and the kind of eyes you want to stare into as you orgasm over and over again."

I blinked rapidly at her as she gushed and swooned over men she adored but would never obtain. Probably.

"I guess he was kind of ... both?" I offered.

"Both!" Ness yelled. This woman needed a volume button!

"Yes, both. He was sweet, sensual, attentive and mind-blowing all at the same time. He has abs! Did you know that? Adam has abs. And not just that, he has one of those hot, deep V lines that dip into his sweats. When did that happen? Did I completely miss the memo that went out that declared my best friend as a hottie?"

Dana shook her head in astonishment. "Our Adam? Are you sure you didn't go blind from that shot in the eye?"

I took her face in my hands, pressing my palms to her cheeks and forced her to stare at me. "I'm not crazy. Adam is a sex god. It's like he was made for it. And he knew all these tricks."

Ness was getting closer and closer to me with every detail. She was a shuffle away from falling off of the sofa.

"Tricks? What do you mean tricks?"

I removed my hands from Dana's face and held them to my chest. Sighing with content, I closed my eyes and remembered every little touch, sensation, movement, and caress.

"I mean, techniques and stuff." Opening my eyes, I was startled a little to find them both inches from my face with grins spreading across their own.

"Go on!" they urged in unison.

"I don't know what to tell you. I can't describe it. It was weird, wonderful, and everything I needed. He made me feel more alive than I have in years."

Ness snickered. "I think a washing machine would do that when up against Brad. Are you for real? I just can't picture

Adam as this sexual animal. It feels too ..." She scrunched up her nose and grimaced. Dana nodded and matched her expression.

"I know it's bizarre, but it's true. Maybe we just never noticed it because we know him so intimately anyway."

Dana laughed. "Yeah, and now you know him carnally, intimately, sexually, and practically inside out and upside down."

I smiled. "I certainly spent some time last night upside down."

Rising from the couch, Ness made a vomiting sound.

"Urgh. It's gross, and I can't even think about it. It's like walking in on your parents having sex. Though in my case, it was usually not with each other."

My smile dropped. "The thing is, now I don't even know how to act around him. I feel so exposed and out of place."

"You were naked together. You can't get much more exposed than that, Charlene!" Dana spat.

I sunk deeper into the cushions of the sofa.

"So what do I do now?"

Ness held out her hand and began counting out my options on her long, manicured fingers. "The way I see it, you have three choices. One, you never speak to him again or even make eye contact."

I shook my head fiercely. "Not an option. Next."

"Two, you go home, talk to him, and try to get back to normal."

I cringed. "If that is even possible."

"Or three, you remain friends, but fuck now and then."

Dana glared at her and sprayed the gulp of tea in her mouth all over the floor. "Are you insane? They can't do that!"

Ness stared at her with confusion. She looked at Dana as though she had just grown an extra head. "Why not? People do it all the time. It would relieve that tension between them, and they both get laid. It's not like they can go back to how it was. Things have changed, and you might as well roll with the punches. What's so wrong with having a fuck buddy? They're hardly strangers."

I sat with my mouth open, staring at her. She was nuts.

"Stop gawping at me like that. You know it makes sense."

I stood and held my hands in the air in total abandonment.

"No. No, no, no. It's not happening. Ness, he's my best friend. We've been through everything together. He's the only guy I've always been able to rely on, and I won't jeopardise that for sex."

She raised an eyebrow at me. "Not even for the best you ever had?"

I walked up to her and jabbed her lightly in the chest with my finger. "Not even if he was the last man on the planet."

She and Dana scoffed. "Yeah, if you say so," Ness remarked over her shoulder as she sauntered toward the kitchen. Running my fingers through my hair, I let out a long and exasperated breath. Dana gave me a sympathetic look.

"What am I going to do, Dana?"

Standing, she wrapped her arms around me and sighed.

"I don't know. But you could start with going home and actually facing him. It's the only chance you have at some sort of normality."

She was right. But how could things ever be normal again? I'd seen his sex face, and he'd seen my orgasm expression. You may be giggling at that, but we all have one. That moment where we lose control; dignity and etiquette go out of the window, and our bodies simply take over. Our features contort, squish, and our eyes roll back in our heads. We make sounds that should only be heard in the wild wilderness of the Amazon rainforest, and let's not forget that smell. Oh yes, sex is so wonderful and intense, but even you know what I'm talking about. The smell of sex—the sweat, bodily fluids, friction, and distinct fragrance of two bodies rubbing against one another. We ignore it while in the throes of passion, but if you're not so into it, I guarantee you will notice that scent immediately. If not during, then certainly after, while scrubbing it off in the shower. I'm not saying it's a bad thing, but you might as well be honest about the dirty and disgusting side of sex. No one can come back from that. Once you've experienced all those things with another human being, you become a part of their sexual chemistry. What is it they say? You're not just sleeping with your partner; you're having sex with everyone they've ever had sex with, too. In this case, Adam was in luck. Sex with Brad had been sterile, clean, and pretty much odour-free. He might as well have been having sex with a steriliser.

With a grunt of anxiety and frustration, I picked up my things, said a quick goodbye to the girls, and headed back to my apartment—back to a pissed off pussycat, the shame of last night, and hopefully, my best friend.

<u>Chapter 20</u>

Sitting at either end of the sofa, Adam and I remained deadly silent. He kept wringing his hands and glancing up at the ceiling. This was painful. Rolling my eyes, I brought my feet up and curled them beneath me.

"So ... Dana and Ness all good?"

At last! He speaks! I shot him the best fake and comfortable smile I could and nodded.

"Mmhmm. They're fine."

He nodded slowly. "Good. Good."

Oh dear God, I wanted to die. This tension between us was tangible.

"I was thinking we could watch a movie or something? Just relax for the evening?" Adam suggested with a slight smile on his face.

I nodded. Jeez, if I wasn't shaking my head lately, I was nodding. It seemed conversation and verbalisation of a yes or no was beyond me.

"Sure. Sounds good."

Picking up the remote, Adam flicked through the endless number of channels before settling on a movie that neither of us had seen before. It was about a young woman who fell in love with a soldier and was deeply romantic. It was full of scenes like kissing in the rain and falling into each other's arms. It seemed a good choice, and as we stayed on our separate halves of the sofa, I couldn't help but feel a sense of … longing. Usually, the two of us would be huddled up with some snacks and making jokes, but this was different. And it was about to get worse.

As the woman and her love were reunited for a brief time while he was on leave, they did the one thing I was dreading. They had sex. Cue the *bow chicka wow wow* music and the classic sensual undressing of our main characters. I was squirming in my seat. Have you ever watched a sex scene with your mum? It felt a little like that. Except, this time, I was uncomfortable for a completely different reason. I was horny.

Adam crossed his legs and sat back in his seat, staring at the screen. The two main characters began rolling around on the bed and caressing one another. I didn't know where to look. I clenched my fists and twirled my hair with the other hand. I needed to seem nonchalant.

Adam cleared his throat loudly and pulled lightly on his t-shirt as though he were a little hot. I wasn't hot. I was on fire. If I didn't expel the flames that were now simmering in my underwear, things could get to a very dangerous level. Adam was watching me out of the corner of his eye. He really wasn't as stealthy as he thought. The moment I turned my head and caught his eye, he immediately turned his attention back to the TV. Not that it really helped because our two stars were now going at it hammer and nail! Was this a movie or soft porn?

Grabbing the remote, I switched it off. "I think we should go out. Let's go out. I'm definitely up for going out. You?" I was in a panic.

Adam got to his feet and adjusted his trousers slightly, blushing as he did so.

"Absolutely. Somewhere loud and full of people. Somewhere public."

I nodded. "Great idea. There's a karaoke and disco place a couple of blocks down that serves cheap drinks every Sunday."

"Just call me Justin Timberlake," Adam joked as he hurried to his room.

"I'll get changed, and we'll go," he yelled over his shoulder as his door slammed shut behind him.

I flopped on the sofa and groaned. Dear God, this was awful. Now we couldn't even watch a racy scene in a movie without getting all flustered and worked up like a couple of sexless teenagers? Grown-ups aren't supposed to have these problems. Sex was meant to be fun, necessary, and at times, totally anonymous!

Adam's bedroom door swooshed as it opened quickly, and he stepped out in a pair of black trousers and a blue shirt. He was stunning. As he moved toward me, I couldn't help but picture his abs, curves, lines, and rocking hot bod beneath. Hell, I was picturing him totally stark naked as he walked across my lounge. Shaking my head, I smiled and then made my way to my own room to pull on a pair of jeans. My t-shirt would suffice for the karaoke bar around the corner.

"Ready?" Adam was beaming at me, scanning my body from head to toe. Holy fuck. My heart beat faster, and I had to gulp hard to find my voice.

"Uh huh," I managed to wheeze. "Let's go tear it up."

* * * *

The karaoke bar was a small, yet full place. It smelled old and dusty, and the décor indicated that it hadn't been cared for or modernised in quite some time. It didn't bother me though as I was simply relieved to be out of the house, out of that awkward silence, and away from the temptation presented via racy and raunchy sex scenes in movies! An older, dark-haired woman was on stage wailing out the lyrics to "Total Eclipse Of The Heart." It was akin to a cat being spade without the anaesthetic. I could only imagine what Jacob might make of it. Placing his hand on the small of my back, Adam gently nudged me forward toward the bar. He leaned over my shoulder and shouted into my ear.

"Let's get a drink."

I nodded and made my way over to the large, antique mahogany bar. A young woman was standing behind it, resting her elbows on the counter. Her bright red lipstick, blonde hair, and thick black eye makeup made her look as though she had just waltzed out of a '70s porno. What is it with porn and me lately? Does *everything* have to make me think of sex?

Adam tapped his hand on the bar in front of her, and she abruptly stood up and beamed at him. Her bright white teeth had smears of lipstick on them, and I noticed Adam trying not to stare. He ordered my usual and a beer for himself, and we located a table not far from the stage. The wailing woman had finally come to the end of her song, and I was sure I heard the entire bar let out a long sigh of relief. Sitting at our small round table, I glided my fingers up and down my glass, collecting the tiny droplets of condensation as I did so.

Another willing victim climbed up on stage, and the music of Ben. E King's "Stand By Me" started up. I rolled my eyes. Why does everyone always choose a ballad or slow song? Glancing at the stage, Adam too rolled his eyes.

"Great, another wailer with a broken heart."

I laughed lightly. "It's Sunday night. Who else is at these places on a Sunday? The winos, drunks, and heartbroken saps of London."

He raised an eyebrow and smiled. "And what category do we fit into?"

I thought for a moment before answering. "The desperately seeking normalcy."

He nodded lightly and looked down at his glass before picking it up and taking a long gulp. He pointed at my half-empty glass. "Another?"

I quickly finished my drink and handed him the glass. "Sure. Thanks."

It was going to take a hell of a lot more vodka-cranberries 'til I would begin to feel more comfortable at this rate. Turning around, I watched as Adam approached the bar. The tramp behind it was twirling her hair and fluttering her eyelashes at him. Dear God woman, have some restraint. He's a customer, not a conquest. Pressing his palms down on the bar, Adam leaned forward to her ear. I watched as she giggled and swatted playfully at his arm. She couldn't have been more obvious. She walked away to get his order, and when she returned, I noticed a couple more buttons on her shirt had *accidentally* fallen open. Her white lacy bra was now fluorescent white under the glare of the UV lamps that hung on the ceiling. She was ridiculous. Surely she didn't think he was interested in a woman who flaunted herself so outwardly.

She placed her hand on his as he handed over some cash. He was smiling at her and speaking animatedly. As she brought him his change, she handed him a small piece of paper. Taking a quick look before slipping it into his pocket, Adam winked at her, took our drinks, and headed back over. He placed my drink in front of me and smiled broadly.

"What was that all about?" I asked.

The corner of his mouth curved up. "Nothing. Cassie was just offering me something that wasn't on the menu. I told her I'd take a rain check."

I cringed. "So that was her number you were slipping into your pocket?"

He pulled out the small piece of paper and handed it to me to read—which I did, twice, and continued to cringe as I did so. "Call me when you want to play doctor." Was she serious? How cliché and completely tacky. He wasn't considering it, surely.

"Are you going to call her?"

He sipped his drink and smiled. "Maybe. I don't know."

I shoved the piece of paper back into his outstretched hand before picking up my drink and swallowing the whole lot. The music stopped, and the mic sat lonely on an empty stage. I needed some fun, and I needed some damn good music!

Standing abruptly, I got on stage and selected my song from the touch screen list. Adam sat at our table, shaking his head and grinning. The song was one of my favourites. Back when I was in college, and Adam in medical school, we had all gone for a wild night on the town. From sundown to sunrise we were drinking, dancing, and singing. Loudly. Anyway, knowing I was a huge Billy Idol fan, Adam had arranged a surprise for me. As the clock struck nine, Dana and Ness blindfolded me and crammed me into a car. I hadn't giggled so much in years.

When I was finally released and the blindfold removed, I was standing outside one of the biggest arenas in London. Adam stood in front of me with four tickets to a Billy Idol Greatest Hits concert. I screamed so loud, I was sure the entire stadium heard me. It was an amazing night. We drank far too much—sang, danced, and yelled for three hours before heading to the nearest bar to begin our pub-crawl back home. I was trashed. Completely hammered, we clambered into a small bar in South London, we were thrilled to discover it had a karaoke machine. The four of us immediately hopped on stage and belted out a Billy Idol classic—the same one that I was about to revive all over again. I wanted to revel in the memory of my friends, friendships, and squash the unsettling jealousy that had settled in my stomach. He wasn't mine. We were friends. That was all. Cassie had every right to hop on board the Adam bus. I just hoped he wouldn't offer her the opportunity.

The tune to "Rebel Yell" started, and Adam's grin widened. His eyes sparkled up at me as the disco ball above my head began to spin. Grabbing the mic, I sang my heart out. I lost myself in the music and allowed myself to get totally carried away. When it finished, the whole bar cheered loudly, and I took a bow in jest. Adam was on his feet, too, cheering, whistling, and offering his hand for me to hold while climbing down from the stage.

"I love that song!" he yelled at me over the sound of people clapping.

"Me too! Do you remember—"

"That concert!" he interrupted. "Of course I do! It was the most fun I have ever had in my life."

I beamed at him. "I had the biggest hangover of *my* life the next day. I must have drunk my liver into a stupor!"

He smiled and handed me another drink. I hadn't even noticed he had gone back to the bar during my performance, but considering my mouth was now as dry as the Sahara, I didn't care.

"I'm buzzing! We should go somewhere! I wanna dance!" I was bouncing on my heels. Adam laughed.

"Sure thing, Dancing Queen. Where do you wanna go?"

I shrugged. "I don't know. Maybe we could ask someone?"

Taking my hand, he pulled me over to the bar and gestured for Cassie to come over. Her cleavage and perky boobs bounced like jello as she wiggled over.

"Come to take me up on my offer?" Her lips pressed together, and I could see the bleed of her lipstick. Attractive, dear. *Really.* I mentally rolled my eyes but continued to smile. Adam gave her an awkward smile before glancing at me. "Actually, we were wondering if you knew anywhere that's open for dancing. A club or something?"

She was practically leering at him! Had this woman no shame at all?

"There's a place a couple of streets over. It's always open. It's kind of retro, though. If you don't mind seventies stuff, then it's pretty cool. Goes on all night, and the drinks are pretty cheap."

Pulling Adam's hand, I urged him to hurry up.

"Thanks, doll." He grinned at her, and she looked like the cat who had gotten the cream. It was sickening. Really, it was.

When we got outside, Adam was laughing loudly.

"You really wanna go and dance?"

I gave him a puzzled look.

"Come on, Charlie. I know exactly what you're doing. You're on a high, I'm on a high, and you're scared to be alone with me."

The thought hadn't crossed my mind, but he wasn't wrong. I *was* afraid to be alone with him. I wasn't sure I could control myself. But he didn't have to know that. "Ha! You wish, stud. You're not *that* irresistible."

He shook his head and snickered. "Okay. If you say so. Let's dance."

* * * *

Cassie had one thing right; it was a cool place. In fact, so many people thought so that it was full to the brim with bodies. Some were dressed in theme with afro wigs, flares, and platform shoes while others, like myself and Adam, were clearly there for the music rather than the theme. And speaking of music, it was disco. Classic, 1970s disco—Bee Gee's, Bay City Rollers, David Cassidy, and many more. I was in heaven. The three vodka and cranberries were warming my blood, and as Adam's hand brushed mine, I knew I needed another, fast!

Making a beeline for the bar, I ordered my drink plus five shots of Jack Daniel's each for Adam and me. He sniffed at the brown liquid before winking and tossing back each and every one in a row. I tried to keep up, but the more I drank, the more my throat burned. Wincing, I looked up at Adam through blurry eyes. I coughed and spluttered. Adam was bent over laughing at me.

"It's not funny. I used to be able to down at least ten of these things in a row. What happened?"

He patted my arm, and his laugh was now a soft chuckle. "No stamina."

I raised an eyebrow. "I think you and I both know I have plenty of stamina."

He blushed and ran his fingers through his hair. Removing his glasses, he slotted them into his pocket. "Come on, let's get another round. "

* * *

Six vodka and cranberries and ten shots of Jack later ... the room was spinning. Adam and I had played every drinking game we knew, and I could see he was also a little tipsy, though he never did seem to get as drunk as I did. The sounds Marvin Gaye's "Give It Up" filled the club, and leaping to my feet, I caught Adam by the hand. "Come on! We *have* to dance to this song. It's my favourite song."

He laughed loudly. "Every song is your favourite song."

I pouted a little, and he quickly came to my side as we made our way onto the dance floor. It was packed with people, and all around us bodies swayed, shimmied, shook, and moved to the music. Adam placed his hands on my hips, and I began to move in time to the rhythm.

I raised my hands in the air above my head causing my shirt to lift slightly and expose my bare skin. Adam's fingertips grazed my hips, and I hitched a breath. I didn't care that I had a muffin top over my jeans. All that mattered was that I was having fun and what's more, Adam was touching me. It was wrong for me to want that. I should have stopped him, pushed him away, but as his hands slid gently up my shirt to my stomach, I couldn't help but close my own hands over his, urging him to hold me tighter. His arms were around my waist as his hips pressed against my behind. His lips caressed my neck, and I moaned gently. I was high on the atmosphere, the booze, and heat I could feel raising between Adam's body and mine.

I leaned my head back onto his shoulder, exposing my neck. He nuzzled it gently with his nose before hungrily kissing and licking my collarbone. My hands swept around his neck, and I fisted his hair in my hands. His teeth skimmed my earlobe, and I bit my lip in anticipation.

"I have to have you, Charlie."

Turning around, I pressed my palms against his cheeks and gazed into his eyes.

"Take me home. Now."

<u>Chapter 21</u>

Lifting my head from the pillow, I rubbed my sore and aching head. Light was streaming through a partially opened window across the room, and as my eyes adjusted to the light, I panicked. The memory of the night before flooded my brain. Sitting bolt upright, I scanned my surroundings. I was in my own room, and … I was alone. Confused, I swung my legs out of bed and staggered to the bathroom. I was still wearing my bra, but the rest of my clothes, including my underwear, were missing. Staring into my bathroom mirror, I winced. Oh crap. I remembered. Adam's hands on me at the club, our frantic exit, and the countless stops we made on the way back from the apartment to grope, fondle, kiss, and almost undress one another. It was a miracle we had made it back without being arrested for being drunk and disorderly or for indecent exposure. Possibly even lewd behaviour… but that's just between you and me.

But what happened when we got back to the apartment was a hazy blur. I remembered taking off our clothes. I remembered giggling, lots of giggling. And I remembered … I held my hand to my mouth and gasped. Oh no. I remembered everything! The sofa, the kitchen counter, the floor, and God only knows where else. I also had a vague memory of Jacob screeching and fleeing from the room, but the details were evading me.

The sound of the kettle boiling in the kitchen caught my attention. Pulling on my work clothes, I inhaled sharply as my arm caught in my shirtsleeve. I had a carpet burn! For real? A carpet burn. I rolled my eyes and held my head in my hands. Great, Charlene. Well done. Another awkward breakfast with your best friend. What is wrong with you? What is wrong with *him*?

Grabbing my jacket, I stormed out of the bedroom toward the kitchen. I was ready for a blowout confrontation, but as I approached the counter, I had the wind taken out of my sails by a sweet kiss planted on my cheek. Turning my head to face him, Adam smiled at me.

"Morning."

He was beaming. He looked positively radiant with happiness … or satisfaction. I wasn't entirely sure. Pulling out a stool, he gestured for me to sit. Watching his every move with suspicion, I lowered myself onto the seat. Why was he so chirpy? Maybe he'd forgotten what we did last night. Maybe he was a little tipsier than I'd thought. Handing me a cup of coffee, a glass of water, and some painkillers, he smiled.

"Sleep okay?"

I eyed him curiously. Reaching for my glass, I raised an eyebrow, cautious of what exactly his game was here.

"I guess so … and you?"

Leaning back against the kitchen counter with his feet crossed and a hand on the edge of the countertop, he nodded as he sipped his coffee.

"Best night's sleep I've ever had. I was pretty exhausted after—"

I flopped my arms onto the counter and slammed my head against them.

"Charlene, what the hell is the matter now?"

I groaned loudly in frustration. "We had sex again! What is wrong with us? Didn't we learn the first time? We said it wouldn't happen again, but here we are at another awkward breakfast."

The corner of his mouth curved into a smile. "I don't feel awkward. Do you?"

And that was the strange thing; I didn't feel awkward. I didn't feel uncomfortable, guilty, or ashamed. Maybe when you've done it once, the rest kind of pales in comparison.

"I ... I don't know what I feel like. I feel ..." I couldn't find the right words, but it didn't matter, Adam found them for us.

"I feel great. I feel rested, satisfied, and last night was the best sex of my life. Last time was amazing, but this time was incredible. I don't know if it's the connection we have already and knowing each other so well, but I really don't think I can go without it, Charlie. So ... I have a little proposition for you."

I picked up my coffee and sipped it, wincing a little as it burned my top lip.

"I think we should keep having sex."

I spluttered my coffee all over the kitchen counter. Grabbing a towel, Adam mopped it up and continued, "Just hear me out. We have great sex. You know you can't deny it. I'm not seeing anyone. You're not seeing anyone, and you keep saying how sex-starved you have been for the past few years. We can stay friends. Nothing has to change we just ... fuck now and then. What do you think?"

I was lost for words. He was actually suggesting we become fuck buddies! Rounding the counter, he stood in front of me and swivelled my seat around to face him. "I know you like it, Charlene. No woman can fake that many orgasms and those sounds you make every time I touch you, I know you're enjoying me as much as I'm enjoying you. I can make you feel sexy again. I can make you feel wanted, desirable, and help you get over those damn body hang-ups of yours. Haven't you noticed how you kind of ... let go when you're with me? Have you been with a guy lately and actually done that? Not worry about how you look, how he thinks you look, or how anything is showing? You even keep the lights on when we're together, and I know you don't do that with anyone else. Think about it. You know what I'm saying is right."

I placed my hands on his forearms and gripped him tightly.

"Adam, you're crazy. We can't just fuck one day then hang out the next. It's not going to work. Look at how awkward things were last night."

He shook his head. "That was because we were still hungering after more. Once we actually set out the ground rules and make an agreement, why does anything have to be difficult or complicated?"

He had a valid point. But we couldn't do this! I'd only ever had this kind of arrangement once in my life, and that was with a guy who lived across the hall from me in college. It was uncomplicated as we hardly knew each other, but he was hot, and at two in the morning, both of us were available for a booty call.

Standing abruptly, I pushed him away from me gently and shook my head. I walked to the sink and emptied my cup. Caffeine was the last thing I wanted right now. I turned around to find myself caged in by Adam. His hand stroked my thigh, his voice whispered in my ear, and he leaned into me.

"Tell me you don't like this. Tell me that it's not turning you on."

I couldn't breathe. The effect his body, touch, and voice had on me these days was insane! Adam and I had known each other forever, and now he wasn't just my nerdy doctor best friend, Adam. No. He was hot, sexy, sexpert, make me moan all night, Adam. I tried to calm my nerves, and I could feel my pulse beginning to race.

"Adam, I ..."

His teeth grazed my earlobe. "Don't deny it, Charlie, you're body gives you away. Just give this a chance. I promise you won't be sorry."

I pressed my palms down on the counter behind me and stared into his eyes. "Just sex. I don't want anything else to change between us."

He nodded. "Just sex. Everything else is exactly as it was before."

Smiling slightly, I urged him to move away from me and grabbed my purse from the countertop.

"Is that a yes then?" he called out as I made my way to the front door in silence.

"I guess you'll find out," I threw back over my shoulder at him.

He chuckled. "I'll come by the office at lunch. We'll go for something to eat and discuss details."

I nodded and held up my hand in a quick wave before heading off to the office. I would need to come up with some kind of rule list before lunch, and I still had a ton of work to plough through on my desk. It was going to be an eventful day.

* * * *

My office felt significantly smaller as I sat at my desk, rifling through a large pile of paperwork. The band from L.A.

was well on their way to being signed, and the stipulations, agreements, and finer details of their contracts were still to be completed. Each had specific requests. The drummer seemed to be the biggest diva in the group, whereas the lead and the bass player were more laid back. Their requests were simple enough, and the company would be only too happy to oblige, but the drummer clearly needed a good and firm punch in the face! I scoured through every line, every detail, and each page was scribbled with notes, highlighted paragraphs, and sticky labels by the time I was finished. And that was only one of the contracts! It had taken me almost three hours. Glancing up at the clock, I bit my lip anxiously. Adam was meeting me for lunch, and there would be yet another form of verbal contract to negotiate. Though that one benefited me directly.

The side door in my office breezed open and in sauntered Regina. Perching herself on the edge of my desk, she grinned. I eyed her with curiosity and continued to search for the next contract.

"What are you so happy about? You look like the cat that got the cream," I remarked.

"Not cream, dear. But something just as tasty. You know that gorgeous new band we're signing?"

I nodded and held up the various pieces of paper on my desk. "I'm vaguely aware, yes."

She smirked. "Well, I just got off the phone with Nicola and Denise, and it seems that they're already on board! They're just waiting on the contracts. How soon can you fax them over?"

I exhaled exasperatedly. "I have no idea. It's the drummer's terms and conditions giving me the most hassle."

Regina giggled. "The lead singer—Oliver, I believe his name is—has told Nic and Denise to ignore it all and issue him the same as the other two. He advises us not to pander to his drama queen needs."

Slamming the wad of paperwork in my hand on the desk, I sat back in my chair and huffed loudly.

"What's the matter with you? You would have thought you'd be relieved to have less work to do."

I rubbed my eyebrows with my finger and thumb. I could feel another headache coming on.

"I am relieved. I've got something on my mind. That's all."

Regina leaned forward. "A problem shared is gossip for lunch tomorrow."

I gave her a half smile. "It's Adam."

She gave me a bewildered look. "What about him?"

I let out a long and staggered breath. "We … had sex."

I waited for a gasp, a look of shock, anything really, but she simply stared at me and raised her eyebrows in what looked like confusion. "Well, everyone in the office knows that, Charlene. They heard it. It was the hot topic of the water cooler for days. What's your point?"

I'd forgotten about our little display. Time to come clean. "We didn't *actually* have sex in here, Regina. We were faking it. Adam said it would give the minions something other than my broken engagement to talk about. And it did."

She sniggered. "So you hadn't had sex then, but you have now?"

I nodded.

"I do not see the problem here, Charlene."

Resting my head back on my chair, I groaned. "He's my best friend! I fucked my long-time best friend. And not just once, oh no, several times. All over my apartment. And now … he wants to keep doing it!"

"He wants to be your fuck buddy? I think I'm following this correctly."

I nodded again. "Yes. He's coming to meet me at lunch to discuss it."

Regina shook her head gently. "Well, I really don't understand what all the fuss is about. Friends can make the best lovers. They know you so intimately already that there's no need for inhibitions or worrying about where the *relationship* is going. It's a win-win situation. You get to spend time with a friend and get laid. Wasn't he good in bed? Is he notoriously bad? Is he tiny?"

I sat up straight and gripped my hands on the edge of the desk, leaning forward as I spoke. "Oh, God no. He's perfect. He's an Adonis in a white coat. And the sex ... wow. I have never been so satisfied."

Standing up, Regina fisted her hands on her hips. "You know, the sooner you modern girls get over the whole *it's complicated* shit, the better. I mean, look at me. I'm married, and I've got more boy toys than I can count. Why shouldn't you have one? It's about time you stopped being so rational and stopped thinking so much. That's your problem. You think too much and feel too little, and I say you should keep feeling Adam!"

I giggled a little. "Yes, but none of your boy toys are also your best friend for twenty years. What if we mess it up, and I lose him forever?"

She rolled her eyes. "Oh, for the love of God, Charlene. If you're not fucking him, someone else will. Would you rather enjoy his pogo stick or have some little tart bouncing up and down on it?"

I suddenly thought of Cassie. I had to admit, I was jealous at that bar. I didn't want him to have her number, and I certainly didn't want him to call her. Was that why I had fucked him? Was it a possessive thing?

"So you think this is a good idea?" I asked her.

She nodded enthusiastically. "I think it's certainly worth trying. Have a little fun for once in your life. Since you and Brad broke up, you've been a different person. You're losing weight, you look great, you're more confident at work, and I can see by the way you carry yourself that you clearly don't miss that douche hole."

She was right. I had lost almost three stone so far and was well on my way to my target weight. I had Adam to thank for that. His strict diet program, exercise sessions in the park, and even the apartment had kept me right on track. The amazing and athletic sex probably didn't hurt either. Maybe happiness was the best diet tool. Maybe just being satisfied in most aspects of your life could do that. Work was going really well. My body was changing for the better. My friends and I were having fun, and I was having mind-blowing sex. Move over Dr Atkins. Dr Fitz had the cure for obesity, and it was a rocking hot sex life!

"Charlene? Hello?"

Regina waved a hand in front of my face and snapped her fingers. "You are away with the fairies sometimes, I swear. So, what are you thinking?"

I pushed my chair away from the desk and crossed my legs. Picking up a pen, I mindlessly nibbled on the end.

"I'm thinking … I'm going to get laid."

Regina threw her head back and laughed. "Good girl! It's about time you had some fun and took some risks. Safe isn't always the best option in life. Believe me."

I smiled up at her. "I guess it only has to be complicated if we let it get that way."

She nodded. "Exactly! Now, go have some lunch, take all the time you need, and if I don't see you for the rest of the day, I won't sweat about it. Though I'm sure you'll be doing enough sweating and panting of your own."

Winking at me, she walked across the office and shut the door behind her.

I couldn't help but smile. She was right. I did need some fun, and if Adam wasn't worried about it, then I shouldn't be either. Glancing up at my office door, I spotted him marching toward it through the glass. Oh God, he's here already. Oh, God. Here we go.

Chapter 22

There is something to be said for the health benefits of sex. It's a stress reliever. A tension dispeller and a serious sleep enhancer. In the three weeks since our arrangement had been finalised, Adam and I had been at it like rabbits. I'm talking hopped up on Prozac, humping bunnies, and I was feeling … amazing! My work was becoming less stressful every day. I was sleeping better than I had in months, and what's more, I had dropped another six pounds. Happiness was making me slimmer! My obsessive need to eat my emotions and swallow my anger was completely eradicated with a few hot and heavy sex sessions with Adam and multiple mind-blowing orgasms.

And it worked the other way, too. Only the previous night, Adam had come home extremely tense and yelled for an hour about his apartment. It seemed the fumigators had caused a slight problem with the building's insulation, and the whole place had to be gutted out and redone. It would be weeks before he could go home again and he'd already been with me for several. I reassured him that he could stay as long as he needed, but it didn't calm his irritated nerves. I got the feeling there was also something else bothering him, but he refused to discuss it. I got a simple, "It's work stuff." And that was it. Deciding that his mood was not welcomed in my apartment that night, I had slipped into a silky nightdress, and as he sat in front of the TV with his shirt unbuttoned, I was on my knees relieving his tension. His hand fisted in my hair as my mouth worked his rigid and solid cock. I could feel the stress and worry of the day washing away from him with every roll of my tongue, and as he thrust his hips upward, forcing himself deeper into my mouth, he groaned loudly. I felt powerful, sexy, and in control. I'd never felt that way before.

After he climaxed, he lifted me onto the couch and reciprocated. Now, usually, I hate oral sex. It makes me uncomfortable. Not only do I feel totally on edge at the thought of being so exposed, but I spend the entire time worrying about the smell, taste, and appearance of my lady flower. Yes, I said lady flower. I know what you're thinking, there was nothing flowery or fragrant about that particular area of the body, but mine certainly opened seasonally!

But with Adam, I just … didn't worry about it. It didn't seem to matter. I lay back as he hooked my legs over his shoulders and licked me like an ice cream cone. Adam had some serious skill. How he'd learned it all and kept it so secret was a mystery. He'd certainly never been given tips from his brother. They hardly spoke. I could only assume that he'd had more practice than I'd thought. There was me thinking he was a quiet, reserved, and sensitive type, and all along he was a sex bomb waiting to explode all over me! Metaphorically speaking, of course.

He was right about my body hang-ups. And it seemed that Adam really was the cure I needed. Every time I tried to cover up, hide myself by wrapping my arms around my body, or even just closed my eyes when he would undress me, he would immediately stop and address what I was doing.

During the couch coitus, I was so embarrassed with him being down there that as his lips trailed over my stomach, I flinched and tensed. Lifting his head, he caught my hands, intercepting my next move.

"Stop it. You're gorgeous. I don't know why you hide."

My throat was dry, and my voice a little horse when I answered him. "Because I have so much jelly on my belly."

He chuckled and placed a light kiss on my belly button.

"If I'm in a restaurant, and I order steak, I expect to dine on a juicy piece of meat. I don't want to gnaw on a bone. You, Charlie, are a feast for my eyes, a succulent sexual fulfilment for my appetite, and if you would just be quiet and stop fighting me, I'm about to enjoy some dessert."

My pulse leapt. Adam always said the perfect thing. He was such a vast contrast to Brad. Brad had always insisted we turn off the lights, and some nights he would even request that I wear a nightshirt or something. At the time I thought he was respecting my body confidence problems, but in hindsight, he just didn't like to watch me wobble around. Not that you can do much wobbling in six and a half minutes. Two pumps and a squirt was pretty much all I could hope for during a night of passion with my germaphobic lover.

But Adam was incredible. All of my inhibitions melted away and I could just … be me. It sounded cliché and completely ridiculous, but I'd forgotten how much fun sex could be.

After three orgasms and a quickie on the carpet, we both settled down to watch TV and talked about our plans for the weekend. I'd promised my mother that I'd visit for my grandmother's birthday in a couple of weeks, and that meant spending my weekend shopping with the girls for the perfect gift. Adam would be working long hours again. His boss really was a bitch, but I was still pretty convinced that she was into him.

* * * *

Sitting at the kitchen counter eating my breakfast, I smiled over at Adam who was sleepily pouring himself a cup of tea.

"So you and the girls are shopping all day, huh?"

I nodded as I shovelled another spoon full of Cheerios into my mouth.

"Sounds fun. I'll be working late so I probably won't see you. If I get in at a reasonable time, are you opposed to being woken?"

He winked at me playfully. I shook my head and pushed my bowl away. "Nope. Well, unless of course, I have company in there. You never know what the day will bring."

Adam's eyebrows furrowed as he looked down at his teacup. "So you're still looking for Mr Right?"

"Of course. I'm sure he's out there somewhere. And now that sex isn't my biggest goal, I can actually think straight for a change."

Walking to the sink, I patted him on the behind. "I have you to thank for that."

He gave me a half smile and nodded gently. Dropping my bowl into the empty sink, I grabbed my bag and headed for the door.

"So I'll see you later?" I asked as I pulled the front door open. He nodded again but said nothing.

"Great. Have a good day."

Closing the door behind me, I couldn't help but feel that something between us had just ... shifted. Trying to put it out of my head, I made my way to the train station to meet the girls.

* * * *

"So the two of you are still banging each other's brains out then?" Ness asked as she browsed a menu. We had been shopping all morning and decided to stop at a local café for some lunch. Scouring my own menu, I tilted my head and pressed my lips together. "You know we are. I don't know why you keep asking."

Dana dropped her menu on the table and rested her elbow on the edge. She leaned her chin against it.

"And things still aren't complicated?"

I shook my head. "Nope. Things are fine. In fact, I even told him that I'm still looking for Mr Right, and he was fine with it."

They both eyed me curiously. "Really?" they asked in unison.

"Yes. I told you, we're friends that fuck. That's all. We're not in a relationship for God's sake. We're adults."

Ness nodded slowly. "And if he happened to also start fucking someone else, you'd be ... okay with that?"

What kind of question was that?

"Of course!" I said a little louder and more enthusiastically than I had intended. "He's free to fuck whoever he wants, and so am I. In fact, he could shag the entire female population of London if he wants."

Dana snorted at me. "Whatever you say, Charlene."

Now I was irritated. "I know you think I'm crazy, and I know you think the two of us are supposed to be destined for some whirlwind romance or something, but life doesn't work like that. I hate to break it to you, but there's no such thing as happily ever after. It's all bullshit. Life is full of disappointments, and you should get your rocks off as often as you can because you're a long time dead."

Ness sniggered. "You are such an idiot. You really are blind, aren't you?"

Slamming down my menu, I glared at her. "What the hell is that supposed to mean?"

Slamming down her own menu, she met my stare. "You know exactly what it means. God, Charlene, you're so busy looking for Prince Charming that you completely missed the hot doctor that's been pining for you for years! You can deny it all you want, but you know that your feelings for each other run deeper than you're both willing to admit."

I shook my head, angry with her and her stupid assumptions. How dare she assume she knew what Adam felt or better yet, what I did? I was not in love with Adam! "You have no idea what you're talking about. If that were true, why the hell would we have stayed friends for all of these years? You really believe Adam is the type of guy to just pine over someone? Especially, someone, he knows he could never have? Of course not. He's not an idiot."

Dana groaned. "Charlene, of course, he would. He's completely besotted with you. Do you really not see it?"

I shook my head. "You're both crazy. Even if it were true, which I'm not saying it is, but if I did have feelings for him, I wouldn't act on them. I'm the queen of rotten judgment, and I've won every award for bad decision-making. I've done the broken heart, falling in love and getting stomped on thing, and I'm finished with it all. Been there, done that."

Ness scoffed. "So we're just imagining the way he looks at you? The way you look at him when he smiles, and how the two of you can't seem to exist without each other? When are you both gonna grow up and own up to how you feel about one another. There's no shame in falling in love! And you two have got it bad. You have for years."

I held my head in my hands. Looking up at them again, I rolled my eyes. "You know what, since you two seem to know me so much better than I do, why don't the two of *you* shop for my gran's gift, and I'll sit here, drink tea, and think about my awful negligence of Adam and his intense love for me. I'll sit here and pine over my unrequited love."

Okay, I was being sarcastic and a little bitchy, but they were pissing me off. There was nothing wrong with the relationship I had with Adam, and their interference was totally for their own selfish reasons. Interfering, nosey, matchmaking, do-gooders!

"If that's how you feel, Charlene, then fine! You made your bed, and now the two of you can go fuck yourselves and each other in it. Just don't come crying to us when the shit hits the fan. You are in love with him. Just say it and fucking deal with it."

Getting up from her seat, Ness tugged on Dana's elbow. Giving me a regretful look, she stood and together they walked away into the crowd of people making their way down the busy London street.

A waitress brought over a small white pot of tea and a cup. I took it from her with a halfhearted smile and poured myself a large cup. This was a nightmare. Not only had I just fallen out with my girls, but I was now in turmoil over Adam. Ness was wrong about him—she had to be. Someone that in love with another person didn't agree to a no-strings and just sex relationship. It would be heartbreaking, surely. But that didn't explain why I was the one with the ache in my chest. My stomach was churning, and my throat was dry. Ness's question was replaying over and over in my ears. Would I really be fine with him seeing some other woman? Would I really just be pleased he'd found someone? The answer was unsettling. No. I wouldn't be okay with it. But that was just because the sex would stop, and I'd be back to my dry spell and poor self-esteem. That was all. I thought. I hoped. Oh, God help me!

Stirring my tea mindlessly with one hand, I rested my chin on my hand as my elbow pressed into the tabletop. Could things possibly get any worse?

"Charlene?"

Turning my head, I gawped in horror. I have to stop asking myself if things could get any worse. Because it seemed every time I did, the universe screwed me over.

"Brad!"

He gave me a small smile, but I couldn't and wouldn't return it. My insides twisted with rage as hate began boiling my blood as it flowed through my veins.

"Hi, Charlene. How are you?"

I glanced around to ensure I wasn't heard and lowered my voice. I didn't want a scene. Reaching up, I grabbed a fistful of his shirt and yanked him downward to me.

"How am I? Are you fucking serious?"

Pulling himself from my grasp, he pulled out a seat and sat opposite me.

"I know, I don't expect you to want to talk to me, but I couldn't just walk by and say nothing."

I glared at him with hatred. "Really? Because I doubt you have anything I want to hear."

He nodded gently. "I deserve that. I do. I did a horrible, horrible thing, and I'm so sorry for all the pain I caused you."

I interrupted him abruptly. "Pain? You think it was pain that I felt? It was a lot fucking more than that! I was humiliated, heartbroken, devastated, and completely betrayed! You called off our wedding, Brad. The day that's supposed to be the happiest in a girl's life, and you did it over the phone! You didn't even have the nuts or guts, both of which I'd like to hack apart with a rusty knife, to tell me to my face that you were screwing some tart at your office!"

He looked down at the table, and for the first time, he actually seemed ashamed.

"I know. I am so sorry. I don't deserve forgiveness, God knows I've learnt my lesson the hard way now."

I gave him a confused but seething glare.

"Aneska dumped me. It seems once I wasn't forbidden fruit anymore I wasn't so exciting. To be honest, I was getting tired of her, too. I was done with the al fresco sex, the social scene, and the endless days in bed."

I held up my hand in disgust. "I really don't want to hear about how the two of you fucked each other into the ground. Thanks."

He grabbed my hand and held it in his, tightly.

"But I know now that I was stupid. I should never have left you. Aneska was just so … exciting and new. But what I had with you was safe, secure, and comfortable. I know I said hurtful things, and I was sure you would never talk to me again, but when I saw you from across the street, I had to see you. You look amazing, Charlene. You must have lost at least four stone."

I scowled at him. "Funny how you notice how good I look *now*. A few months ago you couldn't have picked me out of a lineup. I meant so fucking little to you that I'm surprised you recognise me now!"

He sighed ruefully. "I know. I'm sorry. What I said about your weight was cruel, but it's how I felt, and look what it's done for you. If I hadn't said those things would you have had the motivation to lose the weight?"

Ripping it from his grasp, I slammed my palm on the table. "I lost weight for me! I lost weight because I was tired of being the same frumpy mouse-wife in training that you turned me into! For once, I'm *living* my life and not simply existing. I'm having more sex than I have ever had before, and it's also the *best* I have ever had."

That one hurt him. I could see the disappointment on his face.

"So you're seeing someone?"

I considered lying. I considered telling him about Adam, but in the end, I found myself simply saying, "No."

A distinct look of relief swept over his face. Placing his hand gently on mine, he leaned forward.

"I miss you, Charlene. I'm sorry for everything, and I know I don't have any right to ask you this, but please, if you could just find it in your heart, I would love to see you again. I'm staying with my sister for now until I find a place. I just got here a few weeks ago from Dublin, so I'm sofa-surfing right now."

If he was looking for sympathy, he wouldn't get any from me.

"A sofa is more than you deserve, Brad."

He nodded. "I know. But please, think about it. I still love you, Charlene. I never stopped loving you. Things just got so … complicated."

There was that word again. *Complicated*. It seemed every aspect of my life was complicated these days.

"Go away, Brad. Before I take this teacup and shove it up your arse and ram this teapot down your throat."

He stood quickly and brushed himself down. "Okay. You need time to think about what I've said; I get it. Please call me, Charlene. I'll be waiting by the phone."

He slid a business card toward me with his new address and phone number on it. I glanced at it and snorted. "Don't hold your breath. Actually, do hold your breath. With a little luck, you'll lose consciousness and develop amnesia. Maybe then you'll get out of my life for good. You've done enough damage already."

Nodding, he silently turned and walked away. What a complete and utter nutfucker! How could he take credit for my weight loss and how dare he have the nerve to even speak to me after what he did. It was the first time I'd seen him in months, and he had the bare-faced cheek to beg me to call him! What, now that I was slimmer, he suddenly wanted me again? Bullshit!

My mood was worsening the longer I sat outside the café. Calling the waitress over, I paid her and decided to do some retail therapy. Hey, if I couldn't eat my emotions away anymore, I was at least going to drown out the thoughts in my head with the sound of my credit card screaming!

Chapter 23

By the time I was done drowning my sorrows in a sea of stores, clothing racks, and a brand new Donna Karan dress, I was not only feeling just as stressed as before, but I'd also maxed out my credit card. Don't judge me. We've all had our moments of weakness. She, who has not splurged, impulse bought, or reached for the cookie dough ice cream, cast the first stone.

Time to think. Ha! I'd need a lobotomy to actually consider calling Brad the cactus anytime soon. Throwing my shopping bags on the sofa, I flopped beside them and inhaled deeply. I glanced at the clock on the far wall and was amazed to discover it was almost nine in the evening. My shopping trip and spontaneous dining at my favourite bistro had clearly gone on longer than I had thought. I could hear music coming from Adam's room and smiled. It comforted me to know he was around when I got home. Not only for the prospect of hot sex but also for the security and company. A single girl living in a decent apartment in London, I was a walking target for the right stalker. Maybe Brad was mine. It couldn't possibly have just been a coincidence that he ran into me today.

The sound of Marvin Gaye's "Give It Up" echoed through Adam's door. Grinning, I thought about our dancing. I thought about his hands on me and the wonderful session that followed when we'd arrived home. I was almost giddy with happiness as the memories flooded my mind. His arms around me, his lips on mine, and his deep and soulful eyes gazing into mine. Wait, did I just call his eyes soulful?

Shaking my head, I threw my arm across my eyes. What the hell was happening to me? It was Adam for God's sake. Why did I find myself thinking about him so much? I'd never found myself with so many thoughts of him before. I wasn't in love, that wasn't it, but I was certainly a little … *intrigued* by him. Intrigued, yes, that's what it was. I was just curious and probably a little too comfortable with the arrangement we had. But what if I was wrong? What if Adam really *did* have feelings for me? And not just friendly ones, oh no, I meant the romantic types you only saw in films.

Groaning in frustration, I picked up a pillow and held it over my face. I needed to know what the hell was happening between us, and we seriously needed to talk. Right now. Getting up from the couch, I marched over and opened his door.

"Adam, we really need to—"

I couldn't finish my sentence. My jaw dropped, and my heart plummeted into my stomach. Lying on Adam's bed, with her legs hooked over his shoulders, was Cassie. She shrieked a little, and Adam quickly pulled away from her, grabbed the bed sheets, and rolled off the bed and onto the floor. This, of course, left Cassie totally stark naked! Holding my hand over my eyes, I backed out of the room and slammed the door behind me. I didn't know what to do or think. Hurrying into the solace of my own room, I closed the door behind me and locked it. A second later, the knob was rattling as Adam tried to get in.

"Charlie? Charlie, open the door."

I couldn't breathe. My chest hurt, and I felt sick. Why the hell was I feeling like this? He wasn't mine. I didn't own him. I'd said it myself that he could screw all of London if he wanted to. So then why, in the name of God, did it hurt so much to find him in bed with *her*?

"It's fine, Adam. I'm sorry I barged in, I should have knocked," I yelled breathlessly through the door.

Pressing my palm to my chest, I could feel the rapid beat of my heart.

"Why have you locked yourself in there then?"

I didn't have an answer to that. Not even for myself.

"I was embarrassed, I guess. Just go back to your room and your *plaything*."

Damn it. Did that sound bitter? Because it sure sounded that way as it flew out of my mouth. He banged on the door several times, urging me to open it. I could hear Cassie protesting from the room next door. He stopped a moment and yelled back at her, but I couldn't quite make out what she was saying.

"Charlie, open the door and talk to me."

Storming over, I unlocked the door, and it swung open.

"There's nothing to talk about. You and I are friends. Friends who used to have sex."

He raised an eyebrow and leaned against the doorframe. He was still clutching a sheet around his waist. As though it mattered. I'd seen him naked above, below, and next to me enough times. His modesty had long since packed its bags and hitched a ride to Neverland.

"*Used* to have sex?"

I nodded. "Yep. You've got your new fuck buddy, and I am totally fine with that. It was fun, but we knew it wouldn't last right?"

I was being short with him, and I was sure he could sense that something was up.

"You don't seem too happy about that. Why don't you tell me what's *really* going on? What's really bothering you about this?"

I shook my head. "Nothing." I lied. "I'm fine with it." I did it again. Lying was a new talent of mine, though I clearly hadn't perfected it.

"You're really going to stand there and tell me that you have no problem with this?"

I nodded again. "Absolutely. Now, if you don't mind, I need to unpack my shopping bags and shower. Goodnight."

Pushing him out of the doorway, I slammed it in his face and locked it again. Silence. Resting my back against the cool wood, I slid down to the floor and pulled my knees up to my chest. Fuck. If I didn't think I had feelings for Adam before, then I was fairly certain that I did now. Because for the first time in our twenty year relationship I hated him. It was unfamiliar, and as tears slid down my cheeks, I resigned myself to one simple fact: we'd fucked it up. I knew what I was feeling, but I wouldn't admit to myself. I couldn't. "Say it and deal with it." That was Ness's big solution? I couldn't; if I said it, that made it real, and right now, I couldn't deal with that.

* * * *

I hammered loudly on Ness's door. I wasn't sure if she'd open it, and if she did, there was no guarantee that she wouldn't just slam it in my face again. I hoped she wouldn't. I could hear her grumbling as she approached the door. Please don't leave me out here in the dark. Please, please, please, please, *please*. A wave of relief swept over me as it opened, and standing in her pink pj's and a mud facemask, Ness fisted her hands on her hips.

"Well?" she snapped. Her foot was tapping rapidly as she stared me down. Tears pooled in my eyes, and the moment she saw them, her demeanour softened. Pulling me into a warm hug, she swept her hands up and down my back.

"Oh, sweetie. What happened?"

Pulling away, I swiped at my eyes and let out a sob. "You were right. You can't be friends and lovers. It doesn't work."

She gave me a puzzled look and with her arm around my waist, urged me into the house. As I rounded the door to the living room, Dana got up from the sofa and threw her arms around me. I let out another sob and fell onto the sofa with a bounce.

"You were right. Both of you."

Dana held her hand over mine as she sat beside me on the sofa. "You mean he told you how he feels?" She had a look of hope in her eyes. God, I wish I could have had that hope.

"No. You were wrong about that at least. Adam Fitz definitely does not have romantic feelings for me."

Ness shook her head. "I don't believe that for a second. Where's your evidence?"

I sniffed and let out a long and staggered breath. "She's back at my place. Naked with her feet hooked behind his ears."

That did it. The sobbing, heaving, and erratic breathing began the moment that the image entered my mind. The two of them gasped.

"No way! In your apartment? With you right there in the next room?" Dana enveloped me in a hug as I gently sobbed on her shoulder.

"I came in late. I wanted to talk to him. I was so confused about everything and how I was feeling. I just wanted to try and understand what was happening between us. I went to his room, and I saw them."

Ness was getting riled. "What a dick! How could he do that to—"

I cut her off and shook my head. "It's hardly his fault, Ness. I'm the one who said it was just sex—that I was looking for Mr Right, and that we were both free to shag anyone we wanted to."

She grunted. "So because the steak was suddenly off his menu he decides to dine on some skank's fur burger? Urgh!"

Dana cringed. "As much as I don't like the way she says it, Ness is kind of right."

"No, she's not. I have no one to blame for this stupid mess but myself. I've screwed it up, and now I have to live with it. Adam was not, is not, and never will be mine."

Dana bit her lip and glanced quickly at Ness before turning back to me. "But you wish he was, right?"

I stared at her. "I don't know. I don't know how I feel." That was a lie. I knew exactly how I felt. I just wouldn't say it. Well, not out loud.

"He's not just some guy, though, is he? He's … Adam. He's the one man that's always been there for me. He knows me inside and out, and he still thinks I'm amazing. Where else am I going to find someone who—"

"Loves you like that?" Ness interrupted.

I shook my head gently. "You're wrong. Whatever you think he might have felt for me, he definitely doesn't now."

The two of them held me tightly, and I instantly regretted everything I'd said at the café.

"I'm so sorry for everything I said to you both. Don't hate me."

They chuckled. "We could never hate you. We love you," Dana whispered. Ness nodded and lifted my chin with her hand, forcing me to face her. "Why don't you stay here tonight? You can get some sleep and go home bright as a button tomorrow."

I smiled gratefully at her. "Thank you."

Handing me a blanket, she and Dana kissed me goodnight and left the room, turning out the light as they left. I could hear them whispering in the hallway but couldn't make out what they were saying. I definitely heard Adam's name, though. Adam. Damn it why did all my thoughts have to revolve around him right now? Turning over on the sofa, I tried to get comfy and settle down for the night. There was little chance of me getting any sleep, but at least I wouldn't have to listen to Cassie and her cries of pleasure all night. The thought turned my stomach. Twenty years, it had taken me almost twenty years, a broken engagement and a fuck buddy agreement to realise that I, Charlene Winters, am in love with my best friend. How screwed up is that? It's sick, twisted, not to mention, it's completely messing with my heart and head. I tossed and turned for hours, but I couldn't get to sleep. When the sun began to peek out from behind Ness's blinds, I admitted defeat, got up, and prepared myself for the painful and uncomfortable confrontation that would be waiting for me at home.

* * * *

Walking in my front door, I cautiously looked around. The whole place was silent. Thank God. Maybe Adam was still asleep or better yet, at work all day. I shouldn't have gotten my hopes up because just as I began to feel relieved, his bedroom door squeaked open. Wearing a pair of Adam's boxer shorts and a white t-shirt, Cassie sauntered out of the room and over to the kitchen. *My kitchen.* My fists clenched as I tried to control my irritation. Following her to the kitchen, I closed the front door loudly behind me. She jumped and stared at me, startled. "Oh, it's only you."

She giggled and began helping herself to my carton of strawberries and a smoothie. The nerve!

"Yes, me. You know, the owner of this establishment."

She gave me a confused look. Dear God, was she as stupid as she looked?

"I live here. It's my place," I clarified.

She smirked at me and began pouring herself a tall glass of *my* smoothie. "I thought it was Adam's place. When you came in last night, I actually thought maybe you were his wife or something, but he explained the whole best friend thing to me."

I raised an eyebrow. "Oh he did, did he?"

She nodded. "Oh yeah. I think it's great to have a friend who's the opposite sex. Though, I have no idea how you keep yourself from climbing all over him. He's a hottie, a doctor, and a gentleman."

I know, you stupid little tart, and before you came barging in, he was also going to be mine!

"But anyway, he's still sleeping, and I have to go to work."

My eyes dragged up and down her tiny little body. She was a stick figure. She was more suited as an afternoon treat for the hound across the street than a booty call.

"Oh, I'm going to get dressed, I just don't want to wake him. Could you tell him to call me?"

I gave her my best Oscar award-winning smile and nodded. "Of course. He has your number."

Because I sure do! Tramp. I'm sure your number is tucked away tighter than a stripper's G-string. She bounced on her heels, beaming at me before grabbing her clothes from the bedroom and heading to the bathroom. When she exited, I had to try desperately not to vomit. She was wearing the clothes from the previous night, and in this instance, it was a boob tube and a skirt that was so tiny, it could have been a belt. I like short skirts, I do. I can't wear them, but I like them. And call me old-fashioned, but I also believe that they should be long enough to cover a woman's vagina!

When she finally left, I felt as though I needed to disinfect my entire apartment. It felt cheap, dirty, and I hated it. Grabbing my cleaning cloths and some pine disinfectant, I began scrubbing at every surface.

I heard Adam's door open. His feet shuffled along the carpet as he approached the kitchen. I was now on the floor, scrubbing so hard that my hands were getting red.

"Charlene, what are you doing?" he asked sleepily.

I glanced up, and anger filled my body. He was wearing sweatpants but was totally shirtless. Damn him for being so sexy.

"Cleaning. What does it look like?" I snapped back at him.

"Whoa. Calm down, Rasputin. What's gotten into you?"

Throwing down my cloth, I sat back on my heels and glared up at him.

"What's gotten into me? I'll tell you what's gotten into me! First, I come home to find you in bed with some skanky harlot. This morning, I come home and find her helping herself to the contents of my fridge, and now, I'm scrubbing every surface she's touched because I have no idea where she's been or what horrible and disgusting germs she may have now infected my apartment with."

Bending down, he gripped my arms and lifted me to my feet. "You're nuts. First of all, you said you were fine with us sleeping with other people. Second of all, I'll replace anything she ate and third, she's a woman, not a dog, Charlene."

I laughed at him mockingly. "Looked like a tramp to me."

Adam scowled. "I don't know what exactly is going on with you lately, but I don't like it. Your attitude sucks, and your bare-faced ability to lie to me is really pissing me off, too. I'll ask you again, what the hell happened yesterday?"

I shook my head pulled myself from his grasp. "Nothing. I'm fine. Now if you don't mind, Jacob needs a bath, and I have a ton of stuff to do before I pack for my trip home."

He shook his head in bewilderment. "That trip isn't 'til next weekend."

I skirted around him and walked over to the sofa where Jacob was sleeping soundly. This wouldn't go down well. "Yeah, well, I have a lot of clothes to pack."

Jacob eyed me curiously. Wrapping my arms around him, I heaved him from the sofa. His claws dug into the plush cushions, and he protested loudly. "Come on, Jacob. There's only room for one dirty male in this apartment, and it seems Adam wants that title."

Groaning and muttering under his breath, Adam stormed into his room and slammed the door. *Whatever.* Jacob snarled and hissed as I carried him toward the bathroom. "Don't be such a wuss, Jacob. It's just a bath. Besides, we're going to use Uncle Adam's best shampoo."

Take that, Doctor Perfect!

<u>Chapter 24</u>

Adam and I hardly spoke a word to each other all week. He'd already agreed to drive me to my mother's for my gran's birthday, but I quickly informed him that he didn't have to stay. I was still seething at him over Cassie. I hadn't seen her again since that night, but I was sure that he must have had plans to hook up again. Probably while I was out of town. Hauling my case into the car, he squinted. The sun was bright, and I could feel that spring was almost leaving us and summer would be just around the corner.

"Ready?" he asked as he opened the passenger door.

I nodded. "As I'll ever be."

* * * *

We drove to my mother's in total silence. I had to consciously tell myself not to keep looking at him. I didn't know what it was about Adam driving, but I found it extremely sexy. I wanted to tell him how I felt. I wanted to break this awful tension between us, but every time I opened my mouth to speak, nothing came out. When we pulled up outside the house, my opportunity to talk to him was growing smaller every second. Shutting off the engine, he rested his hands on the steering wheel and sighed.

"Charlene, I ..."

He seemed as lost for words as I was. Exhaling loudly, he shook his head gently. "I should probably get your bag out of the back."

I nodded weakly as he got out of the car, jogged around to the back and pulled out my heavy case. I dropped my head back against the seat and bumped it a few times. This was a nightmare. How could I, or rather, how could *we* have let it come to this? I looked in the rearview mirror and watched as he dragged my case up to the front door. He seemed as frustrated as I was, and as he walked back to the car, his brow was furrowed, and he was stroking his bottom lip with his finger. I'd never seen him act like this. He strolled up to the car and gestured for me to get out.

"I guess I should go then. I'll pick you up in two days?"

"You don't wanna come in and say hi to everyone?"

He held his hands on his hips and swept his foot across the ground, biting his lip with his eyes cast down.

"I probably should. Your grandmother would never forgive me."

I smiled and side-by-side, we walked up to the house. I could hear the sound of people bustling around inside. I distinctly heard the sound of Nadine's voice. Great. That bitch was all I needed to complete my horrible week. Slotting my key in the lock, I took a deep breath and prepared myself for the bombardment. I hadn't spoken to my family much since I had revealed that Brad had dumped me. As the door swung open, my mother was immediately on me. She had hearing like a sonar monitor.

"Charlene! Oh, I'm so glad you could make it!"

Rushing over to me, she threw her arms around me and squeezed me tightly. I went a little rigid. This was still a foreign concept for me. My mother rarely hugged and certainly not me. I looked over my shoulder at Adam who shrugged. Releasing me, my mother stood back with her hands on my arms and beamed. I could see tears in her eyes, and I was beginning to get the feeling that something was up.

"I'm so happy to see you. I've missed you so much. Family is the most important thing we have in this world, you know."

Okay, something was definitely up.

"And Adam! Oh, how wonderful of you to come. You dear, sweet, and amazing boy!"

Boy? If she knew what I did, she wouldn't be considering him much of a 'boy' anymore. She grabbed him and pulled him to her for a warm hug and placed a peck on his cheek.

Again, he shrugged at me. I eyed my mother with suspicion as she let go of Adam and brushed herself down.

"I've done a big spread for lunch. Nadine, Gareth, and Gran are already in the dining room. Come through. They'll be thrilled to see you."

As she wiggled off toward the dining room, I turned to Adam. "I highly doubt that," I muttered.

He gave me a half smile as we followed my mother to the other room. Adam seemed tense. I hated that we couldn't just be ourselves anymore. This lunch was going to be a disaster. Not quite as bad as Christmas dinner had been, but bad, nonetheless.

Rounding the corner to the dining room, I rolled my eyes. Dressed in a long, sleeveless summer dress was Nadine. Her perfect, perky boobs and tiny figure, made her look like summertime Barbie. Gareth was sitting beside her, and as I entered the room, he got to his feet and opened his arms for a hug. Cautiously, I reciprocated. What the hell had gotten into my family?

When Adam walked in behind me, Nadine stood abruptly and practically ran to him, throwing her arms around his neck. "Oh, how wonderful to see you."

I glared at her over Gareth's shoulder. Usually, her obvious flirtation and desire for Adam didn't bother me; in fact, I found it rather funny. But now, I wanted to claw her eyes and hair out. Gareth patted my back gently. "So good to see you, sis."

Sis? Since when was I his sis? If I hadn't been suspicious that something was going on before, I was now!

Nadine released a disgruntled looking Adam and beamed at him before turning her attention to me.

"And Charlene. That's a lovely dress."

I almost choked on a breath. Did the hellhound just compliment me? Furrowing my brow, I pulled away from Gareth and attempted a smile. I don't think I pulled it off all that well. "Uh, thanks. I guess."

I glanced around the room at the enormous spread of food. We would never get through it all, but it seemed to give my mother a sense of accomplishment to have provided such a feast. I smiled at Gareth. "Where's Gran?"

He pressed his lips together and pointed to the lounge. "In there. You should go say hi."

I nodded and headed through the large glass panel doors to the lounge. Sitting in her usual chair, reading a crossword was my cantankerous, witty, and wonderful grandmother.

"Happy birthday, Gran!"

Looking up from her crossword, she gave me a half smile.

"And what's so happy about it?"

I rolled my eyes, walked over, and kissed her on the cheek. She tutted. "It's just another year of getting older, wrinklier, and closer to death. I suppose that's the saving grace. I won't have to be here much longer to put up with these awful family reunions."

I shook my head. "You don't mean that."

She put down her magazine and stared up at me over the rim of her glasses. "Don't I? I had plans you know. Mr McKinney from the bingo hall was taking me for dinner. I even laid out my best pair of knickers for the occasion."

I cringed. "Oh, Gran. Too much information."

She sniggered. "What? You think you youngsters are the only generation that's sexed up? Pfft. I've had more cock than you've had hot meals, my girl. And all of it a darn sight more satisfying, I'd wager."

Eww.

"Besides, I deserve a little excitement after everything that's happened."

I gave her a puzzled look. "What are you talking about?"

She let out a long breath and shook her head. "Your mother is classically the biggest gossip with the biggest mouth in the world, but the moment there's actually some important information to be heard, she clams up! I've been having treatment for cancer, dear."

My jaw dropped, and I stared at her in horror. "Cancer?" It was almost a whisper. My voice was hoarse as tears filled my eyes.

"Yes, cancer. Dear God, have you all gone temporarily deaf? I seem to spend most of my life repeating myself like a bloody parrot these days!"

I shook my head in total disbelief. "When? What type? What's the prognosis?"

She huffed again. "I was a little under the weather, so I referred myself. I was diagnosed with breast cancer. They chopped off the lump, and I've been in remission for about three weeks now."

I was lost for words.

"Oh, for heaven's sake, Charlene. I'm fine. I'm no different than I was before. Except now, I'm more like Miss Boobs in there. I'm stuck with half a tit! At least I had *my* useless lump removed. She's stuck with your brother 'til death they do part."

I nodded weakly. I wanted to laugh, but I couldn't find it in me. Reaching out her hand, my gran held mine in hers. "I'm fine, Charlene. Now, go and ask your mother when we can eat because my stomach is beginning to digest itself. If I must endure a tedious afternoon with you people, I at least want a full stomach."

That time I managed a small smile.

* * * *

Sitting around the dinner table, we were all silent. My mother entered from the kitchen and beamed at us all.

"I'm so happy and grateful to have you all here for Mum's birthday."

Sitting beside my gran, she held her hand over Grans gently. "Happy birthday, Mum."

My gran nodded and immediately reached for a plate. That woman could really eat. Everyone followed her example and began plating from the mountain of food laid out on the table.

Nadine sat back and smirked at me from across the table. "So, Charlene, have you been seeing anyone lately? I saw Brad the other day. He seemed absolutely distraught. He said he was single again and seemed devastated over what happened between you."

Adam shifted in his seat and scowled down at his plate.

I cleared my throat. "I'm fine. I've had a few dates, but nothing to shout about. And I'm sure Brad will be fine. He usually lands on his feet."

Gran snorted a laugh. "And I'm sure it won't be long 'til some other corporate climbing bimbo lands on his cock."

My mother choked and coughed as she took a bite of her sandwich. "Mother!"

Gran rolled her eyes. "Oh, please."

Turning my attention back to Nadine, I grinned wickedly at her. "You don't have to worry about me. I'll be just fine."

She gave me a sympathetic look. "I'm sure you will. Though you must be terribly lonely. After all, it's just you and that cat in your big apartment."

I rolled my eyes. "Actually, Adam's been staying with me."

Nadine's eyes darted to him, and she seemed a little … jealous.

"I see."

My gran nudged my elbow. "I knew it wouldn't take long for you two to hop on the good foot and do a bad thing."

I held my hand over my eyes as Adam coughed beside me and sat back in his seat.

"No, Gran. His place was being fumigated."

She nodded. "And I'm sure you've done a terrific job in helping him pitch his tent at your place."

Oh, this was painful. "Gran!" I snapped. "Please stop."

It was bad enough that the atmosphere between Adam and I was so tense, I didn't need my family to make the air between us even thicker.

Inspecting it first, Gran took a large bite of her sausage roll. "You could do a lot worse, Charlene. I mean, he's smart, successful, caring, and he saved my life. If it weren't for all his long hours, tireless campaigning for my treatment, and dedication to my case, I wouldn't be sitting here. That boss of his would have tossed me on the pile. That hospital will lose a great doctor. America is very lucky."

I stared at her with my mouth wide open.

"What?" she said, staring back at me.

Turning to Adam, I shook my head. "You knew? All this time, all these months, you knew? And you said nothing to me? How could you keep this from me? And America? When did you plan on telling me all of this? After everything we've been through. I just ..."

Tears welled in my eyes and feeling the burn of embarrassment in my cheeks, I pushed away from the table and stormed out of the room. I headed for the front door, pulled it open, and rushed outside. I needed air. I could hear Adam yelling after me.

"Charlene! Charlie, wait!"

Turning on my heel, I glared at him with fury. "How could you not tell me? You know how important she is to me! It all makes sense now—the phone call, your stress over work, and your boss. All this time you were telling me that everything was fine. You were lying to me! You have never lied to me in twenty years!"

He held his hands up defensively. "I couldn't tell you! It's patient confidentiality. I could have lost my job!"

I marched up to him and shoved him hard on the chest. "You really have such little faith in me? You really think I would have let it cost you your career? Well, now I know exactly where I stand. Don't I? You're hiding things from me all the time. My gran, Cassie, what else are you hiding? Fucked Dana or Ness? Maybe you have a secret child somewhere. And America? You're leaving?"

Gripping his hands on my arms, he glared at me. "I have not slept with Ness or Dana, and I don't have a secret child. I was offered a position working in L.A., but I didn't tell you because I hadn't decided whether I would take it or not. I was kind of holding all my hopes on something else. But you made it clear that you and me, we were just for fun."

He was getting worked up, and I could hear the frustration in his voice. "I don't know what you want me to do. You made the rules and then got pissy when I actually met someone."

I huffed at him, tearing myself from his grasp. "I did not get pissy. I was irritated. You could have at least given me a heads up. Or maybe had the common courtesy to wait 'til I was out of town!"

He was getting aggravated. "I didn't know that I had to declare any and all sexual encounters to my best friend. I figured she'd be happy I met someone at all."

I groaned. "Oh, please. I was asking for a little honesty. And since when was the bar hopping, china doll your type anyway? I bet her legs spread faster than a forest fire! "

"What exactly is it that pisses you off more, Charlene? The fact that I was unavailable to satisfy *your* needs or the fact that I didn't tell you I had a woman in my bed?"

I spluttered, and I could feel my anger building. "It's about honesty! It's about the fact that we used to tell each other everything, and these days, I feel I hardly know you!"

Stepping forward, he leaned down, his face inches from mine.

"Ditto! You want to talk honesty? What happened last weekend?"

I shook my head in bewilderment. "What do you mean what happened? I came home and found you in—"

He shook his head and glared at me. "That's not what I meant. You're so fucking self-righteous about whom I do or don't see and what I do or don't tell you, but you're worse.

You set standards that no woman can possibly meet and then, you go and lower your own!"

Okay, now I was really confused.

Stepping back, he raked his fingers through his hair. "I saw you."

I shook my head and furrowed my brow. "What are you talking about?"

"I saw you with Brad!"

Oh. That.

He exhaled slowly. "I was on a break from work and was going to get some lunch. I saw you at the café, I saw you holding hands. It was all very cosy."

His tone was sharp, and I didn't like his attitude.

"So you just assumed that we were together?"

He shook his head. "No, I didn't. I knew you must have run into one another, but I saw the way you were looking at him, Charlene. You can't deny it. You still have feelings for him."

I scoffed a laugh. "Are you serious? You think I want Brad? He cheated on me, dumped me, and jilted me!"

"And that automatically stops you from loving him? You don't just stop feeling, Charlene, I should know!"

I stopped and stared at him. Suddenly things made sense. "Is that why you called Cassie?"

He pressed his lips together but said nothing.

"Oh my God. It is. You saw me with Brad and then called her just to get back at me?"

He growled in frustration. "I was pissed at you! You told me that you were looking for Mr Right. How do you think I felt? I felt used and cast aside. I was disposable to you. So what if I needed to feel a little wanted. I wanted to be needed, and Cassie was very accommodating."

I winced as pain shot through my chest. Tears rolled down my cheeks.

"You think that's what you were? You are such an idiot. I came home that night wanting to talk to you. I needed to know how you really felt because I couldn't do it anymore, Adam. I came home that night to tell you—"

I stopped myself, deciding I'd already made a fool of myself enough over the past few months.

Striding up to me, Adam placed his hands on my jaw and lifted my head to face him.

"That you what, Charlene? Please, I need to hear it."

I shook my head. "It doesn't matter anymore. We're broken, shattered, and irreparable. I don't know who you are anymore."

Pulling away from him, I started down the path, but he chased after me. Gripping my elbow, he spun me around and pressed his lips against mine, hard.

My knees weakened, and I could feel my heart pounding beneath my ribcage. Pressing my hands on his chest, I pushed him away.

"No. I won't do this anymore."

Adam stared at me with tears in his eyes. "Please, Charlene. Just say it."

I shook my head. "No." I began walking away. I couldn't be near him. I swiped at my eyes, trying to rid myself of the tears as they fell. Adam didn't follow me, and I was glad. I could hear my mother calling from the house, but I couldn't go back. I needed to walk, to think, and to calm my frayed nerves. I walked for around an hour before heading back. When I got there, Adam's car was gone. He was gone. And our relationship, in whatever form, was clearly over.

Chapter 25

The apartment felt so bare now. Dropping my case on the floor, I slumped down onto the sofa. Jacob was immediately at my feet, twilling and purring at me. He was after something, no doubt. Whenever I got this sort of attention from my cat, he was usually soliciting either my hand to feed him or wanted to be fussed over. Typical male—thinks he's the most important creature on the planet. Feed him, rub his belly now and then, and he's happy. Getting up, I walked over to the kitchen and filled up his little food dish.

Even the cupboards were lacking. I knew Adam would be gone when I got home, but I didn't know how awful and desolate it would feel without him here. Glancing around, I frowned as I spotted an envelope with my name on it sitting on the countertop. I opened it with trepidation. I wasn't sure I was ready for anything it had to say.

Charlene

I've changed the sheets on the bed. I know you wouldn't want to touch anything that Cassie would have. I've also left £500 on the bed. Use it for bills and utilities. It's my fair share. I'm going to stay with one of the interns at the hospital. He has a spare room, now that his roommate graduated. I'll leave the forwarding address for my mail. I wish you had talked to me. I wish we hadn't ruined everything. But I don't regret a single moment I've spent with you in these twenty years. I'm taking the job in the U.S. I think the distance will do us both good. It's time we found our own way now. But I can't go without telling you how I feel. You might hate me, you might never want to talk to me again, but you have to know ...

I love you. Always have. Always will.

Adam xx

Slamming it down on the counter, I sat down on a stool and held my head in my hands. The phone rang from across the room, and I lifted my head but simply stared at it. I had no interest in speaking to the outside world this evening. The train ride home from my mother's had been torture. After the scene that had played out outside the house, I was too humiliated, angry, and tightly wound to stay. The idea of being questioned by my mother and Nadine was nauseating.

The answering machine picked up and as a familiar voice echoed around my apartment. I rolled my eyes and sunk further into my misery.

"Hey, Charlene. It's Brad. I've been waiting and hoping, well, praying that you'll call. I really want to make amends, sweetheart. I was an idiot. I know that now. I don't want to live the rest of my life without you. Please call me. I just want to talk. I really think we have a chance at real happiness here. Call me."

Urgh. Getting up, I shuffled over and hit the delete button. Just as my finger left the dialling pad, the damn thing rang again.

"Charlene? It's your mother. Pick up."

Great. If I didn't answer, she would only call persistently every hour anyway. I might as well get it over with.

"Yes, Mother? What is it?"

She sighed heavily. "Oh, Charlene. I don't know what on Earth has been going on with you and your life lately, but it seems to be an awful mess."

I rolled my eyes. "Oh really? I hadn't noticed, what with being cheated, dumped, then casually sleeping with my best friend, falling for him, and then discovering he's leaving to go to America."

She gasped. "Oh, Charlene. You silly, silly girl. You are on some sort of self-destructive mission, I'm sure. But that's not why I called. I overheard you and Adam arguing, and he said you saw Brad. What happened? Did he apologise? Does he want you back?"

I groaned loudly in frustration. After everything I just said, that's what she wants to talk about? "Mother, did you not just hear me? I'm in love with Adam."

"Yes, I heard you. I also heard you fight with him and tell me that he's leaving to go to the States. He's clearly not the man for you, my dear. But Brad, he's a steady type. He's not about to jet off across the world. He's stable, and you could do a lot worse."

Was she serious? "He cheated on me!"

She sighed again. My mother could possibly have been using up half of the population's oxygen with the endless sighing she did all day. "I know. But we all make mistakes, Charlene. Goodness knows that men make them more often than we do, but we have to be the bigger person. Do you want to spend the rest of your life alone? I've been alone for a long time; I know what it's really like. Your father abandoned me. Your stepfather up and died on me and then your other one simply changed his mind and divorced me. Life without someone to share it with is empty. I don't want that for you. I think you should at least consider a reconciliation with Brad."

"I have to go, Mother. I appreciate your concern and need to tell me how to run my life, but I assure you, I can ruin it all on my own."

Hanging up, I growled loudly. The whole world had gone mad! I suddenly felt extremely tired. Lying on the sofa, I pulled a blanket over myself as Jacob climbed up and sat beside me. I stroked him gently as he purred into my chest. "At least I have you, Jake. To keep me company, curl up and go to sleep with, and someday to eat my lifeless body as it lay rotting in this very apartment. All alone. Forever."

Tears slid heavily down my cheeks as I lay there and cried myself to sleep.

* * * *

Standing back and staring at my desk, I smiled. It was finally empty. No paperwork, no piles of letters, and no contracts to filter through. I was free to begin a new project at last. Glancing over at the corner of my office, I rolled my eyes. Brad had sent a large bouquet of roses to my office every day for the past two weeks—each with a note and a plea for me to call him. I'd kept the flowers, after all, it was a shame to waste a perfectly good bunch of roses simply because I disliked Brad. I did have to admire his persistence though. On the opposite wall hung pictures of my friends—Ness, Dana, and Adam. Could I even call him my friend anymore?

I hadn't spoken to him since that day at my mother's house, but Dana and Ness had informed me that his flight was booked for that coming Saturday. They begged me to come out with them for a drink to see him off, but I couldn't face it. I felt awful about it and guilt flooded me, but seeing him now, after everything we had said, would be the worst thing in the world. He had a great opportunity opening up to him by leaving, and any contact with me could endanger that. I wouldn't take the risk. Besides, there really wasn't anything left to say. Well, maybe one thing, but I just couldn't do it. Even if he already had.

"Knock, knock."

Turning around, I smiled as Dana and Ness swanned into my office and greeted me with a tight hug.

"Hey, guys. What are you doing here?"

They looked at each other briefly as though looking for an answer. "We thought we'd just drop by and see how you're doing. You've been a little hermit these past weeks, and Dana was worried that you'd been sucked into a black hole or something," Ness joked. I tilted my head and smiled at them both.

"I'm fine. Honest."

Walking around my desk, I sat in my chair and gestured for them to take a seat.

"So, what did you really come here for?"

Dana pressed her lips together. "We thought maybe we could try and convince you to change your mind about tomorrow night. Adam's going away party?"

I shook my head in a definitive no.

"Oh, please, Charlene. The two of you *have* to make amends before he leaves. You just have to."

I shook my head again. "No, Dana. I can't and won't. He needs a clean break, and so do I. It's time we learnt who we are when we're not Charlie and Adam. Besides, I'm pretty sure he would rather not see me on his last night here. It's too complicated."

Ness sighed. "I think you're both nuts. Both crazy in love with each other, but too damn stubborn to just bite the bullet, take a chance, and admit you can't be without each other. Your lives are about to get very lonely. You mark my words."

I gave her an apologetic smile. "I'm sorry, guys. I know how hard this has been on you both. It's not exactly been a fairytale for me either."

Dana nodded. "I know. But you really won't reconsider? He's been miserable and completely and unbearably distant since you fell out. Please, for the sake of my sanity and your friendship, come to the party."

My stomach churned at the thought of Adam's unhappiness. I hated being the cause. It wasn't something I was used to. We had always been each other's reason to smile. I stared at Dana, and she instantly fell silent. "You know my answer, Dana. But the two of you should go. Have fun, get him totally hammered, and make sure you give him the sendoff he deserves. Britain is about to lose a great doctor and an even better man. The U.S. is very lucky."

Ness groaned and rubbed her eyes. "One day I will kill you both. I swear. But if this is really what you decide, then naturally we'll respect it. No matter how much I'd rather just lock you in a room and tie you together. Maybe leave a baseball bat in the corner for you to knock some sense into each other."

I smiled at them from across the desk. "Thank you, I think."

Standing, they moved toward the door but turned at the last minute. "Want to grab something to eat?" Ness offered.

I shook my head. "I have stuff to do. You two go and have fun. I'll catch up with you later."

They each gave me a sympathetic smile before leaving and closing the door behind them.

I looked around my empty office. I should probably get used to that. Silence, emptiness, and loneliness. A small piece of paper on the desk caught my eye. Picking up the phone, I dialled. I had to try; I had to take at least one chance in my miserable life. Maybe my friends and my mother were right; I didn't want to be lonely anymore. I had to talk to him. Now.

"Hello?" his voice purred down the phone.

"Hi, I just wanted to—" I held my hand over the receiver and exhaled loudly.

"Dinner?" he suggested.

"Okay. Tonight? The bistro around the corner from my place?"

I could imagine the smile on his lips as he spoke.

"I'll pick you up at seven. I've missed you, Charlene."

I sighed again. "Yeah. I'll see you at seven."

"Can't wait. Bye Charlene."

"Bye Brad."

Chapter 26

"You're back together?" Ness yelled across the lounge.

"Will you please keep your voice down? He's still in there asleep." I pointed at the bedroom.

"I don't care! I've half a mind to drag his arse out of bed and sling him out of your apartment. Did you hit your head? Because you must be crazy!"

I stood from the sofa and held my hands in the air with exasperation.

"I have the right to make my own decisions, Ness. We went out for dinner the other week and we … talked. He's not perfect; God knows he's been an arsehole, but so does he. He knows what he's done and knows that this is his last chance to put it right."

Dana scoffed at me. "Oh, Charlene. He'll tell you anything to get his feet back under the table. You're not thinking straight. Your heart is broken over Adam, and you're terrified of being alone. That's all."

"And what exactly is wrong with not wanting to be alone? You like being alone?"

She shook her head and stared out of the window.

"Charlene, I *had* the love of my life. I let him slip through my fingers. I've been suffering ever since. You had a chance to be happy; Adam spent the entirety of his going away party staring at the door. He denied it, but it was obvious that he was waiting for you. Now when he calls, it's like he's afraid to ask us about you. I'm telling you, that man is in pain. He's miserable. He works nonstop to keep himself busy, and he's gradually working himself into the ground! I know he's unhappy there."

I looked down at the floor as heartache for him set in. "We would never have worked, Dana."

Ness grunted. "You never tried to find out."

"Well, it's too late now! He's thousands of miles away. Brad is *here*. Right here, in my bedroom, and he actually wants to be with me. He wants to try and make it work, and I owe it to myself to try. I have to know."

Ness shook her head in disgust. "Well, don't expect us to be happy about it. As far as I'm concerned, he's a slimy little slug and always will be. Good luck!" Grabbing her purse, she stared at Dana. "Come on, Dana. I don't want to be here when the nutfucker wakes up."

Shaking her head ruefully, Dana followed Ness, and they left the apartment, slamming the door behind them.

Falling back onto the sofa, I pressed my palms over my face. It wasn't that my rekindled relationship with Brad was a secret, and I was certainly not ashamed. I simply knew my friends, well, Ness would go batshit crazy at me as soon as they found out. I needed time to be sure that this was what I wanted before going … public. I was tired of being alone, pining for Adam, and wondering if I was doomed to roam the planet solo for the rest of my life. Surely being with Brad wasn't my worst option. But right now, it seemed to be my *only* option. Single life clearly didn't agree with me, and I had long since decided to cast it aside like yesterday's newspaper. The bedroom door squeaked from across the room.

"I take it you told the girls?" I removed my hands to find Brad standing in the doorway in a pair of jeans and a blue shirt, giving me a sympathetic smile.

I nodded. "It didn't go so well."

Striding over, he sat beside me and placed his arm around my shoulders, pulling me to him for a hug. "You knew they wouldn't be too happy, but it's not up to them. Is it? This is our life and our choice. You haven't changed your mind, have you?"

I stared into his eyes and smiled. "No. I'm just sad that they can't be happy for me."

He smiled. "They'll come around. I take it you didn't mention the engagement, though?"

Okay, don't judge me, but I may have agreed to marry Brad over dinner. I never mentioned it because it really wasn't such a big deal. It had only happened two days ago. I was pining over Adam leaving, and I'd just watched *The Notebook*. Who wouldn't be feeling a little love sick and heartbroken after that? I'm only human! Anyway, we'd gotten some Chinese and were sitting in the lounge when he dropped to one knee and begged me to take him back. As you can imagine, I was shocked, horrified, and stunned. After everything we'd been through—no, everything he'd put me through—he actually dared to propose marriage! Again! He made promises, begged, pleaded, and even cried. It had to be said that Brad never cried. Not even when his father died. I'm a sucker for a man in tears. You may roll your eyes but have a little sympathy. I was in a particularly poor state of mind at the time. We've all been there.

In a moment of weakness … I found the word *yes* slipping from my lips. He'd been so elated and relieved, I figured, maybe he really had seen the light. Besides, I wasn't exactly flush with admirers right now. And the fact that being alone was also wreaking havoc on my diet was just another reason that my hand slipped into his, and I nodded as he slid a brand new diamond ring onto my finger. I'd been smart enough to leave it on the dresser before the girls came though. They needed time to adjust to the idea of the two of us being together before I would drop that bombshell on them.

"I decided it's best to not tell them yet. It's all still kind of a sore subject for them right now."

He nodded in agreement and placed a soft kiss on my lips. "Well, hot stuff, I have about two hours before I have to head into the office. What do you say I run us a bath, we slip in, and get dirty?"

He winked at me, and I smiled, kissing him gently in return. "Sounds good. I'll be in in a minute."

Leaving me alone in the lounge, he sauntered back to the bedroom. I held my head in my hands. Was I doing the right thing? I didn't want to be alone anymore, but I wasn't sure I really wanted to be with Brad either. I was still hurting and longing for Adam. Maybe that's what was really holding me back. Brad was an idiot, granted, but he loved me, and what's more, he wasn't afraid of saying it. He wasn't about to leave me for a job across the ocean, and he was safe, stable, and comfortable. I knew him, and he knew me. The idea of a new relationship and getting to know someone all over again made me hopelessly tired. I was done with dating. I was done with sex buddies, and I was done with Adam Fitz. He was clearly done with me, too. The thought depressed me. Pushing it to the back of my mind, I looked down at my bare finger. Mrs Bradley Mahoney. I could do this. *Probably.* I would marry Brad and live happily ever after. More or less.

* * * *

"Charlene, this dress is the colour of vomit! Do you actually expect me to wear this?" Ness yelled from the cubicle.

"Yes," I yelled back as I sat in a plush white chair, sipping champagne. Emerging from the changing room, Ness cringed. Her face was contorted with disgust. "This dress is hideous."

She wasn't wrong. "I know, but Brad wanted green for the wedding to complement his Irish roots. Besides, I told you, I'm not bothered about the colour."

She tutted. "Well, you should be. You're wearing the same dress, why can't we?"

She gestured to herself and Dana who was sitting on a puffet stool in a dark green strapless gown that matched Ness's.

"Because this wedding is going to be small. We're not doing the whole big white wedding. It's one of the reasons Brad was so flighty last time. He got the jitters. The idea of all those people scared him. We're just having a small ceremony at the local registrar's office and then an intimate dinner reception with close friends and family."

Ness groaned. "It's bad enough that you're actually going through with this. You won't let us throw you a hen night, you vetoed the idea of a honeymoon, and now you're forcing us to wear these monstrosities that insist on being referred to as dresses!"

I rolled my eyes. "Please, just this once, could you do this and not have to whine, moan, complain and make a scene?"

Dana giggled in the corner. "That would be a miracle."

I walked over and took the champagne bottle and glass from her hands. She'd been slowly and consistently topping off her glass since we'd arrived three hours ago. I was having my dress refitted. I was finally only ten pounds away from my target, and my dress needed taking in a little. It was a glorious feeling.

Slumping down on a chair, Ness crossed her legs and leaned back, smiling at me. I eyed her curiously.

"What are you grinning about?"

She shook her head. "Oh, nothing. I was just wondering if you'd heard from Adam at all?"

I shook my head. "No. Why would I?"

She shrugged. "It's been three months. I figured one of you might buckle and call the other."

I scoffed at her. "Ha! You mean that you were hoping he would talk me out of this wedding."

She pretended to be hurt by my comment. "Would I do a thing like that?"

Dana and I glanced at each other. "Yes," we answered simultaneously. Conceding defeat, she moaned. "Wouldn't be the worst thing in the world to happen. This wedding is, though. Are you actually able to sit there and tell me you're happy? That this is what you really want? A boring, mundane and extremely sexless life. Forever!"

I'd asked myself that question over a hundred times. It had only taken us three months to plan the wedding, and in that time, we were already settling back into our old routine and way of being together. It was simple, uncomplicated, comfortable, and ... BORING. Okay, I admitted it. It was boring. The sex was boring. The conversations were boring, and if I heard the phrase, "Could you change the sheets darling, I think I'd like to have sex" one more time, I was going to hang myself with one of Brad's awful and tacky neckties! But I'd made my choice, and now, I was going to have to live with it, and so were my friends. Exhaling loudly, I got to my feet and stood in the middle of the large dressing room. "Look, I am marrying Brad in three days. You can both be there and stand behind me as I do it, or don't come at all. I can't keep having this fight with you. Adam left. Okay? *He* left."

"Only because he thought he and you had absolutely no chance in hell of being together. He thought you hated him, Charlene. When you didn't call or even go see him, he took the hint. You were just too embarrassed and scared to admit that you wanted him. And he was too stupid to realise that."

Tossing back my champagne, I held my fingertips to my lips. "The decision has been made. This wedding is happening. End of discussion. Now, one of you help me get into this damn dress so that I can make sure I look like a fucking princess."

Dana and Ness both stared at me before all three of us burst out laughing. Falling onto the floor, I dropped my empty champagne glass and tried to catch my breath.

"Oh, what the hell am I doing?"

Dana and Ness, finally able to speak again, joined me on the floor. Draping an arm around each of my shoulders, they smiled, resting their heads against mine.

"I've asked myself that question, but apparently, you're getting married. And we're going to be right up there with you when you say 'I do.' Even if we wish you wouldn't."

Hugging them both, I sighed. "Thank you. I don't know what I would do without you two."

Ness glanced down at her dress. "Find someone else to wear this leprechaun's bride outfit?"

I chuckled. "But you carry it off so well."

She giggled. "Well, I better go and take it off before I rip it off."

I nodded and watched as the two of them giggled and joked as they made their way back into the cubical. It would be fine. I had my family, my girls, and in a few days, I'd have my husband. But what I really wanted … was my best friend.

Chapter 27

Staring at myself in the full-length mirror, I took a deep breath. My hair was curled into perfect, fiery ringlets and held together tightly in a messy bun on top of my head. A silver and jewel-encrusted tiara sat at the front of it and a thin, elegant veil cascaded behind me. My dress was simple yet stylish. Ness had picked it out, and it complemented my shape perfectly—slimline to my waist with a twisting diamond design on the bodice and a flowing white, plain skirt. It was perfect. I looked like a princess, and yet, as I continued to stare blankly at myself, I couldn't have felt less like one if I'd tried.

Today was supposed to be the happiest day of my life. Brad's niece, Adriane, was our flower girl. She was adorable. Five years old and dressed in a little green dress, she tugged gently on my skirt. "You look pretty." She beamed. Bending down, I smiled at her and kissed her gently on the cheek.

"Thank you. So do you."

She grinned up at me. "You're the saddest bride I've ever seen, though, and I'm Irish, I've seen loads!"

She did a little twirl and giggled before skipping away and out of the door. I'd been in the bridal suite of the registrar's office now for over an hour. I could hear people arriving outside. They chatted and laughed amongst themselves. Brad's broad Irish accent was unmistakable. A small part of me had wondered if he'd really go through with it. Would he actually show up? I guess the answer to that was yes. Brushing myself down, I inspected my dress. It was still perfect. Everything was perfect. Except for the fact that I was jittering more than a vibrator! I was sweating; my throat felt dry, and my whole body felt weak. Oh, God. What the hell was I doing? If I couldn't even fool a five-year-old, how the hell would I convince an entire room that this was the happiest day of my life! Simple. I couldn't!

It *wasn't* the happiest day of my life. It was hell, and I was swimming in a sea of regret, anxiety, and downright denial! This was insanity. I couldn't marry Brad. He'd cheated on me, dumped me, and now I was about to walk down the aisle and say yes to forever with a man I didn't trust, love, or even particularly like. When had I gotten so desperate?

I walked around the room, frantically thinking of what to do when there was a knock on the door. Walking in, wearing a stunning grey dress and matching hat, was my mother.

"Oh Charlene, you look beautiful. Are you almost ready?"

I gave her a pleading look, and she frowned. "My darling girl, what's wrong?"

I held my head in my hands and sobbed. I couldn't stop myself. It just flowed out of me.

"I can't do it, Mum. I can't. I can't marry Brad."

She continued to smile and wrapped her arms around me. "Oh, darling. It's just cold feet. You'll be fine."

Pulling away sharply, I shook my head and became more and more agitated. "No! You don't understand. I can't do it! I'm not the same person I was when I met him, and the thought of spending the rest of my life with him makes my stomach churn and my breath catch in my lungs."

"What are you suggesting? You're just going to walk away?"

I ripped the veil from my hair and threw it on the floor. My mother hurried to pick it up. "Charlene, calm down. It'll all be fine. Now is not the time for a meltdown. It's just nerves. Goodness, do you think I really wanted to marry your stepfather? Of course not. I didn't love him. I was still in love with your father. But I had a child to feed, and I wasn't getting any younger. So, I married him, and in time I grew to love him. You have to stop believing in fairytales and happily ever after. They don't exist. That man out there adores you, and he wants to spend the rest of his life with you. He'll take care of you, and one day, you'll look back and wonder what on Earth you did before he came along. I promise."

I stared at her. "Promises are a dangerous thing, Mum. They have the ability to make and break entire lives."

She nodded and gently slipped the veil back into my hair.

"I know. And I also know you'll make the right choice. I have to go back out there. They'll be waiting for me. Ness and Dana told me to give you this. I assume it's a good luck card."

She handed me an envelope and beamed before stroking my face gently.

"You really are beautiful."

I held her hand against my face and snuggled. I needed some comfort, and right now, this would have to suffice. Pulling her hand away, she smiled and left me alone with my envelope. Sitting myself down in front of the dresser, I opened it with trepidation. As I read each word, tears began to stream down my face. My body racked with sobs, and my heart ached. It was from Adam.

Diary Of A Dieter

Charlie

I must have written this letter a thousand times. I hoped so much that you would come to the party to see me off. I wanted to see you, talk to you, and tell you everything that I've been too afraid to say for far too long. Charlene, I love you. From the moment you rescued me in a school gym, I've been besotted. Every breakup, every boyfriend who broke your heart, and every time you smiled at me, I've wanted to tell you just how much I love you. I tried so hard to get past how I felt and move on, find someone, but all of those women just paled next to you. When you told me that you and Brad were getting married, I was crushed. But you were so happy, and just being around you, being your friend, was better than not having you at all. So I said nothing. I should have told you how I felt. I should have been honest. When we made love, it was so much more than sex for me. It was everything I'd ever wanted. You have no idea how my heart broke when you said it was just a means to an end. I never used you. I never wanted anything more than to be yours exclusively. I screwed it up, and now it's too late. I just wanted you to know that everything I've ever done, has only been to protect you and maybe, selfishly, myself too. Don't hate Ness and Dana for this. I made them swear to only give this to you when the time was right. I'm assuming that since you're reading it, they felt it was. I'll always love you, Charlene. You're beautiful, and I've always thought you were the sexiest and most gorgeous woman that ever existed. No matter what size your dress said you were. You're a stunning creature. Inside and out. And I'll miss you every day.

With hope and regret for not telling you sooner.
Adam xxx

Clutching the note to my chest, I held it tightly. I could hardly breathe through my tears, and as I heard the sound of music begin, I panicked. I had to get out! I couldn't marry Brad! I had to find Adam! I didn't care how far away he was, how stupid we'd both been, or how upset I was about to make my family. I was meant to be with Adam, and no wedding was about to stop me.

Opening the door, I checked the coast was clear and hurried across the hall to the bathroom, locking the door behind me. I looked around for a tissue. I need to clean myself up and go out and face everyone. Glancing around, I caught sight of a slightly opened window.

Or … I could just climb out of that, run away, and they would all have to just … get the hint. It was foolproof. Climbing up onto the toilet, I balanced on the seat. Damn thing had no lid. I pushed the window hard, forcing it open. It looked big enough, so gripping the windowsill, I hoisted myself headfirst out of it. Now, I was right about my body fitting through the hole. However, I hadn't accounted for my dress! Pulling myself through, I became stuck as my dress snagged on the lock.

"Damn it!"

The bathroom door rattled behind me, forcing me to still and stay silent. I held my breath for what seemed like forever.

"Charlene? Are you okay? It's Dana and Ness. What are you doing in there?"

I let out the breath I was holding and called back to them.

"Oh, thank God! I'm stuck! Quick, get the door open!"

I heard the rattle of the lock, and Ness asked Dana for a hairpin. That girl could have made a career as a professional thief! I'd once seen her open a car door with her bra wire!

I heard the door open and grunted.

"Charlene, what the hell are you doing?" Dana yelled.

I groaned in frustration. "Will you stop screaming? I don't want to be discovered while I'm jilting the groom at my own wedding!"

Ness made a hissing sound, and I could just make out the long tones of 'yesssssss.'

"Oh, Charlene, I could kiss you! I'm so proud of you! Thank God, I thought I was going to have to wait for the guy to ask if anyone objects and then drag your arse back out!"

I rolled my eyes. "That's so sweet of you, honey. Now, if you don't mind, will you please get me out of here?"

Coming up behind me, the two of them pressed their hands against my behind and pushed. Reaching back I pulled, tugged, and clawed at my dress, desperately trying to get myself free. The distinct sound of fabric ripping caught me by surprise, and as my skirt tore into two pieces, I hurtled out of the window and down onto the ground. I was now covered in mud, in a torn wedding dress, and my hair looked like a bird's nest. To top it off, the heel of my shoe had also snapped. Classy.

Sitting on the ground, I looked up and saw Ness and Dana grinning at me through the window. "Hurry up and go! We'll try and stall them all!" Dana bustled.

Standing up, I brushed myself down and looked around. Everyone was inside, and I could hear voices talking loudly.

My mothers was one of them. She sounded frantic. It was only a matter of seconds before they'd figure out I'd gone and come looking for me. Hobbling along in a now broken heeled shoe, I ran along the pavement, glancing behind me every few steps, waiting to see a crowd of people come pouring out of the registrar's office. I was so busy looking behind me that I found myself suddenly bumping into a solid mass that knocked me on my arse. Sitting on the ground, I held my hand over my eyes to shield me from the sunlight and looked up. Standing over me with a look of both horror and relief on his face was Adam!

"Charlie!" Reaching down he scooped me into his arms and held me tightly. My own arms wound around his back, and I nuzzled my face into his neck.

"Oh, Adam!"

I inhaled him deeply, and tears began falling down my cheeks. "What are you doing here?"

Putting me back on my feet, he stood back and held my arms. "Dana and Ness told me about the wedding. I got on the first flight out here this morning. I tried to stay away and convince myself that it was for the best, but I couldn't do it. I couldn't stay *there* knowing that my last chance to ever make you mine was slipping through my fingers and into Brad's arms. I'm so sorry I made you feel that this was your only option, Charlie. And I know that your wedding day isn't the best time to do this but—"

He paused and scanned me from head to toe. "Wait, did you? Have you? Am I too late?"

I shook my head. "I couldn't do it. I couldn't say yes to him when my whole heart, body, and mind was screaming no."

Pausing, I stared up at him, tilted my head, and smiled. "Wait, were you going to crash my wedding, Adam Fitz?"

He pulled me to him again, and this time he kissed me. He kissed me deeply, passionately, and with a sense of overwhelming love. Gazing down at me, he grinned.

"Damn right I was! There was no way I could let you get away from me again. Charlie, I love you. I've loved you forever, and I *will* love you forever. Just please, don't go back there."

I shook my head. "I won't. I can't. It's done now. They'll all be coming to find me soon. We have to go."

I was panicked, and as I turned around, I could see Ness and Dana as they were pushed out of the doorway by Brad. Their attempt to keep everyone inside by blocking the door had been a temporary reprieve for me, but I could feel the storm clouds moving in. Brad wasn't angry. Oh no, he was seething. Spotting Adam and me a little way down the street, he sprinted toward us.

"You son of a bitch!" he yelled, as his face turned red and he fast approached us.

Moving me behind him, Adam blocked me from his path, and as Brad closed in on us, Adam pulled back his fist and rammed it straight into Brad's nose. I gasped and held my hands over my mouth in shock.

Brad fell to the ground, rolling around and clutching his hand over his bloodied nose. "Oh, my face! You broke my fucking nose, you bastard!"

Shaking his hand out, Adam roared at him. "*That* is for cheating on her."

Reaching down, he pulled Brad to his feet and ducked as Brad aimed a fist at Adams's head. Adam responded with a low blow to Brad's stomach. "*That* is for dumping her on Christmas day!"

Brad groaned and fell to his knees. Standing over him, Adam wiped the sweat from his brow before slamming his foot into Brad's crotch. I was a sucker for a man in tears, but the heaving sounds Brad was making were purely out of excruciating pain. He wasn't crying; no, he was sobbing heavy tears of agony. I was kind of enjoying it. Sick, huh? Adam crouched down and gripped his collar, forcing him to look at him. "And *that*, that's just because you're a dick. You don't deserve her. You never did. I've been waiting a long time to wipe that smug smile off of your face you prick. Now, fuck off, cradle your swollen sack, and stay away from her."

Letting him go, Adam turned to me and opened his arms. I immediately ran into them and held him tightly. Brad laughed breathlessly as he rolled around on the ground.

"You'll regret this, Charlene. Your fat arse is never going to do any better than me. You think this tosspot is going to take care of you? From America?"

Adam moved to hit him again, but grabbing him by the shoulders, I looked up at him, shook my head, and scanned his expression. "Oh my God. Are you leaving again?"

He shook his head and kissed me gently. "Not if you won't come with me."

"Charlene! Charlene!"

I turned to see Ness, Dana, and my mother hurrying down the pavement toward us. A crowd of people were gathering outside the registrar's office, gawping at us.

Turning my attention back to Adam, I shook my head. "I'll go anywhere with you. Always."

Lifting my chin, he closed his mouth over mine.

"I'm your girl, Adam. I always was." I smiled against his lips and pressed my forehead against his. "You've always been so much more than that. Marry me, Charlie."

My mother gasped as she stared at Brad, who I was pretty sure had lost consciousness by now. "My goodness."

Gran stood behind her and laughed. "Ha! Stupid little prick. About time someone shoved his dick down his own throat."

Ness and Dana giggled at her. "Well." Ness beamed. "Answer him!"

Dana was bouncing on her heels as all of them stared at me, waiting. I didn't need to think about it this time. There was no other answer I could possibly give.

"Abso-fucking-lutely!"

Throwing my arms around his neck, I pressed my lips to his. He spun me around and grinned.

"You'll make me the happiest man alive. I promise to make you the happiest woman in the world."

Smiling, I rubbed the tip of my nose gently against his.

"You already have."

<u>Epilogue</u>

Adam and I were married the following spring. We had made the move to the States almost immediately, and Regina was devastated to lose me. However, she did promote me to senior manager at our L.A. office. Nicola and Denise were my new colleagues, and I had never enjoyed my job more. My mother was keen to visit as soon as possible, and the distance was doing wonders for our dysfunctional relationship. Even Gran had made the trip, though she had spent the majority of her time in the countless bars and senior citizen clubs. I was convinced she might actually consider moving out there with us, but the heat was more than she could bear. Thankfully.

Ness and Dana loved the States. I knew they would. Ness was right at home in Hollywood, and Dana was a typical tourist. I had suggested that while there, she look Kieran up, but it seemed to deter her, so I dropped it. The only one who seemed totally unfazed by the whole ordeal was Jacob. The pampered pussy was totally at home in our large, three-bedroom house with its own pool. However, he wasn't overly fond of the Great Dane next door. I would often catch him tormenting the poor animal by marching up and down the brick wall in our garden. But the dog really was his only complaint. Well, that and the week he spent in quarantine before he was allowed to join us from the UK.

The wedding took no time at all to plan, and with the girls, only a Skype call away, it was fairly easy to organise, too! It wasn't the big white wedding that Ness had begged me to have, and it wasn't the formal affair that my mother had pleaded at us to have either. But as we stood at the end of the aisle, in a little chapel in Vegas, Adam was the sexiest groom I had ever laid eyes on. Dressed in his white Prince Charming outfit, he beamed at me. I had opted for a traditional, nylon Cinderella get-up, and my bridesmaids were the Little Mermaid and Snow White. It was the perfect wedding. The perfect dress, place, weather, day, and what's more, the perfect groom.

I'd love to tell you that we lived happily ever after. But life doesn't really work out like that. We had our ups and downs, fights, and disagreements, but does the fairytale always have to be the prince and princess getting married, making babies, and living in a dream castle? Of course not. Our marriage was like everyone else's; we had to work at it. It wasn't magic kingdoms, ball gowns, and pixie dust. It was real. It wasn't happily ever after ... but it was pretty damn close. And as far as I was concerned ... that was good enough for me.

~The End~

Diary Of A Dieter

Acknowledgements

First, I have to thank my wonderful, supportive, inspiring family and partner. Thank you for being there when the writing cave got lonely. Thank you for making sure I didn't over-do it and for taking such good care of my unborn child and me. You kept me grounded and reminded me of what is most important in life. I love you all.

To my friends, you will never know what a crucial part you played in this book. So much of the humour, wit, and fun would not be possible had I not experienced so much of it with you. I love you all deeply and am indebted to you forever.

My beta readers. You are an incredible group of women. You made me laugh and kept me sane! Rhonda, your comments and notes will have me giggling forever. Laura, Kerri, Jen, and Shaina, I cannot thank you enough for reading, discussing and helping me make this novel all it could be. Dana and Vanessa, I am truly touched that you allowed me to borrow your names. I hope I did you justice, and I thank you both from the bottom of my heart for your time and encouragement while beta reading this book. Many a wobble was diverted because of you fantabulous beta ladies!

Madison, thank you so much for all of your support, enthusiasm, and understanding while editing my mass of thoughts! Your professionalism, talent, skill, and eye for detail was amazing, and I would highly recommend your editing services to everyone! You made me smile when nerves set in.

And to you, my fans and readers, I adore you. There is no other way to describe it. I thank you all for your kind words and congratulations on my happy news. I am overwhelmed with how much love and support I have received. You rock.

Find me on Facebook
http://www.facebook.com/authormariecoulson

On Twitter
https://twitter.com/marie_coulson

By Email
authormariecoulson@hotmail.co.uk

Printed in Great Britain
by Amazon

34403475R00163